D0585231

THE DETAINEES

THE DETAINEES

BY

Sean Hughes

First published in Great Britain by Simon & Schuster, 1997
A Viacom Company

Simon & Schuster
West Garden Place
Kendal Street
London W2 2AQ

Simon & Schuster Australia
Sydney

A CIP catalogue record for this book is available
from the British Library

0-684-82081-1

Printed and bound in Great Britain by Butler & Tanner, Frome

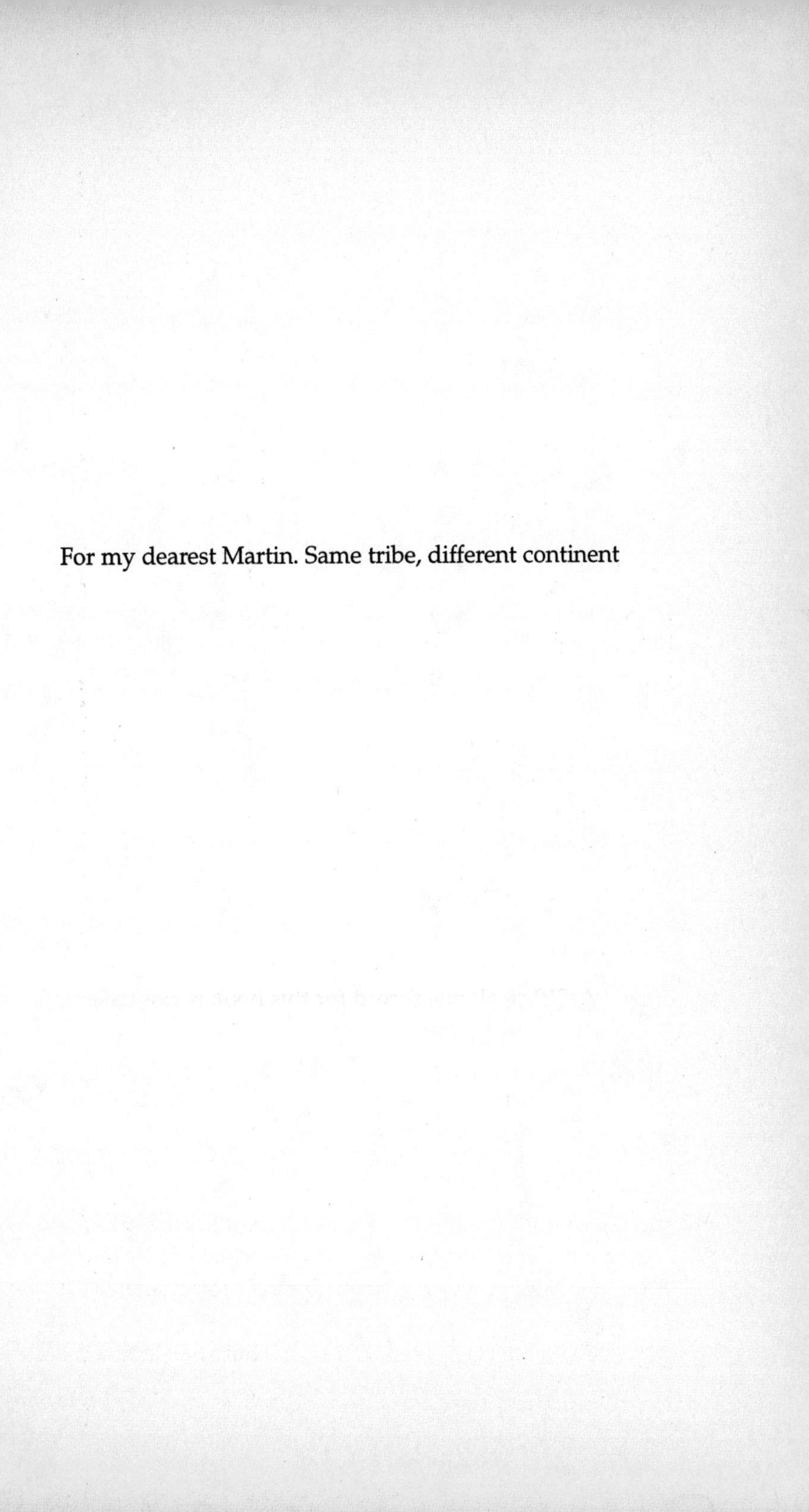

For my dearest Martin. Same tribe, different continent

ACKNOWLEDGEMENTS

Thanks, heartfelt and sincere to Jonny, Martin, Sally, Mick, Hannah, Owen, Chiggey, Marie, Sue, Dave, Matthew, Trish, Mark, Billy and songwriters the world over.

You see through each cloak I wear
Know if I speak without mouth or language.
The World is drunk on its desire for words:
I am the slave of the Master of Silence

Rumi

CHAPTER 1

'What are you looking at, you cunt?'

The preened newsreader didn't answer back. John knew he was in trouble when he swore at the television. He coughed up a sizeable chunk of his lung which came as sweet relief to his wood-dry mouth. He lit a cigarette and contemplated last night's fuck-the-consequences boozy session. He was drinking too much, the hints of decline amassing as he started to look for excuses for his excesses. He had a bulimic approach to drinking, binge and then throw up. Last night it was to comfort himself on hearing that the love of his life, Jodie, was having her first baby. This was the end of an era, the final nail in the coffin of their doomed romance. She was getting on with her life, which meant he had to assess his own; another chance to prise open the fragility of his soul. The hungover brain went into data overdrive and wanted answers. *Why are we so messed up? What is it exactly that we hold so dear? Who can we turn to at times like this? With Jodie out of the picture there's very few left. If I was you, and I am, I'd stop cursing at those newsreaders, because you're going to be seeing a lot more of them from now on.*

John stared at his new friends and watched them take turns telling him about child rapists, mid-air collisions, butchered wives, pre-election government erections, little countries' hunger pangs and the tears of a Di. Here's Jim with the weather: 'It's going to be a lovely day today but don't go outside, it's a fucking jungle out there.'

He considered the idea of being a newsreader, scooping through mayhem every day, having to put on that sombre expression, keeping that particular sad face for the murdered-kid story, and all to the tune of the Queen's proper English. *Show you're human you smug bastard, snigger at another wasted life. We know you don't really care, it's just your job. Don't give us that bland laugh during the feelgood item; the donkey that thinks he's human doesn't put a spring in our step. And don't do that stupid quip when handing over to sports.*

John turned the box off. This was his dog's signal that his master was getting up. Monty licked John out of bed, eager for his walk. When John rose he became aware that he was feeling rougher than he'd thought, but the dog's eyes pleaded and he needed a distraction. He tiptoed out of the door, hushing Monty because he didn't want to wake his doting wife Michelle, who was sound asleep in the next room.

The blinking answer machine wasn't its usual bright self, as if warning that it contained bad news. *Slap.* 'It's Red . . . I'm back. I had awful trouble tracking you down. I'll leave you me number. It'll be just like old times.' He tried to dismiss the impact of the call but only succeeded in making Monty suspicious of all the undue affection. 'Get your coat, Monty . . .' and they were off.

John could never just walk calmly without purpose. There had to be a destination: the village, or a paper to buy; that would do. Monty, never trained, would tug ahead, foraging with his bug eyes. Depending on his mood John would quicken or use the choke. It annoyed him on such mornings that the dog had no commonsense. He wanted to hit him, but he never could. He was never prone to tempers, and would rather curl up than punch. Of Irish stock, poor diet, and born into a narrow-minded town whose pace never gathered momentum, he had a mind that darted, leapt, backturned and somersaulted causing almost daily sharp intakes of breath. The inner voice continually had to chill itself out. Impulses crashed into one another, making for an unlikely walking style. The war in Bosnia was bothering him today. It distressed him that people were able to kill others, that this was deemed allowable.

Closer to home he passed a neighbour. They weren't even at the nodding stage but were cognisant of each other's existence. This stranger was crying, or at least about to. John wanted to comfort him but strode on, imagining scenarios in his head. A possible death in the family had him inevitably thinking of his own parents:

how he expected to get a call any day regaling him with news of one of their demises. He loved his parents, but he didn't like them very much. He was anguished by the limitations of that love, a love that amounted to small talk and the gradual shutting down of communications. On occasion he would try to talk to them, but within minutes he would be irritated into monosyllabic answers, followed by a brash 'Have to go', the 'I love you too' meaningless. The brain brought him back to Bosnia. If he could help there, the nagging guilt might dissipate. That self-sacrifice was the most egotistical of gestures convinced him that this pattern of thought was futile. What really grated was that his parents' happiness could be bought with flowers and money, when all he wanted was a proper chat. It must have seemed to his parents that he resented them for his life itself. His first words had expressed his right to remain silent.

He wasn't a dour child. He could have manic hyper sessions of fun which would tire him out for days, but the cruelty of a working-class family lifestyle shattered him. Home was like a cheap hotel, a place for pleasantries, rules, and Bed and half-eaten Breakfast. School brought about an escape, a chance to voice something; anything. His reports would rush out clichés: 'playing to the gallery', 'could apply himself more', 'finds it hard to concentrate', 'sets fire to other pupils'. That sort of thing. The walk home gave him a chance to mingle desperately with the opposite sex, until the smiling good-byes quickly reverted to the grimaces of a bad telly night in, Red's presence driving him indoors quicker than he would have liked. The front door closed, the huge front door, daunting, leading into cold, tiny rooms, a poxy dinner to be reheated, picked at and binned. Oh blessed Sunday, and the roast, a beautiful meal. Monday, curry with the remains of the meat. It was always on Monday nights that he wished his parents were of Indian descent. Tuesday – spuds, chop and carrots. Wednesday – coddle, a Dublin speciality which not surprisingly has never travelled outside the fair city. Thursday – casserole with an over-abundance of carrots again. 'Mum,' he'd say, 'I hate carrots.' 'If it's good enough . . .' blah blah. Friday – egg and chips, because they were good Catholics with spotty faces. Saturday – shepherd's pie after hoovering all day. *Fuck it, Arsenal drew again. At least Brady scored* . . . roll on Sunday. School lunch every day consisted of cheese. It was understandable why to this day John wasn't one for food. The roast was all he missed and it said a lot about his principles that he had been vegetarian for over ten years.

Michelle was standing by the answering machine when he got home. She seemed excited.

'Red's rung twice,' she told him.

'Who the fuck is Red?' he said, still refusing to acknowledge the voice from his past.

'I have a horrible feeling it's Alan Bulger.'

'Who?'

'You know, Redser. . . What does he want?'

'Why don't you play the message back?'

An over-confident Irish voice spoke to them, little Americanisms pushing through, the speech taken down a gear from its natural Dublin origins.

'John, Johnnie Palmer, you mad bastard, when you gonna ring me back? Listen, com'ere, let's hook up for a drink. I'm home for the next . . .' *small talk, small talk, small talk.*

The number he gave was in Treetown. John obliterated the message and grabbed the note he had made with the number on it, crunched it into a ball and threw it in the wastepaper basket. He missed and had to go over, pick it up and place it in the basket. Michelle stopped herself from quizzing him on his reaction because she didn't know what to think herself. It was such a long time ago; almost forgotten, but never quite erased. She felt a little jittery. John, knowing she was a worrier, appeased her.

'We'll just ignore it,' he said.

He took her hand and led her out of the door. The car journey was silent, as she knew it would be. Radiohead's *Pablo Honey* blared from the state-of-the-art speakers. It was pointless asking him to turn it down because he always played the music loud when he wanted to think. The music balanced out his more overbearing ruminations. Her own thoughts went ascattering, made even more chaotic by John's annoying tendency to shout along with the lyrics.

'I want you to notice when I'm not around, you're so special, so fucking special, but I'm a creep, I wish I was special.'

He dropped her at the clinic. She was early. She was always early if they drove in with Radiohead. Once she was out of sight Monty jumped on to John's lap, licked his face and stuck his head out of the window. It always amused the drivers going in the other direction, to see the dog acting as a permanent right-hand indicator.

John arrived at his premises, a shop and warehouse complex which dealt in the kitschy end of the antiques market for the more discerning punter who harped back to the swinging times. He also supplied the television and movie industry in a props capacity. He employed two craftsmen to restore and modify, while he did the searching and oversaw the whole shebang. His hobby had become a very lucrative business: he was well liked within the trade, and because of its off-beat nature, various acquaintances looked out for bits and bobs for him. The beautifully determined Helen worked in the shop itself. She had one of those cloudy, clear, sculptured faces with dark brown eyes which bubbled out of her face beneath her schoolboy haircut. The look didn't so much say 'fuck me' as 'buy stuff from me'. Now she was indispensable, because nearly every customer fell in love with her. Oh, did I mention she had a French accent?

I should introduce myself. I promise I won't intrude.

My name is Dominic, which you don't have to remember, and I had the misfortune to hear this tale. I am, shall we say, an acquaintance of John's. How can I tell the full story? Surely it would be one-sided. Please allow for a little artistic licence, but I can assure you John didn't want to paint a pretty picture of himself. He kept a diary to which he allowed me access, the one stipulation being that I'm only permitted to write this book in the event that his life is over. Of course he could have made the whole story up, and to cover ourselves you will have noticed it states at the start of this book that all characters are fictional and any similarities to real persons are purely coincidental.

I will fill you in on the minimum of detail about myself. I met John in London at his invitation after he had written to me in praise of a collection of short stories I had published under my own press a few years earlier. This collection was nothing too fancy; the type you see goaties trying to sell in Soho pubs. As you can imagine I was flattered by John's letter. He liked what he described as my attention to tragedy; the tiny tragedies that make up our everyday existence. On first sight I didn't like him and cast him aside. A few months elapsed before a package containing his diaries arrived in the post. I was intrigued, the more so when this was followed by a surprise visit. We got drunk and he started to tell me his story. He frightened me. Do you know that feeling when you're in the company of someone you suspect can be extremely dangerous? I had used imagination to write my fiction and here was a man engrossed in grotesque fact. And yet, as he explained his pain, his actions seemed logical. As the tale unfolded I wanted to get up and change my address there and then, but the bastard dragged me in.

He was aware of the effect he was having and of the risk he was taking in telling me. He had trusted me, something he hadn't done with many people, and he'd given me an out clause by refusing to finish the tale until lunch the following day. There isn't much point in heightening the tension further; as you will have gathered by now, I decided to write the book. My reasons were selfish ones: I wanted to get to the core of the whole grisly affair and in some small way I felt responsible for what he had done. To be fair, I didn't write it. My role was more in an editorial capacity, and much of what lies before you is lifted directly from his diaries. I have spoken at length with Red and with Michelle and have tried to fuse the two sides into one where they appeared to contradict each other. If you will allow me to wish John a less troubled afterlife, I hope he has found peace wherever he is. Now, where were we?

Michelle had polished off the near-tea liquid from the plastic beaker, instantly regretting that she'd accepted it. Her tongue and the roof of her mouth suffered third degree burns, the sour taste lingering, the gritty ingredients remaining in layers on her teeth to annoy her in quiet moments.

The doctor approached, file in hand, handsome bar too many early mornings and midnight crises; hair longer than most, his nod to the anti-establishment. He looked slightly older than fact, the result of giving his home number out to too many patients. Michelle had been in his care for six years, and their relationship had taken on the comfort enjoyed by old friends.

Now that she was down to one weekly visit he felt they had made progress. Michelle had been in and out of therapy since she was fourteen. Finally, her parents had seen it as the only option since a cloud had settled on her which refused to leave. It was never a manic depression. It was a state that had no will, the body moving like a dodgem car, steadily crashing into situations, the mind scarred but unlearning. The psychiatrist had been baffled. He was reluctant to prescribe tranquillizers or anti-depressants, since her body seemed to produce its own. One case-study described her as a completely emotionless person. John had often found her sitting in a room crying without being aware of it. She sat down comfortable in every position and eased her way into the ins and outs of her week. John had enrolled her on many courses to occupy her mind. She'd become proficient at woodwork, textile weaving and origami. Occupying her mind was a part-time job for all those around her. She had recently started learning how to drive, John at last acknowledging the fact that he didn't think she would speed off into the sunset or whatever time of day she drove at.

Dr Smiles ('please call me Tim') had filed more facts about her than she could ever remember but there was still no way of getting through. It was as if she had lobotomised herself. She spoke of Red, and how it would affect John, the crassness of the past creeping back in. They'd been over her formative years many times before. She remembered every instance, yet these memories puzzled Tim. Normally a key event would springboard a cacotopia of recollection where it was possible to fuzzily pinpoint the beginnings of a problem, but not with Michelle. He even went for the other attack of disassembling the past, making events more unfocused; had written a paper – *Harping Back in Denial* – discussing the over-use of childhood trauma in favour of pre-birth memory. In their dream-theory sessions she had an annoying capacity for detailed memory. Here he had struck on the fact that she was obsessive, but only for things and persons within touching distance. This was coupled with the improbable situation that she was living in her subconscious, and was only brought alive by others. It was as if she only lived for her own problems.

'Do you mind if I tape this?' he asked her, not waiting for an answer. 'Tell me about Red.'

'Red was one of the boys in our neighbourhood. He was different to the others. His family had always lived in Treetown. This was before it was even a village, before the council built the various different estates leaving only grassy verges for childhood to take place on. We all descended from these houses and assembled on the field where our parents could see us but dared not go. Being a new town we were the oldest and therefore in charge of this field. There were about fifty of us in all. Of course myself and my sister played with the other girls, until the boys built up enough courage and loin spillage to speak to us.'

'Loin spillage?'

'Yeah, I made it up. I like words, especially makey-up words.'

'But have you thought of this expression before?'

'No . . . they just sometimes come into my head. Anyway, Redser hooked up with a little gang; big little men. They were the toughest in the neighbourhood. Together, I mean. Individually they were all pussy cats. They used to throw shapes and frighten the other kids as they walked around in Doc Martens, tight drainpipe jeans and those plastic leather jackets.'

'Was John in this gang?'

Michelle let out a giggle.

'No . . . sometimes he was on the fringes, but only because of his age. He didn't get on with them. He wouldn't fight, and whenever there was a trouble-free night they would pick on the weakest member of their own gang. Inevitably John would get it if he was around.'

'Why do you think he hung out with them?'

'I suppose because he already had the uniform.' She laughed again. 'Maybe because there was nobody else to hang out with. Ah, you know John, he was an introvert with a loud hailer.'

'And did you know all this then?'

'God no . . . such things wouldn't enter my head, I was too busy having a good time.'

'Would you say they were happy times?' he asked her.

'No . . .' she replied.

'What troubled you back then?'

'Nothing . . . except the normal growing-up pains.'

'So where does Red fit in?'

'Redser was in the gang. He wasn't tough though, he just went along. He was a bit of a show-off. Very loud. He made the others laugh. His dad died when he was young, so he was vulnerable, and seen as an oddity. He used to do impressions for us . . . all the girls liked him.'

'You obviously liked him.'

'I'm not sure. He lost his virginity to me. He said he'd done it before, but he hadn't.'

'What age were you then?'

'Fourteen.'

'And him?'

'Fifteen . . . I think.'

'That was very young, don't you think?' he suggested.

'Well, there wasn't much else to do in the neighbourhood. I'd still be a virgin today if there'd been a community centre.'

'Did you love Red?'

'No . . . it was just practice, wasn't it? It was all very innocent.'

'Did you sleep with all the gang?'

'Most. You make it sound horrible. I used to go out with them, you know what it's like, you end up going out with practically everyone in the area your own age after a while.'

'But they were using you.'

'I think it works both ways.'

'And did your sister sleep with them?'

'No . . . she wanted nothing to do with them.'

'But didn't they lose respect for you?'

'Oh, come on. They never had respect for me in the first place.'

'Didn't you lose respect for yourself?'

'I'm not that hung up on sex. It's just a physical manoeuvre.'

'See,' said Tim, 'this is what I don't understand. You're articulate and intelligent . . . you seem to have a steady grasp of reality, but you seem to let others take control of every situation.'

'I don't know why,' she answered.

'Did they force you to have sex?'

'No . . . that's called rape. As I said, it was all very innocent. We used to camp out in various back gardens. I'd been going out with Redser for two months. We'd kissed a few times and he'd tried to touch my breasts, which was a thankless task as you can see. We had some vodka – he had quite a lot – I remember he was petrified. He retained his cockiness but it was just show, he kept his clothes on until the very last minute and it took him five minutes to undo my bra. Then he kind of fell on top of me and started shoving his mickey in the general direction. I could have told him he was inside there and then and he would have believed me. He came all over my leg and we had to wait another four hours before he could budge again. It was laughable . . . but of course I wouldn't laugh at him. I kept on making affirmative noises about the size of his mickey; you know how insecure men are about such things. Later on I sucked him off. He couldn't believe it. I could hear his heart beat from down there. As soon as he'd come he was itching to leave. God love him, he stayed ten minutes then made up some feeble excuse. I remember as he left the only thing that concerned him was that I wouldn't tell anybody he was circumcised.'

'Do you enjoy sex, Michelle?'

'I enjoy the effect it has on others.'

'Do you miss it?'

'Not really.'

'Maybe we should leave it there for today.'

He saw her out and began to write up his report, omitting the fact that he had a raging hard-on.

John sat at his desk, which was hidden upstairs from the warehouse. The CD player had started to skip on the Tricky album, and it took him a minute before he realised this. He took the CD out, wiped it against his shirt and placed it back in. He started to clear his desk, and absentmindedly poured himself a glass of wine. He never drank excessively, just continually. The mornings didn't bring about a hangover; more a groggy state that left him with a 'can't be arsed' attitude, every action achieved through memory rather than concentration. His morning egg could end up hard, soft, runny; his shave would leave little isolated tufts.

His life had become too regimented. After walking the dog he would drink a decaff coffee which would allow his bowels their exercise. On the toilet he would read supplements of the previous Sunday's newspapers. This was an important ritual since he liked to know what was happening around the globe. It troubled him that he wasn't seeing any of the action. He just let it pass him by, probably a throwback to being brought up in a one-mule town. To the rest of the village he was Christopher Columbus, with his various buying trips abroad, but to him there was nothing glamorous about skirting through warehouses in Neasden.

He popped a mint into his mouth and gazed at a picture of Helen on holiday with her friends. The usual grinning-inanely 'we're all mates' photo. There was always the one leaning in too much, not trusting the photographer, leaving a gap on one side. Did the photographer feel he was the outsider, his presence not recorded? Maybe he just didn't photograph well and always insisted on being the taker. Or was it simply that it was his camera and he was the type who couldn't relax unless he was continually recording the fun? Regardless, John wanted to be in the photo, to be somebody else, to be elsewhere, to have different memories, different ways of thinking. He popped another mint in. He was a cruncher rather than a sucker. As he swallowed the sugar, syrup, vegetable oil, modified starch, colours, E17 and glazing agent and carnauba wax, he noticed the sell-by date was two months past.

Tricky started to skip again. He was in a bad mood. The phone rang. He left the answerphone on. It was Red. He sounded different to how John remembered him. There was still a trace of the old voice which he despised, but maybe he had changed. *It must be ten years.* John resented the fact that Red could still make him feel anxious. He poured himself another excusable glass of wine. Red signed off, 'Hope to hear from you soon, bud.'

'Bud . . .' John repeated out loud to himself. 'What's his fucking game?'

Red hated aeroplanes. He insisted on an aisle seat to give the pretence of not flying. It had always puzzled him how slow they appeared when watching them in the sky. He chatted aimlessly with the passenger to his left, an American businessman, nearing fifty, coming home to Ireland for the first time. The calamity of the IRA having eased with their latest ceasefire had him making up stories of Republican adventures, tales that others had told him in Boston bars.

Red was a likeable man. His freckled face opened up his features, the more so now that his hair had begun to recede. He jittered along, hands, face and legs exaggerating every tale. Talking to him for long periods, you wanted to hold him down. He cajoled the air hostess, uncertain of whether she was being professionally agreeable or whether she might fancy him. He was forever bursting with excitement: he couldn't wait to land on home soil, to let every one in Treetown know that he was back in a big way.

Michelle looked out of the window, willing John home. The stars, so many in the sky, were like an acned face. She got back into bed, but she could never rest when John stayed out late. He did this on occasion, returning home with the sun. No questions were ever asked. He always took the next day off and would often ask her for one of her tranquillizers. She had to stay out of his way because he wasn't able to function. If it rained he wouldn't leave his bed, and she would give him light, healthy snacks every couple of hours. She never knew what he was up to, but she liked nursing him back to stability.

She heard the door open. The dog, confused, went to his bowl. John peered in at Michelle. He looked a state and was sporting a bruised eye.

'What happened?' she asked him.

'I met up with Jimmy.'

He was out of breath. She moved to get up.

'No, stay in bed. I'm fine . . . sorry.'

He went into his own room where he lay on the bed, exhausted but panicky, and started to cry. The never-again resolve lessened his pain but he knew full well it was only a matter of time before he went too far.

Jimmy had never set foot in the house. He was someone John would bump into, be intrigued by and then try to match. He had a capacity for hedonism, but he somehow never paid the price. Whenever John met him he would get so excited that he would forget himself. Jimmy was brilliant company but cared nothing for anyone else's feelings. He always had women, drugs and money with him. And in his company John became equally reckless, but he was a decent guy underneath it all and he suffered as a result. The following day he'd immerse himself in self-hate.

He started to shiver, his body's way of showing disgust, and he knew he would wake with his T-shirt soaked through. He ached down to his bones, and he watched stationary objects move while floaters like amoebas darted around his vision. With his eyes closed, his brain gave him scenarios to fuck him up. Eyes open, he thought of those he hurt. Michelle, he had let her down again. His parents, rising for another day of manual living, pure as the driven snow, all baying for his blood. Suicide was contemplated, every positive thought was quashed. He knew it would pass. He looked at the telephone: he wanted somebody, anybody, to phone and offer forgiveness. If only a tardis-type confession box could appear in his bedroom and for the sake of ten Hail Marys he could start again. But that was no use. He had turned his back on the Church in his teens, impishly at the time; but his devilment had gathered over the years. All that was left of his Catholic upbringing was his deep hatred of Glasgow Rangers FC which went even beyond his passionate love of Celtic.

The rain started to pound on the window, the natural light fading. His bruised face began to throb. This was better; physical pain was a piece of piss. Scabs were always picked to the extent that they would eventually leave little scars. He remembered the heroin experience with Jimmy the night before. He'd been on a downer over the phone calls from Jodie and from Red. He and Jimmy had lost themselves in a squalid flat hidden behind the posh arcade of Grafton Street's shopping delights. John wouldn't inject; not for health reasons but because he hated the sight of blood. He chased the dragon, silver foil and lighter and the golden brown burning. It smelt like baking powder as he inhaled, and he wanted to go home and bake a cake with Michelle.

He was nervous about the heroin and tried to drown his doubts with white wine which their host kept in a cupboard, a screw-off cap and two chipped cups. Within half an hour everyone's eyes were moving like hippopotamuses. Big beautiful eyes filled the room. The longest eyelashes. It was like the defining moment of a good movie where they slow-motion the action so you can really appreciate the scene. He couldn't decide if he was Butch, Sundance or one of the Mexican lackies.

The mental torment which had made him reach for the sachet of oblivion was slowly drifting away, bringing about a smile. All his pain moved into one corner of the room, a tiny pinprick of pain in a faraway place, becoming smaller and smaller until he had to squint to even see it. This was sensational, liminal bliss. He kept hugging Jimmy, thanking him. He thought they should give heroin free to anyone suffering from depression. How dare they keep this from anyone? The murky drug dealers offered the way out. Why did the suits refuse to let people have it? Jimmy was fucking the woman. She looked beautiful. He beckoned John over. No, he was happy to watch. Jimmy was taking her from behind, both slow-grunting, Jimmy savouring her ass, his hands gently rubbing the buttocks. Buttocks wasn't the right word. It was too vulgar. John tried to think of another word but there wasn't one to describe the touching. Maybe handgliding over hills. The ugly floral wallpaper became a fantastic skyline. John started to watch her breasts move with the action; not in a sexual way; his penis was enjoying the buzz too much. The breasts moved like a new piece of technology, the cog in the machine keeping the earth revolving. He looked at her face and was taken aback by her pained expression. He compounded the thought that she enjoyed pain or was simply picking scabs to avoid mental torment. He realised his own pain was still that tiny dot in the corner of the room and it disturbed him that it hadn't disappeared completely. It started to move nearer to him, the room becoming smaller. He noticed the naked light bulb, its feeble wattage, a yellowy despair, leaving coloured blotches before his eyes. Oh fuck, he was coming down and he needed to get out of that flat pronto. He jumped up. 'Get a fucking light shade,' he hollered as he left.

He got into his car. Monty, dozing in the back, was happy to see him. He yawned and moved to John's lap. John was having a major bummer. He'd just decided to go home and ride it out when Jimmy leapt into the car, chastising him, 'What's your problem?'

Jimmy gave him a line of coke and they hit a club on Leeson Street. This perked John up and soon he was dancing with his peers, downing more cheap wine at expensive prices through gritted teeth. Continually bumping against him was a crowd of businessmen in their mid thirties. They were very loud, out-on-the-towners with their bits of spare. Jimmy had disappeared. John listened to the balding bunch talking about their shags, their dodgy deals and their scant regard for the value of money. He couldn't help himself. He pushed amongst them. They stared at him.

'Can I help you, pal?' one asked him.

'I don't think so.'

'Would you mind fucking off?'

'I don't think so.'

They were all a little uncomfortable.

'What do you want?'

'What do I want?' He cleared his throat. 'Well, I was listening to all the shit you were spouting and I couldn't believe it, you know, so to give you a fair chance I decided to get a little nearer, and if you continue in the same manner I am going to ask you to leave this establishment, so let's see how it goes. Arseholes.'

He tried to stare them in the eye but his gaze was focused somewhere around the nose and as he expected he was punched hard in the face. He smiled as they left the building. There was no sign of Jimmy, so he went home.

He awoke at three the following afternoon. Monty lay beside him, also feeling shit. He reached for a cigarette, his head irritated by the movement. His throat was beyond dry and water would be no use. His tonsils had crept up into his mouth in a fit of coughing and he was taken aback to find he was growing accustomed to these sensations. He switched on the television, said hello to his two new friends at the newsdesk and flicked through the thirty-odd cable stations, wondering who they were actually catering for. Maybe by channel-hopping continually he would get the desired effect. Was there a rule in broadcasting that daytime television had to be shit? This wasn't his decrepit mind speaking. Even if he was in a wholesome state he couldn't stomach daytime programming. He turned the set off and couldn't evoke the energy to get up. His body wasn't working yet. He knew he would have to masturbate to kick start his organs. He stumbled towards the en-suite bathroom where he grabbed some tissues and baby oil. Back in bed he summoned his erotica memory before deciding who he was going to fuck: famous person or passer-by. He plumped for famous. It disturbed him that he couldn't get fat Vanessa from daytime television out of his mind. *O fuck me fat Vanessa,* even though it would be like putting a sausage up O'Connell Street. He thought of the Spice Girls but it required too much effort and every time they sang one of their poxy songs his erection would flop. He needed dirty sex, and he knew he was losing the battle when Vanessa turned up in his Spice Girls fantasy, arriving with 'wait for me, loves' while he was drinking champagne with the naked popsters in a jacuzzi. He gave in to his hollow mind and fucked Vanessa up the arse – another little memory which would have to be stored and padlocked and shunted into one of his mind's darker corners, never to see the light of day again. He had already erased the fact that he slapped her a few times during the act.

CHAPTER 2

The airport arrivals lounge was its habitual bustle of palpitating hearts, the detainees passing the delayed time drinking copious amounts of coffee, necks creaking from the constant surveillance of the monitors; the atmosphere punctured by the clear-speaking announcer; the workers oblivious to the heightened emotions of the travellers and their companions. The odd plane spotter sat at vantage points admiring the technological beauty of the flying machines. The arrivees, shattered from the air-conditioned trip, the small talk, the cramped space and condensed food, landed on the black, black tar of home. Many rushed to the terminal to chain-smoke, making up for lost time. Red emerged from the crowd mastering his trolley of luggage while at the same time sticking the two new telephone numbers he had acquired into his wallet. His stern red-faced green-jumpered brother was waiting for him.

'What kept you?'

'Well, we arrived ages ago, but you know I haven't seen Dublin for so long I asked the pilot to circle around a couple of hundred times. He was very obliging . . . And how are you?'

'I see you're the same smart-arse you always were.'

His brother's battered Datsun made most of the noise on the journey home. Peter never had much to say and Red was busy relaxing into all his memories brought on by the size of the streets, the colour of the buses and the Dublin accent. They had never got on. Peter resented Red's travelling – no, he resented his very existence. Even though they both had red hair it was Alan who was given the nickname. With their father's premature death, Peter had quickly had to become the man of the house, giving up an electrician's apprenticeship for a better-paid, menial supermarket job. Of course their mother doted on Red, spoilt him rotten, and took his brother for granted.

Their mother had gradually become iller and rather than accepting her fate she was bitter towards it. The side effects of various tablets had left her with a petty overview. Emotional blackmail was the only way she knew how to get close to others. Others being her two sons. Every soap opera the television could offer made up the rest of her world.

The brothers were comfortable with the silence. Red was happy to listen to the radio, to hear the familiar voices discussing familiar topics. The news was full of the bizarre cheek of one of Dublin's biggest underworld gangsters, nicknamed 'The Duck'. It was coming to light that he'd robbed three banks in the same street this morning in Rathmines, and to take the piss out of the police he had deposited the takings of each theft in the next bank before robbing them back again. The only statement he would offer was 'I don't bank with those thiefing bastards. The building societies give a better rate of interest.'

This made Red, like most of the population, chuckle out loud, punctuating his laughter with shouts of 'fair play'. Peter turned it off.

'I don't think it's funny. He's just another bollox who thinks he can get away with the easy option. What about the people who work hard for their money?'

Red sighed.

'You know she's dying,' Peter said.

'There's no need to exaggerate . . . she's just going through a bad patch.'

'Wait until you see her. She's old beyond her years.'

'You're such a fucking wanker, Peter.'

'I just thought you should be prepared. And for her sake let's keep our differences to ourselves.'

'These differences you talk about, I don't have a problem with you. You're not my older brother any more, so don't pull that shit with me . . . Look . . . you're my brother and I love you. Why can't you just accept that?'

'Let's just keep it under wraps, okay?'

'Ah, whatever.'

Red knew they were approaching Treetown as the

value of houses decreased by the mile and pebble-dashed facades came into view. He couldn't contain his snigger when he saw that the town sign had been graffiti-ed with the letters 'tree' markered out and replaced with 'under a rock'.

They pulled up at the kerb, and Red was bewildered that his mother hadn't come to greet him. He opened the front door, surprised that his key still fitted. Peter started unloading the car, resigned to his role as chauffeur once again. As Red entered the sitting room the smell hit him; nothing he could pinpoint, but it was the smell he'd despised, the one that had probably driven him to emigrate. There was still no sign of his mother. The curtains were drawn and tiny pieces of sun squeezed into the room, throwing shadows on to the shabby furniture. He felt compelled to open the curtains but didn't think it was his place. Instead he switched a light on and his heart sank.

Everything was as he had left it, and this freaked him out. The mantelpiece's prize possession was the windmill house which turned when you wound it up. He had brought it back from Amsterdam after the school outing which had been his first trip overseas. When he had told his fiancée about his house he had reminisced about the windmill. He would have been terribly disappointed if it had not been there, but seeing it standing proudly gathering dust, it made him face his past. He wound it up and the windmill slowly did its circle as the three musical notes sheepishly accompanied it. The light only lit the middle of the room. He had to squint to reveal the corners. Peter shut the front door.

'Have you been up to see her yet?'

'Just getting my bearings . . . Oh, here, hand us that bag. I've got some presents.'

Rummaging through the contents he dug out two hundred Silk Cut and offered them to Peter.

'Gee thanks, a packet for every year you've been gone . . . If you'd read my last letter you'd have known I'm trying to give up.'

'Well sell them, then.' He showed him the beautiful silver necklace he'd got for their mother. 'What do you think?'

'It's quite a necklace.'

'Do you think she'll like it? She could wear it for those special occasions.'

'Yeah, like when she comes downstairs.'

'Look, are you trying to put a downer on things? You're so selfish.'

'Me? Alan, she's been bedridden for four months. Necklaces are the last thing on her mind, specially one that was grabbed in Duty Free. Maybe if you'd been here she wouldn't be in the state that she's in now.'

'Well, I'm here now, so shut up.'

Red made for the stairs. It got progressively darker the further up he travelled. His mother's door was closed and he gently pushed it, hoping to see that smile that lit up both their faces. She lay on the bed, mouth open, snoring loudly. He barely recognised her. He was rooted to the spot, his legs losing their power. His eyes filled up as he tried to remember her as she used to be. He wanted to wake her and hold her and tell her everything was going to be alright but he bolted for the door, regretting the fact that he had come home at all.

He hated himself for having such thoughts but he didn't feel part of this any more.

As twilight ushered the lunatics onto the street, Red wanted to join them. He felt alienated from his own culture. Instead, aghast, he did that typical Irish thing. He ran to the pub.

The Treehouse Inn was sought out by the seasoned drinker and was devoid of the underage moustachioes. It lay in a compact site, its own car park encompassing a betting shop: a fantasy island for those who could never afford a foreign holiday. Its lounge was large, with enough nooks and crannies to shout out individual conversations, its nod to tradition being the bar area where contemplative old drinkers welled up over hazy golden eras. Red made his way to the lounge, nervous of familiar faces he might bump into, wishing there was a little hut he could go to first where you could get tanked up before facing the social onslaught. He took a deep breath and walked like a cowboy into the saloon. He half expected everyone to go quiet but was relieved to find televisions blaring out Dolby surround-sound football from all corners. He hung his head and instinctively pushed towards the counter, and then he spotted an old friend, Patrick O'Neill, with a group of noisy lads all shouting at the telly.

He grabbed his Smithwicks, cleared his throat, got his face into smiling position and prepared to become good old Red.

'Zebedee you old cunt, how are ya?'

Soon Patrick, after the initial shock of hearing his old nickname, had Red in bear hugs, head locks, leap frogs

– the two of them were a proper Chinese State Circus. The football became mere background and Red had the time of his life. Patrick agreed to meet up with him the next night and paint the town with Red.

Next morning saw the sheets of the single bed scattered around the room. Duvets hadn't reached Treetown yet and grown men had to roll up into the foetal position to get any comfort from their childhood beds. Red felt a numbness in his leg. The electric blanket was one little luxury he had missed. Even though it was mild late summer, the electric blanket always went on, purely for the joy of that initial contact with the sheets, the toasty sensation which the body soon grows accustomed to.

He contemplated yesterday's events. A slight hangover, jet lag and the continuing numbness in his leg curtailed any concentrated thought. The idea of facing his family had him gently going back to that secondary sleep where the subconscious bullies its way into the conscious, laying on those fucked-up banality tales with just enough truths for you to question their reality. He was at a bus stop with his brother: they had reverted to children. Bored of waiting for the bus, they played that game of pretending to wave at car drivers as if they knew them, only to change the wave to a brushing of the hair as they waved back. One driver stopped and a big hairy no-face-feature dream character got out and started dragging Red into his car. He pleaded with his brother to help him but the bus had come and Peter wanted to get on. All he would say was 'you know him, you know him, go with him.' Everybody on the bus was urging Red to go with the faceless man who had his huge hand around Red's upper arm. He woke to find his brother poking his arm with a cup of tea.

'Are you getting up?' Peter asked him.

'What time is it?' Peter looked at Red's watch on the dresser.

'According to your Omega here it's gone midday. . . Listen, Mum is getting up for lunch, so make an effort. This is a big deal for her.'

'Yeah,' said Red, 'okay.'

'. . . And open a window, it stinks in here.'

Red was perplexed that Peter reminded him of their Da. When his brother had left the room he reached for the tea, delighted that Peter had thought his watch authentic. He noticed that the numbness had gone further up his leg, and started to panic. *Oh shit, cancer of the leg, I'm going to have to get it amputated. No more sports, I'll be wheelchair bound, fuck – that's my life over.* He put his hand under the one remaining sheet that covered him, and as he reached down he jumped, the cat's sudden shifting culminating in palpitations for both of them. The cat fled, and Red had to laugh. He had forgotten all about Dana, the fat family cat, named after the singer because she ate all kinds of everything. She must have been sleeping on him all night. He tried to call her to him but she didn't want to know. She hadn't aged very gracefully either. What was it about this family? They'd obviously cleared the attic of paintings a very long time ago – Tir na n'Og it wasn't.

Red washed himself in the tiny bathroom where the Guaranteed Irish soap and toothpaste were put to use. He went back to the bedroom looking for a jumper. The sun shone outside but there was a chill sweeping around the house. He wondered if the house rule was still no heat on until dark. He could hear faint noises coming from the kitchen. He couldn't stomach food at the moment and the whiff of hamburger only made him nauseous.

'Honestly Mum, I think he'd prefer something lighter,' Peter was bargaining.

'Nonsense, they're always eating them in America. We'll all have one, he won't want any of our junk, he's used to better things. Don't burn them, Peter. Here, get that jar of gherkins out of the fridge . . . don't put them on mine.'

Red was deep-breathing as he tiptoed down the stairs. His scalp started to tighten and his hands were trembling. He opened the door. His mother had her back turned, and she was still in her dressing gown. Her hair was longer than he expected and had kept its natural blonde colour. Maybe last night was exaggerated, because she looked good from the back. He was starting to perk up. Peter spotted him and was about to blurt out when Red motioned for him to remain hushed. He sneaked over and grabbed her around the shoulders, pressing cheek to cheek.

'Did you miss me, Mum?'

'Ah, Alan.' Her voice was croaky.

She turned around, beaming. They were face to face. His expression held the smile but his eyes showed his shock. His beautiful mother, for whom he had undying love, was an old woman. He avoided her gaze. It was a sight that would remain with him forever: this frail creature whose posture was slipping, hunched there in a tatty old dressing gown and run-down house shoes, smiling with joy; her eyes caved in, jaw dropped, mouth crooked, the lines blurring her face; youthful hair falling to where her shoulders used to be, neck-veins and bones protruding, barely enough flesh to hold the head up at all. Yet the focal point of this horrifying image was the necklace he had given her, shining and sparkling and wanting to get off this hideous body.

Red's head swam. He had to sit down because there was a fair chance he was going to collapse. *Don't say it Peter, don't say it Peter.* He knew Peter was about to say it.

'Doesn't the necklace look great on her, Alan?'

'It really suits you, Mum, you look . . .' he couldn't muster the word beautiful '. . . great.'

'Ah, stop it you two. Come on, let's eat, and Alan can fill us in on what he's been up to . . . is burgers alright?'

'Great.'

His mother struggled with her cutlery and kept looking at him with immense pride, occasionally fingering the necklace, feeling like a princess. He knew he should draw happiness from the fact that she felt like this. He was also aware that at some later date, after her death, this scene would bring a teary joy to him; but for now he wasn't able to cope with this much reality. He wanted his mother back. If only someone was responsible for her state then he could go and seek revenge. He would kill the person who had done this to her. He felt bitter towards life's microscopic tragedies. His head was confused. No rationale could explain the depth of his depression; a deep hatred of life, self, mother, brother, burgers, small kitchens and God. He was crying.

'What's wrong, son?'

He hugged her, fell onto her lap, felt the skin and bone and kept repeating 'I love you Mam, everything's going to be alright. I'm back, anything you want I'll get you, everything is alright.'

She patted his head gently, like she used to when she was looking for lice.

'I love you too, son, everything's alright now. We're all feeling emotional, but I'm really tired. I'd better have a lie down.'

It was one of the moments that you can never be prepared for; the aftermath, the clumsiness of sniffling and having to get off his mother's lap while Peter looked on in embarrassed silence, broken as he handed Red his burger.

'I see you still can't handle your drink,' he said.

Dana at least was happy, knowing she had three burgers to look forward to, with a side order of gherkins.

Red walked out of the house and purposefully strode towards the local shopping complex which had been his teenage hangout. His mood lifted momentarily and he wondered if his name was still emblazoned on the shopping centre's roof. The complex came into view, a SuperValue market with an arcade of assorted shops which were forever changing. The only four permanent shops were the Italian chip shop, closed for repairs for a month after the last World Cup; a newsagents, where he'd mastered the art of pilfering; the chemist, with its window display of the latest development in Prozac and of course the ever expanding video shop which now took up the space of three units. The other shops which were *en vogue* for the time being were a furniture store, a boutique, a menswear shop, a unisex hairdressers and a coffee shop. The local paper was currently trying to guess what the bankrupt electrical shop was going to become. The 'Everything for Under a Pound' store was a favourite.

A gang of fourteen-year-olds were hanging out of an abandoned shopping trolley listlessly shouting away their energies, spinning each other around before it was time to go home to their vows of silence. Red wondered which one was playing his role. He saw the boutique with a 'final reductions' sign Blu-tacked to its door. As he entered the shop he had to concentrate on the push or pull dilemma. Having overcome this obstacle he didn't browse but went straight to the assistant behind the counter and asked for the most expensive dressing gown in stock.

'Any particular pattern?' she asked.

'I'm sorry, I'm not very good at this shopping lark. I'm just looking for a bit of quality. It's for my mother.'

She moved towards a rail.

'This one's a good seller, eighty percent cotton.'

'Haven't you got anything one hundred percent cotton?'

'There's not much call for it around here.'

'Well, whatever's the best then.'

'You haven't changed much, have you, Redser?' she said.

He was taken aback and looked at her more carefully,

moving his head back slightly whilst squinting his face up. A big smile erupted.

'It couldn't be . . . Gillian?'

She nodded.

'Jesus, last time I saw you, you were . . . God . . . you were fourteen.'

'I'm not immune to that ageing process yet, you know,' she laughed.

They were soon sitting in the coffee shop next to the stench of the deep-fat fryer, one of the management's subliminal efforts to ensure that nobody stayed too long. Gillian was twenty-four, married with three kids, still living in Treetown.

'Are you not married yourself?' she asked him.

'Nearly. I've got one of those "fiancées". We're going to get married next year, she's coming over in a few months.'

'An American?'

'Irish descent.'

'I suppose none of us were up to your standards?'

'You said it, wha'.' They laughed.

'I always thought you'd end up with my sister.'

'Michelle? God, how is she?'

'You don't know?'

'How would I?'

'She got married to that John Palmer.'

'John Palmer . . . you're joking. John and Michelle. . . there's an unlikely couple. Any kids?'

'No, they only married a couple of years ago. She went to London for a while. We don't see very much of each other – you know Michelle, always keeps herself to herself – but they're doing very well. He's got a big antiques business. They live in a huge house out in Blessington.'

'John and Michelle, eh?'

'If you ask me, they're well suited. Neither of them is the full shilling.'

Red sat on the hard-backed chair beside his mother's bed waiting for her to wake up. Night was creeping into the room and he was dozing off, which was the nearest he ever got to meditation. Once he had visited a Buddhist monk in Boston, not to reach any spiritual highland, but because they gave out free food. He'd arrived in Boston with little more than his charming forward nature and the priceless addresses of some distant second cousin and a maiden aunt. A couple of the Treetown old-boys had settled there a few years before and they came in handy for the social side of things. He thought again of the monk. He and Mark, his 'lifelong-bestest-new-friend-in-the-world' had gone along to fill their bellies and mock. Red had never shaken off his Catholic upbringing and had a healthy disrespect for others' beliefs. As far as he was concerned, the Buddhists believed in reincarnation ('handy at plane crashes') and spoke in riddles, which they deemed wisdom. He and Mark had joked on the street about asking where the meat was, but the cheerless mood that greeted them stifled the laughter. He had giggled at his granny's funeral while holding the casket, and the more the daggered stares entrapped him, the harder he found it to suppress the uncontrolled noises. At the wake he had had to force himself to cry to let the gathered congregation know he too had feelings.

He had gone through the same emotions at the temple, which was essentially a semi-detached house in suburbia. The head Buddhist looked as if he was at the end of this particular life, propped up by his two disciples who sat adoringly one on either side of him. It was odd to be sitting in a semi-circle in the lotus position surrounded by religious artefacts with incense and candles burning brightly, all for a sandwich. The deal was that you meditated for an hour and then you ate. The local hobos were also wise to the food scam and knew it was always warmer there than the doss-house. One of them sat on the only chair available, nursing his hangover. Occasionally he would look at the others, never quite making it to the lotus position, hiccuping and apologising at regular intervals. The monk was tolerant of his guests and, like all the deeply religious, had condescending views on the uninitiated. After Red had complained that the food was rubbery, causing outrage, whenever he got a pain thereafter he suspected they'd made a voodoo doll in his likeness.

It made him feel worldly that he'd experienced other cultures than just the Treetown way of life. He loved Boston, but it never felt like home. He was ready to come back, but this time on his own terms. He wanted to start his own business, make big bucks and then OD on the simple pleasures of Dublin which he had pined for. He'd started to question whether Treetown was really the right location, but then his mind cracked open – if the kids are apathetic, surely he could give them some enthusiasm, lead by example, start up a sports shop, set up local teams, get some events happening . . . *Yeah, fuck it*. Watching all the miniature Reds roaming the area saddened him. I'll make a go of it, he thought, his eagerness spilling over; afford them opportunities, open their eyes.

His mum kept on sleeping. He looked hard at her when it dawned on him that she looked like an extra from *Star Trek*. He couldn't wait and shook her awake, filling the room with his excitement. He told her all his plans, heralding the news of his fiancée.

'Yes, Mum, you'll love her, her name's Mary Beth, it was love at first sight. It wasn't an easy courtship, but all is fair in love and war and now we're inseparable. She's coming over in three months, there's a couple of loose ends to be sorted, but once things start moving . . . and Mum, she can't wait to meet you and to tell you the truth I don't think it'll be long now before you're a grandmother.'

He was in top gear now.

'No, listen Mum, I want you to get better 'cos you're going to have your fair share of baby-sitting to do. Yeah, there's going to be big changes around here, you're going to be so proud, Mum, you really are.'

'I am,' was all she could muster. But hey, it was a start. Red handed her the new dressing gown and kissed her on the cheek.

On his way out she asked him to turn on the television which was an old black and white portable. He made a mental note to buy her a new one, a colour one with a remote control, maybe even a flat screen with surround-sound and Ceefax.

He was buzzing now and rang up directory enquiries, found out John's number and left a message. He was going to make a night of it with Patrick. He spruced himself up, dabbing flashy aftershave behind his ears. Some of the flaky skin came off but it didn't bother him. The house had a perfect rosy feel to it. He skipped into the bedroom, narrowly avoiding a puddle of Dana's vomit, and called for Peter, laughing, 'There's some gherkins need clearing up.' He put on his favourite jacket, a fake designer label; a tight black number which always made him feel like a Reservoir Dog. He looked into the mirror, shot his own reflection with his pretend gun and stated in a broad Bronx accent '. . . If you don't do what I tell you, I'm gonna get this fuckin' phone, I'm gonna ram it up your ass and I'm gonna call you on the fuckin' hour.'

The taxi dropped the likely lads off at St Stephen's Green. Red was amazed by the cosmopolitan air of his reinvigorated Dublin. Patrick pointed out new pubs and shops but he wasn't much in the way of a guide as he rarely left Treetown himself. Red watched the various blocks of people, the shattered, going-straight-home lot, the pitching-in-for-one-for-the-road crowd and the charged coming-in-to-town-for-the-night brigade, all manoeuvring around one another. It dawned on him how fast Dublin people walked. For a city that was world-renowned for its laid-back attitude, they sure were in a hurry to get there.

The plan for the night was a couple of swift pints, a meal, a few more pints and then a club that sold pints. They ended up on South William Street. The big purple sign of an Indian restaurant beckoned, but priorities in order, the red exterior of Peter's Pub was the first port of call. Inside, it was a simple affair, a small L-shaped room curved by the bar itself, a few lonesome drinkers spread around the outer benches, newspapers on the tables, waiting for the pub to get busy. That there were two barmen on duty meant this was inevitable. Patrick ordered some drinks and the older barman served him with a friendly 'hello' and a nod and a wink to affirm the quality of the beer. Red circled his surroundings, eyeballing where they would sit. Patrick forced him to have a Guinness, even though he hated the stuff. 'A pint of plain, a pint of plain is your only man,' was Patrick's mantra for the night. The hummable mutterings very quickly gave way to uproarious devilment. It was as if half the population of Dublin had followed them into the pub, smoke weaving in and out of any remaining spaces as all the participants began talking shite.

Red squeezed past the rocking counter standers and made his way down a darkened stair to the scuzziest of toilets. He struggled his way back to Patrick, doing the *excuse me, sorry, smile* walk. Patrick was reflecting on Manchester United's chances for the championship with another don't-pause-for-breath conversationalist. It was a straightforward encounter as they kept agreeing with each other. *He needs to spend; can't rely on the youngsters; Cantona looks uninterested; Cole was a waste of money; Giggsie's a bit of a playboy, and thick with it; Schmeichel's nose is getting redder; Keane's arse is getting bigger;* ending on the song 'By Far the Greatest Team the World Has Ever Seen'.

They enjoyed the chat but were disappointed that there wasn't a smidgin of new information to be gleaned. Patrick tilted his shoulder towards Red by way of letting the stranger know the talk was over. A quick 'see you later' sufficed. The bustle of the crowd kept edging the two of them further into a corner. After four pints of Guinness neither of them felt like eating. Red was getting drunk and was having problems keeping up with Patrick's half-pint sups. Red was a good drunk, loud but friendly, and he was doing most of the talking. He would start off with a question and then take off into a story while Patrick often interrupted by taking the piss out of the little American phrases that popped out willy-nilly. It dawned on Red that they were having the same conversation they'd had the night before, more or less word-for-word. He thought that Patrick must be one of those repetitive drunks, but he drew a blank whenever he tried to steer him on to other topics.

Soon there were occasional silences as they started looking at the women in the pub. Leering followed, then their penises wanted a quick stretch. Their chat consisted of size of tits and ass and various shared experiences. Patrick, being long-term unemployed, stopped buying drinks. Red, wise to this, started getting them all in, always ordering when Patrick had a half a pint left to avoid embarrassment. They were suddenly both very drunk: Red, louder and unbalanced; Patrick, silent and steady, his eyes intensified. Red felt uneasy and tried to lighten the tone.

'Michelle and John, eh? Who would have thought? He's done very well for himself, own business, big house. Do you ever see him?'

'Stay well away from that mess,' warned Patrick. 'He's fucking bad news.'

'Yeah? What do you mean?'

'He's a fucking nutcase.'

'Why, what happened?'

'He just gives me the creeps. I want nothing to do with him, and I'd advise you to do the same. Look at yer one over there, fucking gorgeous or what? Her tits defy gravity.'

Red turned around too quickly, bumping into a guy walking past, lost his balance and spilt the guy's pint.

'Sorry, bud, let me get you another,' he offered.

'Bud?' the bumpee laughed. 'Where do you think you are? New York?'

He called over to his mates who were standing nearby.

'Me bud knocked me pint!'

They cackled with glee. It was obvious that they were spliffed up, which relieved Red, since he knew he was in no danger.

He insisted, 'Can I get you another?'

'No, no, buddy, let me get you one and extend the warm hand of Ireland to our well-travelled friend, and also . . .' he began to play to the gallery '. . . by way of thanking you for those many years of enjoyment you have given me with your quality television. *Little House on the Prairie, Highway to Heaven* and all those other programmes which starred the fellow who died of cancer.'

The group was in fits of laughter now, as was Red. When he said, 'I'm actually Irish,' the laughter became uncontrolled, infectious. The bumpee was doubled up holding his chest, his spare hand blindly looking for some sort of a handle, when a size ten Doc Marten boot landed in his face. The atmosphere twisted 360 degrees as Patrick was savagely kicking at the floored man who was screaming for help. Blood splattered indiscriminately. Red, feeling sick to the stomach, was too shocked to do anything. It was probably only thirty seconds before the older barman grabbed Patrick in a headlock and dragged him out onto the street.

Red stayed with the victim, concerned for his welfare, but the barman asked him to leave.

Shaking, he said, 'Sure.' He knew he was going to throw up. Crashing into walls and skipping steps he made it down the stairs, and poured eight pints of Guinness into the toilet. His heart was pounding, his eyes watering. His body remembered the last vicious mêlée he had encountered, the one where he had been the aggressor, the one he was desperately trying to forget. After five minutes, he resembled a human being again, and he had to leave because the smell of piss was so overpowering that he felt it could comatose him.

After a nightmare journey home, desperate for his electric blanket, he was confronted on the doorstep by his brother's pained expression. Peter slowly removed the cigarette from his mouth and spoke.

'Mum's taken a turn for the worse.'

CHAPTER 3

'B*rassneck, I've just decided I don't trust you any more . . .'*

John had the volume in his car cranked up to distortion levels, windows closed, air-conditioning on, fag in mouth and dog on lap. Monty was used to the noise but a little pissed off about the window. He kept on rubbing his nose against it, leaving bits of saliva and dog-breath on the pane. John looked at him.

'Monty, I know the sun is shining but we have to leave the windows shut. The other villagers haven't got our appreciation of The Wedding Present's more progressive side.'

They were parked by the main bus stop, waiting for Michelle to disembark from the 65B. Monty was sniffing at the picnic basket on the passenger seat. This was his Rubik's cube and he wouldn't rest until it was solved. John was ecstatically happy. A lovely afternoon lay ahead – a picnic by the lake on one of the last summery days of winter with his favourite woman, dog and music. His highs came from those sudden moments when you look at your life from an outsider's point of view, like watching a play and being moved by a scene and loving all the characters involved. He didn't like the sun, but he loved daylight. A dream would be to fly across the different time zones so that it would be continual day. He knew from experience not to analyse his happiness but to freewheel with what Spalding Gray had called the perfect moment. He wanted to hug the world, but settled for Monty. The dog interpreted this as his master wanting his face licked, which he did, whilst continuing to take sneaky looks at the basket situation. Michelle's bus moved into view. John got out and led Michelle by the hand as she got off.

'Madame, if I may.' He opened the passenger door for her and she turned down the music while Monty acted on his best behaviour as he followed the food basket on to the back seat. John jumped into the car, kissed Michelle and started the engine with the Haircut 100 lyric, *'Is it down to the lake I fear'*.

Michelle loved it when John was in one of these moods and tried to follow suit, but she was always melancholy after visiting her parents. She was not as depressed as she was when in their company, but the mix of relief, fact and afterthought topped by the sleepy sensation a long bus journey causes left her deflated.

'Well, how are the Goebbels?' John asked her.

'As expected.'

'And their offspring?'

'Gillian's fine.'

'And her offspring?'

'Her kids are fine.'

'And tell me, have they had any offspring?'

Michelle chose to ignore his sarcasm.

'And the gossip?' he went on.

'Patrick O'Neill is missing two weeks now, they're starting to fear the worst.'

'He probably forgot to take his address with him and can't remember where he lives. He should have had it tattooed on his arm.'

'Don't be so cruel, John.'

'You wouldn't have it any other way.'

Monty was lying in the back doing his dead dog impression.

John asked, 'And how is our best pal Red?'

'I thought you didn't want to know about him.'

'I don't . . . So how is he?'

'He's getting rather friendly with Gillian actually.'

'Good, get him off our back.'

'She says he's hoping to take up the empty unit at the shopping arcade.'

'The fool.'

'Everybody's a fool to you.'

'Are we having a row?'

'Sometimes you're just so ungiving.'

'Look, I know I'm supposed to go all quiet now, sulk, trade insults . . . but let's nip it in the bud. I'm sorry for everything, including apologising too flippantly. There's no point in taking it out on each other because we were given dodgy gene pools.'

'You've an answer for everything, haven't you?'

'Oh dear. I somehow don't think our moods are going to find that middle ground, so it looks like it's you and me today, Monty. "While we're at it, there are a couple of things I'd like to mention," barked Monty. "I don't like the way you pet me when I'm asleep, it should be a two-way thing, you're selfish, and also I don't like water so don't even think of throwing me into the lake, okay?"'

John's impression didn't raise the smile on Michelle's face that he had anticipated. Silence followed, but that was acceptable because the scenery made it impossible to have negative thoughts. The lakes on either side, the taken-for-granted greenery, getting ready to cover and resow for spring. The overall view gave every indication that the place would be something really special next summer. Michelle admired the beauty as well but she wondered whether she'd be alive to see next year's growth. She quickly wrestled such thoughts aside, out of harm's way.

John was heading for a quiet rocky spot which they'd come to consider their own, regardless of the three-foot-high graffiti that screamed out 'Nicola rides everyone in Booterstown'. As they criss-crossed the steadily narrowing lanes to the tranquil place, they were taken aback to come across a group of policemen and divers, with boats and nets in the lake and a gruesome display of assorted paraphernalia on the shore. The Gardai had blocked the path to their hideaway. Michelle perked up and started rubber-necking, imagining worst-case scenarios. John's only comment was 'these policemen take their fishing very serious, very serious indeed.' It made Michelle laugh. John was on a roll.

'I think I was reading about this. Yeah, the killer fish, they've been trying to catch him for years. I just hope they don't get the wrong one – I know I might sound fishist, but they do all look the same . . . What shall we do?'

'Let's see what's going on.'

'No, that's morbid. If you want some action I'll hire you out a Chuck Norris film when we get home.'

Suddenly a flurry of activity erupted as the Gardai began to drag their prize from the lake. Michelle was mesmerized, but John found it unsettling. He started the car, reversed quickly and sped away. Michelle kept on looking back. 'It looks like a body,' she squirmed. The Gardai surrounded the netting, making it impossible to identify any of the shapes.

'Come on Michelle, leave it. You'll read about it in the papers soon enough.'

Monty sensed the tension and started his little body tremors without ever taking his eyes off John's face, waiting for his instructions.

Back home, Michelle kept looking at her watch, waiting for the 6.01 News. The picnic basket lay open on the kitchen table, the pretty display of food only partially ruined as bits of cheese, scallions, plum tomatoes, French bread and hummus were picked at and dipped into. Monty hated the atmosphere but knew he was in for a left-over feast. John was keen to see the News but he disliked Michelle's obsession about local mayhem. The television could not be turned on until 6.01 because John couldn't bear to hear the Angelus, the one minute of bells that gave the people of Ireland an opportunity to pray and rejoice in their God.

It was the leading story: a body had been dredged up from the lake. The Gardai suspected foul play, but there was speculation of suicide. That was enough to keep Michelle transfixed for the night. She waited for details. No name was given, just that the body was female and in her early forties. As the report ended, the telephone rang. They both jumped. John usually let the answerphone act as go-between but this time he felt an urge to answer. It was Helen, her voice frail and broken, trying to say what she had to say with the minimum of fuss. She wanted two weeks off work, and John obliged. Despite his concern he knew better than to question her. He tried to calm her but he could tell that she just wanted to get off the phone.

'See you in two weeks,' she told him, and hung up before she could hear his gentlemanly answer: 'Take as long as you like.'

John went into his study, opened a bottle of good wine, and blasted out the Fatima Mansions – his mufflers to the outside world.

As Michelle got ready for bed she popped her head round the door and wished John goodnight with the information, 'They've found another body.' He didn't react and she quickly pulled the door shut. Knowing she wouldn't have any need for her book tonight, she picked up one of her monthly magazines from the endless pile.

Sean Hughes

John was away with himself. His favourite chair aching his back, he absent-mindedly took out his various savings accounts, his high yield bonds, his Peps, Tessas, national savings, pensions, and life assurances and tallied them up. It surprised him to find that he was a millionaire; that is if business and property values were included. This didn't please him. Money was no more than an amount in an account. He didn't dislike money but he despised people's attitude towards it; the respect it bought from un-monied types, the regular invites to parties and events from people to whom he had only the tiniest link. Occasionally he would go along to see what he was missing and would always hate the fact that he enjoyed them.

He never looked down on their attitudes. He knew he had no right. He loved to meet new people, to embrace the brief flirtation, but he was always aware that this was as good as it got. It was when he had reached the mature age of seven that he first realised people were rubbish and started to phase them out of his life. Moments like these only came about when he remembered that he hadn't been able to replace people with anything else. He supposed that Monty came closest, and yet he was never a comfort. He seemed to surround himself with creatures of need. Monty nestled his head on John's lap. His problem was his sense of self. Rescued from a dogs' home, he had no self-esteem, and always thought he was a smaller dog than he was, which made for the ridiculous situation of his constantly jumping up on to John's lap only for half of his body to slip off. John let him do it, hoping he would eventually suss out how stupid he was, but if he was fair, he loved the warm feeling of the dog on his lap, much like a hot water bottle on continual call.

John opened a second bottle of wine. He would have been an alcoholic of long standing by now, only his body would not let him. His body was a well-oiled machine, unkempt, unfit, lungs coated in nicotine, energised by the most basic of foods, but functioning. If ever he drank over his body's limit, out it would regurgitate. This was a little unflattering for a well-to-do, mature, stalwart member of the community. He would find himself on somebody else's toilet floor, curled up, shaking with half breaths, doing the death rattle, caressing dust; the brain alert but unforgiving, vomiting into a pool of self-disgust. All the time he'd be eavesdropping on the good and proper people downstairs who were partying tastefully and decently, laughing wholesome laughs, chatting for the joy of it, flirting with just the right etiquette while all the time their bodies were taking in the poison with grace and decorum. No doubt even their hangovers could be sniggered away the following day with sheepish grins and allocated winks.

He picked up a refill jotter and started to scribble. *Work fulfilling – no one to share it with. Friendships – unfulfilling and unbinding. Family – nuisance. Dog – dopey love. Sex – meaningless. Religion – non-committal. Michelle – sheepish. Life – take it or leave it.*

It occurred to him that he needed a huge overhaul. It would probably take joining a cult to sort himself out or at least to come to his senses. That was all a bit too much effort, so buying a few existentialist books would have to suffice. John was always able to push himself away from the brink of despair by belittling his own life. He had learnt never to expect too much, and so he was never disappointed.

It was four a.m. and he'd wasted himself on pointless musings. He tried to sleep, but he couldn't. Usually when he was over-tired, familiar voices would echo in his head. In his youth they would freak him out but now they comforted him with the hint that sleep was imminent. Tonight, however, he was on his own. He kept on having to open his eyes and edge a dent into the pillow.

Seven a.m. and he was still roaming around the house. He looked in on Michelle. She was peaceful. If only there were more local murders. Her face had kept its youth, a little girl's face made all the more charming when she wore those big Elton John glasses, the ones that he'd worn to distract people from looking at his lack of hair. On her they gave the impression of a little face about a foot back from the glasses. She was long-sighted to the extreme. She had always slept like a queen, perfectly at ease, while John punched, kicked, shouted, farted, sweated, snored and contorted his face into every conceivable ugly expression, and yet he was always the one most refreshed in the morning.

He left her to enjoy her respite and shuffled into the kitchen. Monty appeared out of nowhere, his sense of smell connected to the speed of his legs. John started to fry an egg and turned on the radio, concentrating on neither. The News homed in on the latest lake developments: two bodies, unrelated; one had been in the lake for up to five years, the other more recent. John took the news in in shorthand, facts unassembled, just enough to get the full picture, until Patrick O'Neill's name came up as one of the bodies. He thought that he'd misheard. He hoped he had. He had no time for Patrick, but nevertheless he was still at an age where death was not meant to be part of his generation's agenda.

Had he jumped or was he pushed? In an attempt to deflect the true horror John ordered a wreath for Patrick's mother and, for the hell of it, a bunch of flowers for Michelle. He felt a tinge of guilt which he tried to dismiss. The thought of attending the funeral, which he knew would be expected of him, sent an air of despondency around the room. Knowing it would take place in Treetown blew out a couple of thousand braincells more.

Treetown was out in force to gawk at the area's first suicide, for that was indeed how Patrick had met his maker. No foul play was suspected. The rain kept the bemused to curtain-twitching. The Mass was the sombre affair it should have been, made more agonising by the smell of wet coats drying quickly in the heated church, condensation rising, the fake stained-glass windows being denied their spiritual aura as they took a battering from the downpour. The priest, unduly doing his duty, had nothing of interest to say to the bereaved bar the usual tottle. At least Christ seemed suitably fazed on His crucifix.

Patrick had left a sister and a mother and average juggling skills. Those of his age and ilk who had remained in Treetown stood in a group, heads down, wearing black jackets last seen out in force ten years before when the Treetown youth had succumbed to Goth culture. Red stood among them. He noticed the cuff of his sleeve was frayed and toyed with the thought of buying a new black jacket before his mother's funeral. Peter kept him company. Red, having been the last to see Patrick alive, was bombarded with questions at the reception. The house was crammed with people and sandwiches, Mrs O'Neill's hand being constantly shaken as commiserations were offered and accepted. Hushed conversations unfolded in little circles as groups of mourners looked for their social peers, finding common ground as booze was downed.

John had yet to turn up, but his parents were there, both small people. John looked like his dad, which both of them resented. His mother rarely left the house and seldom drank, so she wasn't in her element. As people became less guarded, she became more sensitive. It would definitely end in tears. They clung on to Michelle, who had her own parents to contend with. They questioned her about John, trying to acquire any information they could from her since he scarcely ever told them anything of interest. All she could mutter was that he was running late, and that he'd arrive soon. Fortunately both sets of parents tolerated each other and could ramble on about whatever it was that parents talked to each other about for the accepted period of time.

The reception started to become too raucous and seasoned funeral-goers felt that the time was right to ferry the revellers down to the pub. Michelle was getting agitated by John's non-appearance and constantly had to answer for him with 'Ah, you know

John.' She was put out when Patrick's sister Estelle retorted, 'Well, the point is, we don't.'

The pub atmosphere eased the gloomy mood and it was now accepted as a celebration. Those who felt the need to joke and laugh no longer felt stifled. Soon the more affected were promising never to lose touch with their renewed acquaintances and formations abounded, the musical-chairs part of the evening over; no more table-hopping as each group huddled together, close-knit, the chemistry right. One such assemblage consisted of Michelle, Gillian, Peter, Red and Gummy, whose parents had moved back to Dundalk just as he himself was becoming a Dubliner. This wasn't untypical in the emigration-injected Irish nation. The continual search for peace of mind was high up on the list of necessities alongside economic means. The Irish were the nomads of Europe, sprinkled and infiltrated into every corner. After all, it's easier to be Irish outside Ireland.

As full pints left no space on the tables, the bonding session began. They reminisced about their teens, oblivious to the fact that it was the one summer they were focused on. The one summer when everything appeared right in hindsight. Of course there were songs and television programmes and, to a lesser degree, world events which had been shared moments. But what made it special was that at fifteen years old their responsibilities were trivial and their parents had let them off the leash. Freedom in Treetown was camping out in each other's back gardens. Their elders thought the kids were loving nature, battling the elements, kissing the earth; but to fifteen-year-olds it was about losing your virginity, fighting strangers who dared to step on your patch, being cruel to cats, going on the rob, smashing windows, getting pissed, letting the air out of tyres, sniffing glue and publicly humiliating at least one of the less muscular members of the party.

The more sensitive in the neighbourhood tried the camping lark but found they had not built up enough testosterone for such forays. If the camping was paradise, the free gaff was nirvana. This was allowed by the more trusting parents whose son had managed to talk himself out of the two-week family caravan holiday to Wexford. He was given the keys to the house, instructions, and money to stick in his pocket which would barely fit alongside the erection of excitement and anticipation. This was more civilised. A group of eight; four boys, four girls; an older brother's trip to the off-licence and the night was in place. Monopoly was played, until enough courage was summoned to play 'spin the bottle' and give you your chance to kiss a girl in the hope that you would click and be sorted for the summer.

Unfortunately, news of a free gaff spread like sheepshit and come three a.m. the bad element turned up. Either you let them in or you had your windows smashed. They would take the best girls, and your girl, the girl you had been chasing for months, the one you treated like a goddess would turn to you and say 'I like you as a friend.' You watched as the girls let sweaty, dirty hands braille their bodies and you listened as wet passionless kisses smacked on to your angels. You, the gooseberry, got to share the hard nose breathings which filled the air. The bad element, bored with the totty, would insist on a chaotic outdoor adventure. You would go with them, hoping that you would return unscathed, thinking the shared bravado had brought you closer to the thugs, only to find half your possessions gone in the morning.

Laughter rang out as Peter, being the eldest, confirmed tall stories of the older generation which the youngsters had tried to outdo when they came of age. Each generation always went that one step futher. Red, having been away, had the more heightened memory. John didn't feature in any of these tales and Michelle soon stopped sneaking looks at her watch and fell under the spell of their reconstructed adolescence. There were no long pauses or embarrassed silences as everyone listened to the capers, storing up their own, ready to jump in when the time allowed. Other tables were visibly jealous until a crowd started edging towards them, not daring to interrupt but wanting to be a part of it nevertheless. As chucking-out time came, somebody asked who was responsible for the Golf Club tuck shop robbery. No one had ever taken the blame, because the cops had been called in.

'I was,' Gummy proudly admitted. 'Well, me, Estelle and John.'

'John?' Michelle exclaimed.

'I know, I couldn't believe it myself.'

'Crafty fucker,' said Red, in between sips. 'What happened?'

Gummy went on. 'It wasn't planned. There was a bunch of us out camping, and after a chase the pigs were called and we all split up. We ended up by the Dodder, out of breath, in a field, when this mad horse went for us. We legged it and ended up at the golf course. We thought the heat would still be on in Treetown so we stayed out a little longer and it was absolutely fucking freezing . . .'

'But it was summer,' Red interrupted, wanting the full facts.

'Yeah, how long have you been away? It's freezing every fucking day.'

They all laughed, and Gummy continued his story.

'John noticed a small window open in the clubhouse and we decided to go for it. Estelle, being the smallest, was nominated as she could fit through and then open a bigger window for the two of us. She crawled in and started rummaging about but then this huge fucking alarm went off. She looked at us and there was panic in her eyes. We just cracked up, laughing uncontrollably. She made a dive for the window but because she was freaking she couldn't get it together to get through. Me and John were still laughing, even more so now because we were shitting it as well. So we're there, she's pleading for help and we're trying to pull her out. I've got her head, John's got her arms but we have no strength because of the laughing, and the alarm is getting louder. It took us about ten minutes to pull her out and like idiots we ran down the golf course.'

'What was wrong with that?' Gillian asked.

'It was dewy and we left a trail of our footprints more or less all the way home. You know that's when Estelle got her nickname.'

'Which one?'

'Stretchy, 'cos she grew about two feet taller that night.'

The barman began to collect the glasses and gently tried to get rid of them. Everyone started to make a move. Michelle worried about John again. She was annoyed that he hadn't shown but the story had endeared him to her. She thought he'd better have a good excuse but she hoped nothing was wrong and she didn't know how she was going to get home. Peter offered to drive her, since he hadn't been drinking, and after five minutes of gracious non-committal refusals she accepted. Red proposed that they all drive up to John's place and have a bit of a laugh. Michelle, the worse for wear, couldn't resist. They got a take-out from the bar and all piled into Peter's car and laughed their way up to the mountains.

They arrived at the house in mid-song. It was the old Squeeze classic, *Cool for Cats* – with the lyrics changed to *cruel to cats, crueeel to cats*. Michelle, seeing the kitchen light on, was livid. The revellers staggered towards the front door. The house looked sinister at night, surrounded by evergreens whose branches made creepy noises in the breeze. Occasionally a light would flicker along the mountain and the stars looked further away than they actually were. Michelle and John had fitted a security light on the front porch. Gillian needed the toilet, as did Red, so he decided to piss in the bushes. He reeled around in the darkness until he tripped over a shovel and fell on some freshly turned-up soil.

'Fuck it,' he thought, 'here will do fine.'

The others were already in the hall. There was no music or barking. Michelle took the lead as the gang crept behind her making drunkenly loud keep-quiet attempts to seem orderly. Gillian was pointed in the direction of the toilet. Michelle entered the kitchen determined to give John a tongue-lashing, but everybody shut up when they saw his face. His eyes were swollen, and he was seated awkwardly by the table, wearing his funeral clothes. He looked up, not in the slightest bit moved, and stared towards the group without taking them in. Michelle's face dropped.

'What's wrong?' she asked him.

'Monty's dead.'

The others edged towards the door. Michelle tried to approach him but she knew that wasn't what he needed. To stop her coming any further John spoke.

'He saved my life.'

He started crying then, weeping, breaking down. Gillian entered and stayed by the door as she heard John half-breathe his story with no control on pitch.

'It came out of nowhere. I slammed on the brakes, Monty was on my lap. He took the impact between me and the wheel. He was crushed . . . he let out such a yelp. I crushed him. I killed my own fuckin' dog! He didn't even die immediately. . . He was looking at me, wondering what to do, he couldn't breathe, and he just kept on looking at me, wondering what I was going to do. . .

'He was so helpless. I held him in my arms, I could feel his broken bones and his tongue kept coming out to try and catch his breath. As I petted him he was so frightened, his eyes kept on closing . . . as if I was going to hurt him, imagine? Then he started fading, his eyes staring at me, all the time never taking his eyes off me. He was shaking all over . . . and then he was gone. I buried him in the garden.'

Red burst into the room, paused, and with a comic's timing, loudly shared: 'Hey! Did somebody die in here?'

CHAPTER 4

John seethed for a week after the death of Monty. Michelle, trying to comfort him but failing, withdrew into a feebler state. The gravity of the outside world was eroding both their safety barriers. John crutched brandy, Michelle Temazepam. They spent most of the day shedding skin in separate rooms. Fazed and dazed, brimming with energy and fatigue. Michelle waiting for John, John waiting for a breakthrough.

John couldn't get Red's face out of his mind. Initially he felt nothing but pure hatred, recalling Red's childhood cruelty, memory upon memory colliding, all coming too easily. It occurred to him that he didn't have a single happy consecutive twenty-four-hour period in his youth. He tried to think positively. He thought of birthdays, but the pressure of enforced fun always turned them on their side. Once his mother had bought him a Teardrop Explodes album, but it wasn't a surprise, because she'd asked him to write down the details for her. She would play the game of pretending it hadn't been available before handing it over, and he'd feign amazement. His mother would give him a look of love, and endure the increased volume as she prepared his favourite dinner, *pomme frites, traditional style, with a touch of seasoning overwhelmed by delicately turned ova . . .* Yeah, egg and chips. This was a pleasant enough memory, but three hours later his record player had found itself locked in his father's wardrobe for nothing more than a clash of moods. John never felt hard done by. He held a negative view towards people because he'd experienced their inherent weakness, their lack of love. Having indifference or hatred battered into him in his formative years had left a wedge in him rather than a dent. It depressed him that he carried an overnight bag of his father's traits into his own rounded life.

As a child he'd been pushed out into the sun on the pretence that it was criminal to be indoors on sunny days. Squinting and nervous, head hung low he would attempt to mingle, with a friendly grunt at the less-scary-looking children of the community. Then there was the shock of meeting people outside his own lineage, the chit-chat, the mischievousness, the bonding, until he was permitted entry into another house and then the sudden dawning that his family wasn't the standard model and the hoping that he was adopted or would be allowed to live with another family.

There was a side to him which he implicitly despised but which he had to surrender to, a side which prohibited his enjoyment of any situation. Once, on impulse, the occasion being nothing more than a spring in the step, he went into a bakery and bought four cakes for his family. This surprised him, because he had never had a sweet tooth. He felt undiluted happiness as he took on the role of mother for a while. He skipped home with his box of cakes, convinced that the gesture would raise his family's spirits. The scene was set as he handed his puzzled mother the package. Beaming in between puffs on her cigarette, she called the rest of the family into the kitchen. They circled, Dad wondering what John had done wrong, resigning himself to dishing out punishment. His older brother Paul, wondering what his role was to be, acted nonplussed, and to get in on the game of generosity heralded, 'You pick first, Mum, you pick first.'

The cakes stood to attention, the chocolate eclair hinting at the lovely gooeyness inside, the meringue hiding its pearl of cream, the doughnut as ever reliable and the jam tart, the supermodel of the cake world, curvy, perfectly formed and way too pretty to eat. Mum chose the meringue.

'I want that one.' John could not believe what he had just said.

Paul seized his opportunity. 'Don't be so selfish.'

'I want that one,' John repeated.

His mother, having no drama in her life, hammed up her role.

'I won't bother with any of them then.'

John, totally losing control, grabbed the meringue

and tried to cram it into his mouth. His father, unaware of the tension, picked up the jam tart and walked back into the sitting room, more concerned that he had three up on a yankee. Ten minutes later his mother was crying in the kitchen alone, but making sufficient noise to be heard. Paul went and comforted her, a smile on his face. He was Mum's favourite, and it hadn't cost him a penny. Without anyone noticing, he had eaten two of the cakes. John sat in his room with his headphones on, hating his favourite music.

Was his family to blame? Probably, but he took that blueprint everywhere with him. He must have seemed a normal boy when he was with outsiders. This joyless revelry. He joked and larked with others, but he recognised its hollow sound. Reprieve upon reprieve from the frightening density of thought. *'Love was the only thing,'* he mused: not the going out with a girl, the pictures and the hanky panky, but the giving of one's soul. Saturday nights were spent in his bedroom, where the crackly stereo volumed full lives. It was the experienced old man in the corner, and John relied on him and on chocolate fingers for solace. He was never content just listening to the music; he wanted to do it himself, he wanted to be the wise old man in the corners of other rooms. He only ventured down to make tea, but the din of Saturday night television would rush him back upstairs again. The mix of caffeine, cocoa and nicotine left him uncomfortable, little flurries flying around his bloodstream when all he wanted was numbness. He would fight off what he considered to be normal growing pains while other fifteen-year-old boys were desperately trying to fondle the neighbourhood's more developed breasts.

He thought of Peggy, his one true love. Peggy had everything going for her bar her name. John met her in Superquin, a supermarket where he worked part-time. It was at the pricier end of the trade where you paid that little bit extra to shop with a better class of person. He was pushing a trolley of milk into its display unit one Friday night when she appeared out of everywhere. All else around her blurred. As she spoke the surrounding customers became her backing singers: all his senses blew open and he knew the meaning of head over heels.

'What aisle for mushy peas?' she enquired.

What he wanted to say was *you will never have to eat such miserable foods again. I will take you away and we will hold hands and I will cater for your every need. You will never go without and I will arrange it so that you will never have to ask for anything. I will intercept your thoughts so you will have what you want before you even know you want it.* Unfortunately he was struck dumb, and he came across to Peggy as the weird bloke who just stared at you when you asked him a question.

From that moment on, he gave his life to Peggy, and what did he get in return? An appreciation of God. He noticed the smiling sun, the revitalising smell of freshly cut grass. He started seeing his dad's point of view; hope in his mother; the freedom of dance, the intricacies of table football, the fullness of cheese, the acting talents of James Brolin, kindness in strangers and the crunchiness of brussel sprouts. She would never realise the effect she was having. Every rejection life cast at him would be countered by 'there's always Peggy.'

Sundays became the dreariest day, since he had to wade through until Friday before he could snatch a glimpse of his purpose in life. He would run into work fifteen minutes early in the hope of being able to clock in at the same time. Of course this love brought about its own anxieties, since part-timers were renowned for lasting just one week before wanting their teenage years back. A week of sleepless nights lay ahead of those first seven days. He had to take two days off school because he felt sick. When he saw her again the nervous exhaustion had his legs shaking. He couldn't eat. Acid was being mass-produced in his stomach, his normal work-friendly chats had become a nuisance and he would gladly have slaved for free. In this state he was useless anyway.

He subtly stalked her for the weekend. If he saw her going towards the storeroom he would dash out the boxes of butter in record time, convening a meeting in the darkened engine room. Out of breath, he would try to appear cool as he strolled past with the empty boxes, ready to give that firm but casual nod. *Yes, she smiled at me, that was enough, I can die now.* John worked out a plan of campaign, strategy after strategy; retreat, attack, fold back, regroup and on it went. If he'd have joined the army, he would have made the rank of General. For the first few weeks he was happy with nods, cultivating a 'he's-a-friendly-guy' status. He painstakingly gathered information about her. He had to go gently here because if one of his workmates got a sniff of his intentions, he would be continually slagged, his bottle would go and he wouldn't be able to be himself – an awkward misfit at the best of times. After two months he started discreetly bumping into her on the way to work, gradually working up to walking the same way home, adding three miles to his journey. The next stage was to make sure their lunch breaks clashed, no easy feat, and then delicately pushing his humour onto her. When he made her laugh he knew he had a fighting chance. Although he wasn't by nature conniving, he made sure to be nice to her closest friend who was always glued to her side. This wasn't easy, since she was a bit of a joke to the workforce, blessed with over six feet of body, topped with a large mound of curly blonde hair. It wasn't surprising that she'd been nicknamed 'Big Bird'. Martin, John's second-in-command, was his only confidant. Since Martin was no use at being a teenager either, he played along. That is, until it transpired that Big Bird fancied him (and no, he wouldn't do a kamikaze job for John). Big Bird had invited the two of them to her free gaff along with Peggy. When Martin refused, John gave him an unconditional discharge. His last call of duty was spilling the information that Peggy's sister was mentally retarded, or, as they said in Treetown's book-reading population, a spa.

John swallowed the information hard, but it gave him more resolve. He went to bed that night warm in the thought of their future, picturing Peggy and himself having their own handicapped child and how it would bring them closer together. He would do anything for Peggy. He didn't see it as a sacrifice; the idea filled him with joy. She had changed over the weeks, become more relaxed and outgoing, turning into something of a catch. The campaign continued with longer conversations, more frequent bumping-intos, a little eye contact, until six months down the line another friend of Peggy's, not Big Bird, approached John in the canteen and told him, 'John, Peggy wants to know if you would like to go out with her.'

Oh, the elation. He pinned the Purple Heart medal onto his chest and rose above the ground, levitating and embracing the whole canteen. He stretched out his arms, shook hands, had his back slapped, lit a cigar, kissed everybody and announced over the supermarket PA system, 'John and Peggy are a couple.' He imagined how well their names would look together on a car visor, started making a shopping list for Mothercare, fantasized about the two of them as grandparents rocking away with achievement on chairs in the porch. He came back down to earth with the biggest smile on his face and bellowed a resounding 'No.'

And that was that. From that moment on, he never trusted himself again.

John began to cry, a heaving of waste. He had cried once before in his adult life, and for much the same reason. A build-up of sorrow kept at bay by alcohol, hangovers taking precedence over the real problems. A night spent with a couple whose lifestyle he did not envy, but whose simplistic crusades he pined for: their acceptance of the norm he knew he could never have, their mundane dilemmas; he wanted them. Where others in his position would look down on them with their knowing nods, he couldn't. The snobbery of superior knowledge and better standards of living sustained them. The all-encompassing thought that both of them were wrong, and rather than comfort, they should agree to differ, shake hands and part had John choking with sentimentality. This acceptance he could deal with, but when he passed his study and saw a picture of his mother aged fourteen it was too much for him. Tears of anger came. Her eyes were full of hope and expectancy. She had been cheated of that life and granted instead the hell-is-earth philosophy so many Catholics welcome.

He cried his mother away that night, she never knowing or being present when they were at their closest. Now he was crying for himself, his own recognition of being cheated of that life. He didn't want to live at this moment and he needed to blame somebody. But who? He started at the beginning. Adam, why did you have to fuck Eve? He fast-forwarded to modern times, looking for his own pre-lapsarian bliss and sought out his own serpent, searching for that moment when he understood the pain of existence, the point at which he became frightened. He tried to fight it, he didn't want to know, but it was Red who was to blame. Red who had persecuted him in his childhood. He wouldn't have minded if it had been straightforward bullying, strong against weak; that was standard practice. But Red was weak too. They should have been friends. Together they could have fought back. John remembered each incident when Red had tried to gain brownie points off people he was better than, by humiliating him. The punching, the name-calling, the throwing into water, the taking off of trousers all done to the background of laughter and sniggering. John, scared witless, brave by his mere attendance, had hope for Red. If only he could get him alone then they could talk and Red would succumb to humanity. *Apologise, young man, and we will run off at once, doing good deeds.*

His chance came one winter night. John had bought a cheap bike because he could never outrun the thugs. He was cycling back from Martin's house after a night of fantasy talk in Martin's bedroom, during which they had fantasized about not having to be in Martin's bedroom. He turned a corner and spotted Red strolling purposefully home, fag in mouth, hands in pockets. At first John shuddered, almost falling off his bicycle. Then he eased on the brake in case Red wanted a chat, a chance to start their relationship proper. As they approached each other, John let out the friendliest 'How a' ye?' he could muster. Red looked at John disdainfully, pulling hard on his cigarette, took it out of his mouth and with finger and thumb in the appropriate position, flicked it straight into John's face.

He hesitated to see if he had hit the target, and then, satisfied with his bullseye, he shaped his way home. John scrabbled with the burning cigarette, trying to keep the motion of the bike going, whilst all the time he was in a state of shock. It was decision time. Did he stop the bike, get off, tell Red he can't do that to another human being and take a hiding while getting his point across? Or did he cycle home deflated? John cycled home, knowing he'd just experienced the biggest regret of his life.

'Fuck it,' he thought, 'I'll ring Red, let's get this thing sorted once and for all.' As he dialled the number, the gloom lifted, and he wasn't frightened any more.

He looked in on Michelle. She was dozing, but his excitement lifted her.

'You know Michelle, we've been playing this all wrong, hiding away like this. We've got to enjoy life more, we've got money and our health.'

'Have we now?'

'That's what I'm talking about, Michelle, that attitude, it's dragging us down . . . I think we've come to an impasse. The past is the past, we're going to start treating ourselves . . . How about a holiday?'

'A cup of tea will do fine.'

'I suppose it's a start.' John left the room half-smiling. '. . . By the way, I'm having dinner with Red tomorrow.'

Michelle was delighted that his mood had brightened but she didn't believe a word of what he was saying and she knew that neither did he. It worried her that his attitude had changed so suddenly. He had a habit of bullishly forcing new ways onto himself and then she had to be there to pick up the pieces when he realised he hadn't got it in him after all. First frustration, followed by resentment, ending in resignation. She admired his attempts but they vexed her, too, and she was always happy in his failure. It gave her a chance to play her part. The role of the last arm around him when all else failed. She knew she was being pathetic, but stronger still was the knowledge that it suited her. It was a good state to be in, resting between the hell she had been through and the one that was waiting around the corner.

But what if he succeeded, had no need for her; what if they started drifting apart? She needed him muddled and she was determined to keep him that way. She knew she was being selfish, but at the same time she convinced herself she was protecting him. It was what she termed a catch-11 situation, where two negatives amounted to a positive. She didn't love John; she loved what she and John had together. It could never be a true love. It was impossible for it to be a normal love because she owed John so much. He had saved her life, he had taken her in when the existence she was leading had been subhuman. He never reminded her, never asked for a pay-back, he just accepted her for what she was. She had long ago given up on the idea of their falling in love; but she didn't like the way he treated her sometimes as his pet, compassionate but with no depth of feeling. They did enjoy some tremendous moments of tenderness, but because it was so nearly perfect she sometimes pushed too hard, prodding at John, trying to get a reaction, hoping that everything would neatly fall into place. But John wouldn't risk a confrontation. He would rather be trodden on than raise his voice. She heard the unforgettable sound of Tindersticks coming from the other room. There was John listening to his miserable music, singing along forever out of tune to words he did not understand. Nothing made him happier.

She smiled, knowing that he could never change.

CHAPTER 5

Peter took the food tray away from his mother. She'd picked at the meat, played with the mashed potatoes and ignored the carrots. He left it on the dresser and pulled the curtains closed. Mrs Bulger was officially finishing daylight. He turned on the television, picked up the tray and left the room. Not a word was spoken.

Downstairs Red lay slumped on the couch reading an old copy of *Shoot* he'd found in the attic. He noticed that footballers in the eighties had a lot more facial hair. He supposed it was to make up for the general lack of skill. There was a focus on Steve Daly, Manchester City's new signing, breaking what was then the transfer record fee. His eyes were strangely sad, as if he were bearing the weight of the money on his shoulders, and he looked as if he was about to wink, camouflaging the fact that he didn't think he was up to much himself. Peter strode by with the tray. Red looked up.

'You're not binning that, are you?'

'No. I was going to put it in the fridge and serve it up to her tomorrow.' Regretting his flippancy, Peter tried to express his concern. 'She hardly touched it.'

'I'll have it.' Red jumped up.

'I thought you were meeting John for dinner tonight.'

'Ah well, you know, we'll probably end up not eating. You know what it's like.'

'The thing is, I don't. I barely get out of the house any more.'

He handed Red the plate as he started to assemble the assorted pills his mother took after her evening meal. Red was busy milling into the dinner as if it might disappear before his eyes.

'You're always moaning, you are,' he said, not quite in between mouthfuls. 'You're turning into a little old biddy. And before you start, yes I know you're looking after Mum and you're sacrificing your life' – here he put on a whining voice – 'but let's just lead our own lives, okay?'

'Someone's got to do it.'

'Have they? Think about it, Peter. You were the older brother, you should have been the one to go away. Maybe it's in your nature to be a stay-at-home. Maybe you'd be like this even if Mum wasn't sick.'

'You've got some balls!' Peter was indignant. They stared at each other. 'We've got a selective memory, have we? Have you forgotten that Dad died when I was fifteen, and Mum started getting sick four months later.

I suppose that was when I should have travelled the world. But I couldn't, could I, because I was too busy washing behind your ears.'

'And I'll tell you something else, Peter, you were shit at that as well.'

'Everything's a joke to you!'

'Would you ever fuckin' lighten fuckin' up. Everything isn't a joke. I know you're dying to get all this off your chest, but I'll tell you this, buddy, you're not doing it with me . . . Why don't you take a vacation? You don't have to go far, the bottom of the garden would do . . . Or watch the holiday programme . . . but do *something*, for both our sakes, because if you don't stop, there's going to be a mercy killing. Now here, give us those pills, I'll take them up to our Klingon. You relax, kid, kick off those shoes . . . Maybe you should take one of these yourself.'

From the bedroom door, Red saw his mother gazing towards the neon blue of the television set. Either she was getting smaller or the bed was getting bigger.

'Medication time, Mum.'

She efforted out a half-smile.

'May I suggest, as a starter, a couple of these red ones? They rest on the palate, gently releasing a sense of well-being . . . and they go particularly well with Treetown tap water. And then as your main course, one of these big blue ones, with a couple of the teeny-weeny green ones to befriend it on its exciting journey around your bloodstream. And then, and only if you are up to it, for dessert this lovely multi-coloured capsule. *Bon appetite*.'

He handed her the tablets and kissed her on the

cheek, knowing he had done his job. As he closed the door on the way out he sighed the silent sigh of solitude, the one that has to face up to the bare facts. He was figuring that his situation couldn't get any more disturbing, pushing pills down the corpse-like love of his life, when through the door he heard his mother let out an extremely loud fart. He deflected his gloom as he always did by joking to himself: 'At least we know she's still alive.'

Getting ready to go out, he decided on a light jacket, since it seemed that the sun had no intention of going to bed. He was a little apprehensive about meeting with John after his faux pas over the dog, but he imagined a quick apology would put them back on a level footing. Going to say goodnight to Peter, he found him in front of the television, fag in mouth and curtains pulled. He couldn't stop himself. He drew the curtains, looked at Peter and pointed out of the window.

'There's a big world out there, brother. Why don't you check it out?'

John sat at the little Greek Tavern on Wicklow Street. He had purposely arrived twenty minutes late because he hated sitting alone in restaurants but frustratingly he was still the first one there. He picked the table nearest the door so that he could make a quick getaway if necessary. He had what was almost a phobia about restaurants: whenever he was on his own he always felt the other diners were feeling sorry for him. He ordered a bottle of house red without looking at the list and got out his copy of the *Evening Herald*. He had half a gram of Charles Stuart Parnell on his person and was toying with the thought of doing a line, but he was jumpy enough as it was. He didn't have his own dealer. He didn't need to: Jimmy would always throw him his scraps. Once Jimmy had taken him to see his dealer, Diamond Dave, and John got the shock of his life when he realised he'd gone to school with him. He'd never got to know him because Dave had left school when he was nine to work in the family business. His four brothers had all been killed in gangland feuds and his dad was a man about town, procreating all over the city, desperately trying to make up the numbers. One visit to Diamond Dave had been enough for John. He reckoned he'd rather do without than meet up with him again.

The restaurant was becoming busy and John lifted his head every time a movement went by the window, waiting to see the crop of red hair skip through the door. He tried to read the paper but he couldn't concentrate. Instead he began to eavesdrop on the couple at the table to his left. A besuited, besotted man, his body language signalling a first date, leant too far in to the table and was asking the kind of questions you might find on a survey. It was obvious she was keen on him. She played with her feet, releasing them from the stilettos, giving them little rubs. She laughed at any semblance of a joke he told and was wearing a strong perfume. John recognised the scent from Helen, who dabbed a little on now and then, but he figured this debutante must have spilt the bottle over herself. The smell was so overpowering that John was afraid he might get sclerosis of the liver, and when she excused herself and went to the toilet, he prayed that it wasn't to put more perfume on.

In her absence the guy slumped back in his seat, wondering what topics to bring up next, second-guessing how he was doing on this dating game; irked at having to put on his courting persona, counting the days until they could relax in each other's natural postures and laugh about the stupid things they will have said to each other before the night's end. He caught John looking at him and stared back. John put his head in the newspaper but instead of reading he started clocking the diners to his right. He took an instant dislike to them. A plastic couple, both of them blonde, with expensive casual clothes and handsome, well-toned bodies, they didn't speak a word to one another. John imagined they had won each other as a prize and were determined not to let each other out of their sight. It puzzled him what they could possibly talk about. Surely they couldn't get by with no more than the odd 'it's your go on the rowing machine'? They didn't seem to be enjoying their food, even though their combined salaries dictated four meals out a week.

Tiring of them, John forced himself to concentrate on the newspaper. The waiter came with the wine, and dispensing with the formality of tasting filled the glass more or less to the brim. It troubled John that the waiter saw him as a pisshead.

'Come on Red, where are you, you fucker?'

The *Herald*'s headline story was the latest gangland slaying, an ongoing battle between two rival gangs whose main occupations were dealing drugs and competing for the silliest names for their members. They had the Penguin, the Goose, the Duck, the Pigeon, the Robin and the Raven. John laughed to himself. No wonder they never got caught. The Gardai shouldn't be checking out the pubs or the clubs, but the parks. The rest of the page detailed the latest impassioned outburst from The Cranberries' singer Dolores O'Riordan.

'Sorry I'm late.'

John was taken aback. He urged Red to sit down, shook his hand, touched sweat, felt stupid and avoided eye contact. Come on, think of something to say, get off on the right track. He took a huge gulp of wine and offered to pour some for Red.

'Have they got any beer?'

'I'm sure they do.'

John called the waiter over. Red's face suddenly crunched up.

'What the fuck is that smell?'

John saw that the woman on the first date was back in her seat, laughing that laugh which makes women's hair move around in sexy positions. It was only then that he smelt the guy's aftershave, which was just as strong as the woman's perfume. Christ, if they held hands there might be some sort of chemical explosion. He lowered his voice.

'It's an oestrogen and testosterone imbalance.'

'What?'

'Perfumes. . .' He eased them into their discourse. 'I see that Dolores has sussed that war isn't very nice, and wouldn't it be great if we all just got on.'

'Yeah, but she's a great singer that Dolores.'

'She's a fucking knacker.'

'They're great ambassadors for the country. They're very big in America.'

John looked Red in the eye.

'So are drive-by killings.'

'That's just the blacks though. Don't get me wrong, I'm not a racist, but some of them are animals.'

'Yeah, as opposed to Irish criminals, who all seem to be birds.'

'What?'

'Nothing . . . Are you hungry?'

'Starving.' Red studied the menu.

The waiter stood over them, notebook at the ready.

John said, 'I just want a starter. Can I have some pitta bread and hummus with a green salad but no cucumber.'

The waiter jotted down the order, muttering under his breath, 'I'll book the family holiday with the profits from that one,' and looked expectantly at Red. It was John's first chance to have a good gape at him. He watched Red's eyes dart around the menu. He looked puzzled by the choices, and John felt a little compassion towards him.

'Er . . . I'll just have the lamb kebab.'

'Salad?' The waiter's question was automatic.

'Do you do chips?'

The waiter, nodding, asked if he wanted ketchup. Red said yes, missing the little joke. He ordered his beer and the waiter was gone.

'Is the lamb any good in here?' asked Red, trying to steer the conversation away from confrontation.

'I wouldn't know. I'm vegetarian,' John couldn't help sneering.

'God, you've changed.'

'I hope you have, too.'

'Listen, I'm sorry about your dog. I'd no idea, I didn't mean any offence.'

'I know, I know.' John stopped this line of dialogue. 'So what has you back in Treetown?'

'Well, to be frank, I missed the place . . . I know it's a shithole, but it's my shithole. And as you know, me mum isn't very well.'

'How is she?'

'Well . . . not great.'

'It's not one of those situations where she was holding on until you got home, is it?'

'I reckon she wants to live long enough to see if Ken Barlow from *Coronation Street* will ever get married again.'

They both laughed.

'I can joke about it,' Red went on, 'but it gets me down. You know half the time I don't think she knows who I am . . . I just want to have one proper chat with her before she goes. Not small talk; just a chat.'

'About what?'

'It doesn't really matter.'

'I know what you mean. I've tried with my mother but it's—'

Red cut in. 'I don't suppose I'll get the chance now.'

John felt confused. He had found himself warming to Red, but now he was affronted by his rudeness. It reminded him again of his teenage years, never being given a voice, and there was Red thinking he could stamp all over him again.

The waiter came with the food.

Red smothered his kebab with every available condiment and launched great chunks of lamb into his mouth. John daintily dabbed his pitta bread into his hummus, thinking he could do with a line of Parnell.

He made the mistake of asking Red a question. Red, oblivious to his own eating habits, was a loud mouth-open chewer who answered the question mid-chomp leaving John to watch bits of lamb and saliva all over his tongue and teeth. Some flew out of his mouth and on to the table, and one even ricochetted off the side of John's face. Disgusted, he wiped it off with as much subtlety as he could muster. Appetite gone, he excused himself and went down the spiral staircase to the toilet.

Seeing that it was a one-cubicle affair, he had to work fast. He shut the door behind him, got the wrap out of his wallet and chopped out a line with one of his credit cards. The wrap was made up from a page from a pornography magazine, which indicated the sleazier side to Diamond Dave's personality. Happy with his line, he licked the credit card clean, immedately getting that stingy buzz on his tongue. He got out a twenty, rolled it up and snorted up the cocaine, or whatever it was that Jimmy had deigned to sell him on this occasion. For all he knew it was probably a cocktail of speed, ajax, suppositories, talcum powder – and, with a bit of luck, your actual cocaine. The hit came quickly but as always when he took it, the substance went right through his system and immediately he needed a shit.

'Right time, right place,' he muttered as he lowered his trousers.

As he sat there he summarised his meeting with Red so far. He didn't hate him as he'd feared he would. Now, he just didn't like him. They didn't have much in common. If Red knew what he was doing right now he'd more than likely shop him to the cops. He knew Red didn't like him much either. He was only looking for a free meal, and John was in no doubt that Red was using him to see what he could gain.

When he got back to the table, Red had a toothpick working away between his teeth.

'I've taken care of the bill. And don't worry, I've ordered you another half bottle of wine.'

'Thanks.'

The Parnell was working overtime. Thank God he had the wine to balance it out. He abhorred being wrong about Red . . . maybe his intentions were innocent after all, maybe his badness was going with his hair. Hold it, hold it, here it comes. . .

'How's business?'

Bingo! That's it. It's money he wants.

'Grand,' he answered. 'It tends to run itself these days.' Normally he'd have stopped there but the teeth-gnashing drug activated the chattier part of his brain and before he knew it he was giving Red the rundown on all his business affairs. Red's nodding was just enough to keep him going, but it was clear that he wanted to swing the talk around to finding out specifics.

'How did you actually get started?'

John poured himself another glass of wine. The waiter was looking at him, Jesus it must be so obvious that he was on drugs, he must be able to tell. From meek newspaper reader to Murray Walker in less than half an hour.

'I got a part-time stall on the Dandelion market . . . remember, the one off St Stephen's Green?'

'Did you see U2 play there?'

'No. I never went to see any of the bands, they were all shite, as I'm sure U2 were then—'

Red interrupted him. 'They're great ambassadors for the country, them boys.'

John gave him a dumbfounded look and carried on with his story: '—but I've met at least five hundred people who remember being among the sixty-odd heads who were actually at the gig. Anyway, I worked on a stall selling pop badges but the bloke at the next stall, Jim, had a nice line in knick-knacks and we'd always have a laugh together. When they closed down the market, he took me on as his assistant. I started going to all these antique fairs and I could see straightaway that you could make a killing. I learnt the trade very quickly. Jim loved the travelling salesman bit, going from town to town joining up with various markets. He loved all the rapport. I stuck it for two years before every bog town began to mingle into one. It was all right for Jim, he had a little sweetheart in every town. . .'

John paused for breath.

'Yeah, but how did you start?' Red enthused.

'Fuck me, it's not just the Parnell,' thought John, continuing his business history.

'I built up a lot of contacts and I realised the real money was to be had if you had your own premises. I heard of an area near Blessington which was renowned for its antiques, and I found there was a site for sale. I took the gamble. Well, the bank did. I'd come across a young craftsman, Jason, who could restore practically anything back to its former glory, so we started specialising in repairs as we gradually built up our stock.

'Now, the thing about the antiques business is that it seems like a nice bunch of old men doing it as a hobby . . . but if you cross them you're fucked. They'll blacklist you, and you'll find it impossible to get any stock. I approached all the other dealers, told them not to worry, that I was going to get into the kitschy end of the market, that I wouldn't encroach on their space . . . I had to go to England for supplies at first. I knew this bloke in Manchester who was buying up old funfair equipment, and I just went for it. I bought jukeboxes, pinball machines, old space invader machines, table football games, halls of mirrors . . . anything I could get my hands on. The other shopkeepers started to see me as a blessing. Because my shop looked interesting it brought a lot of trade into the area. Not browsers either but people with disposable income, a lot of young execs who never had a childhood, and now had big houses to fill. So they bought childish stuff. Then they'd look around the other shops and buy the odd bit of furniture. It had a great name too. John's Antique Emporium.'

'Nice.' Red nodded.

'I was soon accepted . . . The others liked me, they began to tell me about the better deals, until I started doing similar stuff to theirs.'

'Is the mark-up on them incredible?'

'No. No, the trick is to bump up the price, letting them haggle you down to the price you really want. They think they've got a bargain and go home happy, and tell all their friends. The other trick is to let them play with some of the games . . . especially the browsers, because they always feel obliged to buy something.'

'What, like a pinball machine?'

'Don't be stupid . . . Candles, greeting cards, bits of tack, there's a fifty percent mark up on those kind of items. They're your bread and butter . . . But don't tell me you're interested in my business. What's on your mind?'

'Well . . . I'm hoping to get my own little business going and any advice would be appreciated.'

John felt good. Red needed him, was turning to him. He remembered the cigarette incident, but let it pass.

'I'll tell you what, I'll go to the jacks and we'll continue this conversation over the road in the International. It doesn't get too crowded, and Paddy pulls a good pint.'

'Sounds good to me.'

They were in the pub within five minutes, John one line lighter, Red munching crisps. Red told John his dream of owning his own sports shop, his ideal location being the spare unit in Treetown's shopping centre. He had a bit of a plan, setting up lots of local teams who would need to be kitted out. Free memberships to sports clubs where he could supply the equipment. Discounts to all local activity clubs. John reckoned that Red was being naive. His instinct told him it was a losing proposition. The units were continually changing hands; there must be something amiss. But he gave practical advice and said he'd do a bit of phoning around.

Red was banging on about the community. 'Involve the community and the community will involve you.' It sounded like he'd spent too many nights in Boston's republican bars. John encouraged him to get all the trade magazines, go to some sports fairs, and do a deal with a big supplier in return for a guarantee to only use their brands. He told him about the cheap Asian cash 'n' carrys in Manchester, and warned him that he'd need plenty of cash up front. There was the cost of the leasehold – they would want a three-month deposit at the very least –; the cost of fitting out the shop – the suppliers would want cash on delivery on a new venture – all on top of your actual day-to-day running costs.

Red was frowning like an impatient child who wanted the answers now.

'How much do you think I would need?'

John did some quick calculations which his cocaine-addled brain was only too pleased to produce.

'I'd say at a rough estimate, you would need forty grand . . . Can you manage that?'

'Phew! Barely. . . If the bank backs me fifty-fifty – but that would mean throwing in everything.'

'And you've got that kind of dosh hanging around? What is it you did in America? Painting and decorating? I'm obviously in the wrong business.'

'I worked my bollox off over there.' Red sounded slightly uptight.

'Why don't you bring in a partner? You know, someone who knows the business.'

'This is something I want to do on my own. I don't want to be answerable to anyone.'

'To be fair, that's not what being your own boss is about. There's more ass-licking to do than you'd ever imagine.'

Red, ignoring him, went into dream mode.

'You know I'm getting married,' he said.

'No, I didn't. Congratulations.'

'Yeah. Mary Beth. She's coming over in three months' time and I want to have everything settled by then.'

'What, you're going to live in Treetown?'

'It's as good as anywhere else!'

'All I'll say is I hope you've warned her.'

'She's from the sticks herself. She knows the score.'

'Where'd you hook up with her?'

'She worked at the office. It's funny, she was seeing this other Irish bloke at the time . . . but I was nuts about her, and then I found out she felt the same about me.' He paused and gazed away. 'I'd do anything for that girl, and she for me.'

'Did she dump the other guy.'

'All's fair in love and war. Do you want another one?' Red enquired, quickly changing the subject. John signalled to Paddy who went to work on a couple of pints. While they waited he looked at the counter which was covered in flyers. One of them caught his eye.

'Fuck it! I don't believe it! Red, look, The Wedding Present are playing the Mean Fiddler tonight.'

'Who're they?'

'They're brilliant . . .' Getting no response from Red he started gesticulating, 'Guitar band? From Leeds?'

Red, still wrapped up in his sports fantasy, looked blank.

'Do you fancy it?' John asked him.

Red wasn't too sure.

'It'll be a laugh. Trust me, they're brilliant.'

'Fair enough. I'll take your word for it.'

They downed their pints. John made a quick visit to the little boys' room where he finished his pack, and they decided to walk to the gig.

They walked along George's Street, John half a pace quicker, quarter Wedding Present anticipation, quarter drug intake. Red was having trouble keeping up, the food and the booze demanding stability. They passed a gang of fourteen-year-old baggies trying to sell their dodgy Es. The triangle of trendy pubs they passed were packed so tightly that the bouncers were forced off the pavement on to the street.

As they approached Wexford Street, the pubs and the shop fronts grew shabbier. The Mean Fiddler stood out with its nod to modernisation and its bright primary colours. The bouncers kept an orderly queue and joked among themselves but even their laughter had an aggressive tone, belying the fact that they weren't called bouncers any more but rejoiced in the name of crowd liaison officers.

Safely through, John shepherded Red straight up the stairs to the music venue. The long bar was emptying as the band had just come on and there was the usual surge toward the stage, leaving no chance of getting near the front, which annoyed Red because that's where the toilets were and he was bursting for a piss. As usual, it took about three songs before the audience decided on their positions. The die-hards pressed against the stage, moshing in the pit. Loyal fans stood behind them, not dancing, but wanting to feel that they were part of the occasion. Then came the older ones edged against the walls, wanting a good view of the band but not prepared to participate; a mixture of thirty-year-olds and shrieking violets and the small-time hacks desperately hoping that someone would notice their blatant scribblings.

A handful of chatterers remained at the bar for whom it was just a night out, a social gathering with background music. Red was happy to stay at the bar but John insisted on being a wall-leaner at least. He knew most of the songs and half-danced the dance of the non-dancer: head moving, feet tapping, the bulk of the body remaining motionless. Red swayed a little, secretly thinking, *'Where's the fucking tunes?'* Every time the band struck up a number John would recognise it and smile at Red, over-compensating for what he suspected was Red's lack of enjoyment. When his favourite songs came on he wished that Michelle was by his side. He could have trusted her to enjoy it.

Gradually those at the front left little pockets of space as the moshers came out like war casualties, shattered and sweating, surrendering to their better judgement. John kept nudging the two of them forward until they reached the fringes of the action, helping to throw the odd die-hard back into the fray. The breakthrough came when the band launched into one of their old chestnuts, a song called 'Kennedy' which was impossible not to get excited by. Big jingly guitars, pounding drums and, hold it, a chorus to sing along to. The crowd erupted, the second tier mangled into the front and Red, seeing his chance, pushed John into the pit.

He did it for all the wrong reasons, not in good humour but to cause pain, hurt and humiliation. John was flung in sideways and completely lost his balance; and as he fell he was terrified of being crushed. At all the gigs he had attended he had never moshed because it looked too frightening. His head went down into the sea of Doc Marten boots. His vision impaired, he was close to blackout when a huge pair of tattooed hands grabbed the front of his jacket and pulled him upright. On his feet, John looked at the skinhead and hugged him. Both of them were smiling and in the middle of their embrace they went colliding into the other movers and shakers. The pushing and shoving was forceful but gentle; grins and winded expressions abounded.

John moved into the core of the group, lost in music. It was when he got to the no-man's-land of the front that he realised why the centre had been so cramped, for at the stage stood four crowd liaison officers, five foot by five foot, their arms folded and do-not-dare-to-touch-me expressions on their muscles. This brought the dancing community closer together as they restrained the hurling, losing control of their balance, trusting the other participants to catch them. Crashing into strangers, knowing they would be cushioned, the distressed ones helped, and all of them submerged eventually with the bruises of passion. It was naked and tribal and though it was alien to John, he adored it.

He spotted Red standing back safely, looking smug, laughing at what he believed to be John's misfortune. For more than three numbers John stayed in the pit, leaving it only when his T-shirt was soaked through. He couldn't wait to tell Michelle about the exhilaration he felt and decided not to waste any of the tiny energy he had left on the reasons for Red's manhandling. He could wait until the morning before deliberating on his verdict on the new Red.

Back at the bar they had one more pint as the band finished their set, John having to do so to regain his normal body weight. John couldn't get the smile off his face, while Red just smirked, still thinking he'd played a cruel trick. He kept repeating, 'How's the back?' and laughing. But John was busy nodding good-byes to his new tribe.

CHAPTER 6

The doctor wrote out Michelle's prescription. He'd decided to double the dose. Years of medical school were made redundant, alternative remedies made all the more pertinent, because the chief complaints of the modern era were in the head. Of course the illnesses made themselves known to the body over a period of time, but it was frustrating for any doctor to have to wait until that stage before they could act. There was nothing physically wrong with Michelle beside the fact that she was unwell. And saying 'pull yourself together' wouldn't suffice.

Michelle lay on the bed feeling helpless while this one rambled on about high blood pressure, taking it easy and various other empty words of comfort. He was her fifth new doctor this year. She never told them of her past ailments, thinking it would prejudice their analysis, and she was concerned that they always came to the same conclusions. The seach for the right doctor continued. In the kitchen John tried to fill him in on some of the background, but the doctor was honest enough to admit to John that he didn't think he'd been a great help. He told him that Michelle had demanded new tranquillizers, and this shocked John since she had never been reliant on them before. He and the doctor eyed each other, both scared to bring up the subject of suicide.

'It's not really her style,' said John.

The doctor pursed his lips.

'To be on the safe side, I'm going to give her duds, a course of pills which have the desired effect on certain people but are actually harmless . . . What you can do, John, is watch out for her. She's feeling fragile, but treat her as if there was nothing wrong. If you can change her daily routine it would be a help. Anything that can take her out of herself. I have to go . . . I'm sorry I can't do anything concrete, but . . .'

As John showed him out of the door, the doctor noticed that he was limping.

'What happened to you?'

'An old dancing injury.'

'You stick to jiving. Good luck,' he said, clasping John's forearm.

John closed the door, picked up the post and began preparing Michelle's breakfast. Michelle sat up in her bed, not knowing whether or not she'd get up today. She flicked on the television. It was that time of the morning when each station had a studio discussion about life's little problems. *I'm too fat, my husband is having an affair, how do I tell my parents I'm a tranny*. She hated herself for thinking it but she found all the participants ugly and their problems only made them more repulsive. She found it ironic that none of these people who were trying to talk their troubles away had anything remotely interesting or informative to say. What was the point of these programmes existing or these people existing, what was the point in anything?

Her despondency panicked her and immediately she threw two pills down the hatch, shutting out the day. Her depressions came out of the blue and quickly. A combination of thoughts could unlock her adrenalin. Her vision darkened as if the coat of her brain had split and it was oozing out into her senses, rational thought hidden away waiting for the all-clear while the out-of-control microchips did laps of honour all over her psyche. She was deep-breathing when a knock on the door startled her and John walked in with the breakfast tray, a dopey smile on his face.

'It's come to knocking now, has it?'

Michelle didn't mean it, she hadn't the energy for a row, but it just seemed to be the appropriate thing to say.

'I thought you might still be dozing.'

He put the tray on the bedside table. Tea, scrambled eggs, apple juice and a single yellow rose snipped from the garden. He started to tell her about last night but he couldn't get the excitement across because she wasn't responding, and his story petered out, dying an early death. She picked up the tray and started nibbling on the eggs, and John turned off the television.

'I was watching that,' she lied.

'I've got a surprise for you.'

Michelle loved surprises. She tried to keep up her guard of indifference but she couldn't resist getting excited.

'What is it?'

John held up a twelve-inch envelope.

'It came this morning.'

He hadn't opened it, but he knew from the postcode exactly what it was. He tore it open to reveal a book.

'It's Dominic Richards's new collection.'

Michelle's eyes widened a fraction of an inch. He presented the book to her.

'It's called *Buckets in Spades*.'

He sat on the bed beside her while they studied the cover. It was an illustration of an object shaped like a hoover covered over by an old carpet in a modern sitting room. Carefully Michelle started to flick through the pages. She knew from experience the book was shoddily produced and would fall to pieces unless it was handled right.

John had stumbled across Dominic's first collection on one of his buying trips to London. He'd been intrigued by its title – *My Parents Were Born In London And All I Got Was This Lousy Book*. He'd enjoyed it, and since that first read, Dominic's books had become John and Michelle's little secret. They'd asked to be put on his mailing list, and whenever one was published they read it out loud to each other.

'Read me a story, John.' She handed him back the book.

'I have to get to work, sweetheart . . . Why don't we read it tonight when I get back. It'll be something to look forward to.'

'Just a little one . . . please.'

'Alright, then.'

John had turned to the contents list to find the shortest story when he came across the dedication.

'Listen to this, Michelle . . .'

'A man gazes up at the stars and feels tiny all his life. He thinks the stars are tiny too. Another man reaches for the stars. He lives just long enough. This is dedicated to all those who do. . .'

John re-read it to himself a couple of times, taking it in. A rush of ineptitude engulfed him. The quotation and the tranquillizers had eased Michelle away from her pain. He found the appropriate piece.

'Are you ready?'

She nodded.

'Right. It's called *The Good Doctor.*' He looked at her again, making sure she was paying attention.

'READ!'

'Okay.'

He took a deep breath.

'The Good Doctor Mard had just come out of theatre after another successful insertion of the thumb-sized heart pump – the Jarvik 2000. The press and the balding hospital bigwigs were waiting for him to clean up and recuperate before they could start their official back-slapping ceremony, but Doctor Mard was having none of it. He sneaked out of the back door, forsaking cheese and pineapple sticks for a relaxing night

under less harsh light in front of the television. Prolonging life for others had become his life . . .

'Michelle. . .' He looked at her and she was starting to doze off. 'Shall I finish it later?'

'No, no, read on.'

She was losing her battle for consciousness. She tried to perk up as a child does when allowed to watch the late movie only to fall asleep during the opening credits. John read on.

'His selfless attitude gave him peace of mind. Uncomfortable chairs fitted themselves to him, blustery winds combed his hair, sobriety made him merry and simple foods had his taste buds dancing. A ring on the door had him inviting in two MI5 agents, who asked him to accompany them. The car journey was silent but the route was familiar. Soon he found himself back at the cardio-thoracic department of the hospital. Doctor Mard was asleep on his feet when he was informed that a member of the Royal Family needed urgent heart surgery. He was handed the case history, graphs and X-rays and told to prepare for the operation. The heart had been carefully monitored since the first signs of deterioration had shown themselves six months ago and now it was functioning at a third of its capacity. The doctor was dismayed. He knew the heart could not hold out much longer. But the surrounding tissue damage meant there was no way it would hold up to the surgery either. He knew there was every chance of chronic immunosuppression, and the heart was so small that a supraventricular tachycardia was likely. But he kept this to himself. He did not feel it was his place to tell the country that a new heir to the throne was imminent.

'The operation was set for two days' time, and sinister men told Doctor Mard to go home and prepare for his most

important task. But the morning of the operation brought a new complication in the form of Doctor Mortimer, a distinguished and egotistical heart surgeon. The downmarket papers had splashed his name all over their front pages, insisting that the Royal Family should be treated by one of their own, someone of British extraction and not a Spaniard, a man they referred to with sickening racist undertones as "Doctor Ar-Mard-a". Doctor Mard himself was relieved, hoping that this would be the end of the story. But the Royal Family were insisting that he perform his duty.'

John stole a look at Michelle and was disappointed to find her sound asleep. He put the bookmark in its place and left the book on the dresser.

He got ready for work, intrigued by the story and looking forward to reaching its conclusion later that night. He loved Dominic's stories. There were always a few lines which stuck with him. *The Good Doctor* seemed to be about content over style, and he wanted to know how it ended. One of Dominic's constant themes was the battle of the individual against the state. He tended to give the authorities Pyrrhic victories, but he never allowed them to break down the individual's heart. *Yes, maybe that's what he's getting at. The surgery is the metaphor for the state's lack of heart, and how they need the individual to restore it.* That was what he loved about such writing; it took him away from the mundane, allowed him to jump for the stars. Dominic had a habit of letting his heroes' inaction move the world around them. It was a purposeful inertia, rather than a willingness to let fate take hold.

Soon he was driving to work, his brain spilling out splendid ideas, a Philip Glass CD helping to keep his head in the clouds. He felt privileged. Today was going to be a good day. He let drivers out in front of him, gave pedestrians right of way, afforded cyclists lots of space and made no attempt to overtake buses. His only wish was that Monty could be beside him. It wasn't so much a sadness as a remembrance of shared moments. He parked in his usual spot and greeted strangers with knowing looks. In a corner of the warehouse four of his staff were cuddled around a box inside which five kittens were huddled, crying and full of fear. Jason explained that he'd never had his cat neutered, and lo and behold, this was her second litter. His huffing and puffing didn't ring true and his sense of pride gave the impression that he had fathered them himself. He wasn't able to keep them, though, and now he had to get rid of them, or as he put it, he was looking for good homes. He asked John if he'd like one, but John insisted he wasn't a cat person. He'd never been able to fathom their appeal. Jason, turning salesman for the day, stressed the urgency in choosing one, since Helen had already opted for two.

'Helen's back?'

'Yeah, she's in your office.' Jason pointed before going back to dote on his abundance of kittens.

Helen had cleared all the debris from the desk, as John had let the place go a little in her absence, and was typing out the itinerary for his trip to London. She tensed up when he entered. John, having an idea what lay ahead of him, gave her a big bear hug of a welcome from the back, his chin resting on the top of her head. She put her hands on his and they stayed like that for a few seconds without uttering a word. John could feel her stiffness and whispered into her ear that everything was going to be okay. She thought her two week cryathon had dried her out, but she had kept a secret reserve for public outpourings. This tender moment, this slight caress pushed her emotions to the limit and the tears that she had promised herself would not come came anyway.

John held on to her not knowing what else to do. Softly he started to massage her back, but her sobbing made their positions uncomfortable. Instead he got down on his knees in front of her and took her face in his hands, kissing away the fallen tears, stopping the flow towards the corners of her mouth. He waited until her body stilled and then looked into her eyes, darting from one to the other until he focused on her left pupil.

'Don't blame yourself, Helen,' he kept repeating until it finally registered.

'It's not fair John, why did he drag me into this?'

'Cos he was selfish.' John was aware that for over a year Patrick O'Neill had tried to badger Helen into a relationship, threatening her that he'd take his own life if she turned him down. It had started when John had given Patrick a menial job at the business. He hadn't done it as an altruistic gesture. He'd despised Patrick, and wanted to watch him grovel for his pittance, a payback for all the kicks that Patrick had given him for looking at him the wrong way in their youth. Patrick had been very much of the punch and don't bother asking questions later type. He'd left school at fourteen to start as a butcher's apprentice, until the powers that be had realised that Patrick and knives were not a good combination. He had idled ever since. The only thing that made him stand out in the dole queue was his juggling skill, with which he bored the pants off everyone he encountered. It wasn't that he was a waster: he was just very stupid.

At the warehouse, he was the butt of every practical joke. Helen, feeling sorry for him, was compassionate, and poor beguiled Patrick misread all the signs. John himself never got involved in the jokes, which were sometimes cruel, but he enjoyed them nevertheless.

The classic trick which the staff played on all the new boys was especially sinister. Gary, Jason's assistant, had a replica gun, and he and Jason would don balaclavas and wait outside the delivery door at the back of the warehouse. It was Patrick's job to let the deliveries in, but this time when he opened the door he was grabbed around the face by a big gloved hand, a gun was put to his head and he was ordered to hand over the day's takings. The rest of the staff hid in the background watching the joke unfold. Gary and Jason were a little apprehensive, because Patrick was always boasting of his black belt in karate. But Patrick's reaction shocked them all, since he begged for mercy until he fainted.

That was when Helen first became tender towards him, and he got it into his head that she fancied him. One night in the pub after work he confessed his feelings to John. Patrick's cockiness had John telling him that he suspected Helen felt the same way. With John egging him on, Patrick got the bit between his teeth and began to channel all his efforts into wooing Helen. At first this amounted to little more than sweeping around her desk, continually staring at her. Helen started to feel uncomfortable with Patrick's presence, which left a burning sensation on the back of her neck. He soon became obsessive and started turning up in Helen's garden at all hours of the night. John had no option but to give him his marching orders, along with the warning that he wasn't to trouble Helen any more. Patrick's way of dealing with the news was to do five thousand pounds worth of damage on his way out.

John told Helen about his responsibility, half to get it off his chest and half to diminish his sense of guilt. He'd never expected that Patrick would actually take his life, and assumed that he must have had other serious problems to want to end it all.

'But that's where you're wrong, John. He came up to my house the night he killed himself.'

John's heart stopped and then quickened.

'What did he say?' he asked, his mouth drying.

'He pleaded with me. He said he'd do anything for me and he just couldn't comprehend why we couldn't be a couple. I was pretty scared but I asked him in and tried to explain . . . but he just kept repeating "why couldn't it be like it was?".'

'Jesus. He didn't, did he?'

'He got it into his head that you were trying to break us up.'

'The guy was just deluded.'

'I sat him down for over two hours. I said anything I thought might help. I think when I told him I was gay that it was finally getting through to him that it wasn't going to work out between the two of us. That was the odd part because then he seemed to accept the fact. He became very peaceful, hugged me and left. He must have thrown himself into the lake straight after.'

'Maybe it was an accident?'

'They found rocks in his pockets.'

'They do say that when someone decides to commit suicide an inner peace takes hold of them, as if they're resigned to their fate. But that's the point, Helen. It was his decision, not ours.'

'I know. But I can't help feeling it's my fault.'

They meditated on their positions until John broke the silence.

'Look, it's all in the past. There's nothing we can do, we better just get on with . . .' he paused '. . . our lives.' Helen made to leave, and he added, 'Oh, by the way Helen, *are* you gay?'

'You didn't know?'

'It never occurred to me.'

'What about that time you bumped into me at Reynards and I was kissing that woman?'

John smiled wryly. 'I thought you were just good friends.'

Helen gave him a look of disbelief.

'I'm a lot more innocent than you'd think, Helen.'

Her parting shot was 'That I can't believe.'

John was reeling from Helen's admission. His understanding of his fellow human beings was taking a bashing today. He looked at his messages. There'd been one from Red first thing that morning. John had forgotten about him, had hoped for a Redless day. He thought of Patrick again. He hated the idea of somebody taking his own life. He was aware of his own involvement, but he felt no remorse. He hadn't liked the guy, and figured he was better off dead.What sort of life would he have had anyway? He hadn't even left a suicide note. That last defiant act had been the only way he knew how to express himself. A final boot in the face for his family and friends. John contemplated his own character. Was he a naturally cold person, or was he storing up hidden guilt that would ambush him during a crisis? Regardless, he decided to get on with the day.

He began with a session of staring into space, letting his thoughts go unhindered until one jumped out to end his period of inactivity. He went to his phone book and looked up a business acquaintance of old who was now the property unit manager of the Treetown shopping centre. Simon O'Donnell was a brash man known in the business community as the 'fella with balls'. John dialled his office where the answering machine clicked on and Simon's loud, confident voice boomed out: 'Busy, Busy, Busy. Try the mobile.'

John had to ring three times before he could catch the number and even after his third attempt he wasn't sure if the final digit was a one or a nine. He rang trying the one, assuming he'd made the wrong choice when a soft hushed voice whispered, 'Hello?'

John reciprocated with his own whisper: 'Is that Simon?'

Another subdued answer: 'Yes it is, who's that?'

'It's John, John Palmer.'

Simon's voice brightened a bit. 'Hello mate, how are you?'

'I didn't think it was you. You were so quiet.'

'Yeah. Yeah, I'm in the cinema at the moment. I'm watching *Some Mother's Son*.'

In the background, John could hear Simon being hushed.

'I'm sorry, Simon, I'll ring you back later.'

'No, it's alright. It's shite anyway. I'll just pop out and get a better reception . . . What can I do for you . . ? Yeah, yeah, I'm going . . . They all die in the end, have you not studied history, wanker? . . . *Hello, John, got a new motor* . . . aaghh!'

'I was just wondering, are you still managing the Treetown shopping centre properties?'

'You're not interested in that old rubbish, are you?'

Simon had a contagious vocabulary of business-speak which one couldn't help copying. John was no exception.

'Why? Is it a definite non-runner?'

'It's fucking Dodge City, me auld flower.'

This was something coming from Simon who was reputed to make 150K a year, had a big house out in Howth and drove a brand new BMW, while every second cheque you received from him was guaranteed to bounce.

'What's the scam?'

'I can't really say on the blower, you never know who's listening . . . but touch and bargepole if you get me drift.'

'The units do alright, yeah?'

'It's the location. Easy prey. It's a piece of *caca milas* for the cowboys . . .'

'What do you mean?'

'Overalls and tennis players. I'll say no more. Why the questions?'

'Has anyone shown an interest?'

'As it happens, I got a call today. Sports shop he wants to open up. Very green.'

'Was his name Red?'

'Yes. Yes it was. He'd be amber when I'm finished with him,' said Simon, bursting into uproarious laughter.

'What's the going rate?'

'One K, calendar month.'

'Bottom line?'

'Seven hundred.'

'Listen, do me a favour. Offer him the family and friends . . .'

'Six hundred? He'd better be a good friend.'

'Go on, it's no skin off your nose.'

'I'm telling you, if he's a friend stay well away from it. It's a complete mare.'

'Simon, I have my reasons. Call it an experiment.'

'You're a contrary fucker. As long as you know he's going to get his fingers burnt, and I mean, literally . . . I'll see what I can do . . . Oh, listen, I know where I can get my hands on a load of cheap videos if you want them.'

'Simon, I'm in the antiques business.'

'Yeah, I know. But these are vintage.' Again Simon laughed at his own joke.

'Later, Simon. I owe you one.'

'Yeah, later. Oh, by the by, we never had this conversation, right?'

And Simon was gone. People were invariably taken in by his charm, even when he was ripping them off. He always left them with a smile on their faces. Otherwise he'd have been run out of town a long time ago. John put down the phone and tried to figure out what the hell he'd been on about in the conversation that had never taken place. Simon had never been outside Dublin in his life, but somehow he'd picked up his share of cockney barrow-boy business acumen all the same. He spoke in a code which was a law unto itself but after a few airings it wasn't too difficult to work it out. *'Overalls and tennis players,'* John repeated to himself. He wrote the two words down and tried to solve the puzzle.

'Fuck! That's it. It's a protection racket.'

John was about to get on the phone to Red when it rang. Sure enough it was Red himself, bursting with enthusiasm for his venture now that he'd spoken to Simon O'Donnell. He told John all about the three-month deposit, the monthly rent of twelve hundred pounds – John kept in his snigger – the minimum year lease; until he ran out of breath, finally finishing with a 'What do you think, John?' John told him that he'd made enquiries and that under no circumstances was Red to take up the lease. Red, downcast, demanded to know the reasons why. John replied that he wasn't at liberty to say, and again advised him against it. Red was umming and ahing when John surprised himself by asking Red if he wanted to have dinner with him and Michelle at their house the following evening. Red accepted, they made arrangements and then Red launched into his sports-shop-speak once more until John, restating his position, was forced to be openly curt to get him off the phone. Peace at last.

He contemplated what he had just done. He'd never formulated a plan, but one was falling into place. If he had divulged the information at hand, would that have put an end to it, he wondered? He thought of *The Good Doctor*, and wondered if his own inaction would spur events to a conclusion. He couldn't make out whether he'd done a good thing or a bad one. Instinctively he felt that he'd made the right choice. Michelle sprang to mind. Perhaps inviting Red to the house might force her out of her slumber, albeit momentarily. He spent the rest of the day sorting out his VAT returns, the powerful mood of the morning helping to stave off the tedium. As he prepared to go home, satisfied with his half day's work, Jason popped in to say goodnight, a tiny black and white kitten peppered with ginger tucked between his arms. John surprised himself again by announcing he'd take it. It was becoming one of those days when he just rolled along with life, asking questions only as an afterthought.

He took the kitten in the fold of his arm and tickled its stomach, crooning at it, 'Who's a pretty boy?' When Jason started to fill him in on the dos and don'ts of cat care John, feeling suitably patronised, barked 'I know how to look after animals.' He decided on Chris as a name because the kitten moved its paws like Chris Eubank jabbing. Jason pointed out that Chris was actually a female.

'I'll call her Chrissie, then, after Chrissie Hynde.'

Unruffled, he put Chrissie on the front seat of the car. She was petrified, and wouldn't stop squealing while John made inane chatter to try and appease her. He petted her as he sang, *'You've got to stop your sobbing, oh, oh . . .'* He thought of Monty again and how he used to sing to him. It brought a smile to his face. He missed walking Monty and the way he'd never allowed anyone else to pet him. In the park, people would call him, hoping for some friendly interplay, but Monty was having none of it. He'd stay by his master's side, overplaying his devotion to ward off the strangers' affections. John stopped at a convenience store and bought ten tins of cat food.

He sneaked quietly into the hallway expecting to find Michelle still in bed. Instead he could hear her rummaging around in the kitchen. The aroma of cooking puzzled him. Michelle hadn't cooked a meal in over a year; it wasn't one of her specialities. He dropped the cat food by the stairwell and gently put Chrissie down.

In the kitchen he was amazed to find Michelle had laid out dinner. Lighting a candle, she told him to sit down. She had made a garlic loaf which took pride of place at the centre of the table, and she dished out a vegetable casserole bubbling with natural smells. John sat down, forgetting about Chrissie, more concerned that he wouldn't have an appetite for Michelle's unexpected culinary offering.

She scooped out generous helpings for each of them, while John feigned delight at the food, his stomach tightening. For his first mouthful he went hunting for a potato. Cutting into it was a struggle, which didn't bode well as he lifted it to his mouth. It was underdone, but he tried to keep smiling as he bit into it: a minimum of chewing and he managed to swallow it down.

Oh fuck, the carrots are next.

Michelle asked him for his approval.

'Lovely, Michelle. A little underdone, maybe. But very tasty.'

Michelle looked hurt, but what could he do? Hers must be just as hard. Surely it wasn't a stroke of bad luck that had landed him with all the uncooked lumps and besides, she would sense it if he lied to her.

He took a small carrot and swallowed it whole. It stuck in his windpipe and he had to leap up and grab some water from the sink. As it went down he could feel it crashing into his abdomen, banging into all his vital organs as it went. He felt physically sick. He stood spluttering by the sink, apologising, laughing, all the while gulping water. He heard the sound of crying and was about to remonstrate with Michelle that she couldn't break down like that at the slightest grievance, when he turned to see Chrissie sitting on her lap, uttering little screams which were louder than he'd have thought possible from such a small creature. Michelle was too busy caressing the kitten to recall that they'd been at the beginning of a row. He went over to the females and tussled with them.

'Her name is Chrissie, I thought you might like her.'

'Oh, she's gorgeous.'

Michelle was mesmerised as she practically smothered her. She'd had two cats as a child and was forever hassling John to let her have one. John recollected why he disliked cats when Chrissie dug her claws into his arm. She twisted free and went scampering out of the kitchen, roaming from room to room, looking for the house's darkest crevice where she could contemplate her future.

Michelle began to make out a list: cat litter, tray,

scratching board, flea pills, spray, collar, nips and toys. John sucked on his little cut. Suddenly, without warning, Michelle jumped up and hugged him and kissed him on the lips, telling him over and over how much she loved him. Happy with the sentiment but embarrassed by the attention, he gently loosened her grip and tried to change the mood.

'So how much of *The Good Doctor* do you remember, sleepy head?'

He touched her cheek with the knuckle of his finger.

'Oh, it's great. It's terribly sad when that Doctor Mortimer starts that smear campaign and the Good Doctor is forced to retire.'

'No, no, stop it, Michelle,' he protested, blocking her mouth.

She was puzzled.

'I haven't read it yet.' His voice was raised.

'Oh. Sorry. I assumed you had. I finished it this afternoon.'

'What?' He couldn't hide his disappointment. 'Michelle, we always read them together . . . What were you thinking of?'

'I'm sorry . . . This morning's a haze. What can I say?'

'Say nothing, your life's a fucking haze. I'm going off to finish it now.'

'What about your dinner?'

'I think we both know it could do with another couple of hours in the oven. I'll eat it later,' he said as he walked out.

He found the book tossed carelessly on Michelle's bed, another little bubble of dissatisfaction to be stored up against her. He went to his study and poured himself a glass of red wine, settling into his comfortable swivel chair, deep-breathing his fumery away. He picked up the book and tried to recapture his earlier enthusiasm but the words just stared back at him. He was still having trouble forgiving Michelle. He shut book and eyes and concentrated on the inside of his eyelids.

Michelle busied herself the next day tending to the kitten. She went to the village to buy what Chrissie needed and made a quick call on the local vet to make an appointment for her jabs. It being Saturday, John lazily finished reading the previous Sunday's papers.

Red arrived late for dinner. Peter had driven him up and John had invited him in, but he'd refused. Red had a big smile on his face and what looked like a huge bottle of champagne clutched in both hands. Awkwardly shaking hands with John, he seemed reluctant to let go his hold on the bottle, and John caught a glimpse of the magnum of cheap fizzy wine.

He ushered Red into the sitting room where Michelle stood self-consciously to attention, her inelegance pushing her hands into invisible pockets. She approached and air-kissed Red on both cheeks. John poured them all a glass of wine, pleasing Red by choosing to save the bubbles for later. Then he excused himself, saying that there were a few minor adjustments to be made to dinner. It was simple fare: a pesto sauce, fresh pasta, a few herbs and a generous portion of garlic; melon with honey and mustard dressing to start.

Michelle toyed with Chrissie while Red pottered

around the room, paying particular attention to the record collection. She asked him to pick a CD. Red searched for something he'd actually heard of. The sweet ambient sound of Talk Talk's *Spirit of Eden* was cut mid-song to be replaced by U2's *October*. Red took the liberty of boosting the volume and 'Gloria' blasted out around the tranquil house. He told Michelle of the times he'd seen them live, pre Live-Aid, just as Bono was perfecting his short-at-the-front and long-at-the-back look, the one that made him look like a hairdresser. He didn't like the later stuff, what he termed 'the old spiritual bollox'.

John was still ambling around the kitchen mixing the honey and mustard. He had tired of this album but he still looked forward to hearing the harrowing tune of 'Tomorrow', the song where Bono first showed signs of being more than a flag-waver in leather trousers. John contrived to time the starter to coincide with the end of the song. The tune began with uillean pipes before Bono's voice streamed in. He hadn't listened to it in years, and maybe it wasn't as he remembered, because Larry's military drumming came crashing in instead. After a minute he realised that the gobshite had skipped it, and the following track, because he reckoned them too slow.

He beckoned the two of them into the kitchen. He poured more wine and told them to tuck in. After a half-baked sign of the cross Red gave the impression of never having seen a melon before in his life. As he took his first bite, John remembered his disgusting eating habits. He tried to concentrate on other things, pretending to put the final touches to his pasta.

Michelle didn't seem to notice. Red was in full gallop about how U2 were great ambassadors for the country but they should have kicked Adam out when he was done for drugs. He added that it didn't really matter as Adam was British anyway and was never really one of us. He nudged Michelle to confirm her as his accomplice. Once he had finished his starter, well ahead of the others, he picked up a fork and with the spoon in his other hand he started drumming the table. John gulped down a full glass of red wine and decided oblivion was the only state to be in to get through the night.

The three of them got steadily drunker. During the pasta, Red took the opportunity to slag off all the Italians he'd met in Boston. Then he got in his expected pop at vegetarianism: 'A meal without meat is like settling for masturbation instead of sex.'

John couldn't be bothered to argue and anyway, he wasn't the converting type. A cheesecake was placed on the table and Red ate half of it, a cream moustache resting on his upper lip until Michelle pointed it out to him. On his last bite Red said it was time to open the champers. Popping open the bottle, he made an inappropriate cheering noise. He waited until the three glasses were full, announced a toast, had a quick sip before he put down his glass and did a drum roll on the table.

'You are now looking at the proud leaseholder of unit four of Treetown's rather splendid shopping centre, which will from here on in be named Red's Sports Emporium.'

Michelle and John offered their congratulations.

Michelle went as far as to pat him on the back. Red spotted John's disapproving look.

'I know you said I shouldn't take it. But I really think I can make a go of it.'

In between gritted teeth John grunted sarcastically: 'Well, I hope you have as much luck as John's Antique Emporium.'

Red ignored the comment. His enthusiasm was unabated.

'. . . And wait for it, I managed to talk that eejit Simon O'Donnell down to eight hundred a month . . . so I'm well within my budget. He's a nice bloke, that Simon, but half the time I haven't a fucking clue what he's saying. Still, he seems straight enough.'

John assumed that Red had been so annoying that Simon hadn't been bothered to give him the full reduction. To his relief Michelle kept the conversation going, asking all the banal questions that need to be asked on such occasions. He busied himself clearing the table, the perfect distraction as he thought things through. So Red was going it alone, was he? Still thinks he's a big shot . . . He knows best, does he? As he washed up, it niggled him that he hadn't got to the core of Red's soul; it was all so superficial. He still wasn't sure why he was allowing Red into his life. It was a ridiculous situation. He didn't like him, why not just make him disappear from his life?

But from his heroin experience he knew that Red, like his pain, would remain a pinprick getting bigger from time to time. Big deal, so Red didn't take his advice. Leave it, orchestrate a row, avoid one another . . . He could hear Red and Michelle enjoying a joke about homosexual Jews. What could they have in common? Then Red's voice piped up:

'Here John, another glass of wine over here.'

John wanted to tell him to go fuck himself but the sheer abruptness of the request forced him into carrying out the menial task. Momentarily he was the little boy being ordered about again. He even felt his nerves jangle as they had whenever he'd bumped into Red as a youth. He put it down to his wayward imagination. He took another huge gulp of wine and announced he was going to roll a joint. This made Red twitchy: he had obviously never smoked a joint before. But when he saw that Michelle was also participating, he grew calmer. They retired into the sitting room. Red found an old Police album to which he proceeded to sing along. Michelle lit the joint and soon she too was singing. Red took two quick toots of the joint and relaxed when he realised pink elephants weren't appearing before his eyes. Before long they were each away with their own thoughts, interconnecting and dispersing.

John was upset that Michelle and Red were getting on so well but at the same time he was pleased that she was able to come out of herself. As the hashish seeped into the brains, bullshit was coming out of the mouths. Snippets of profundity started them off on free association but they'd need a sieve to find any grains of pure intelligence. His fears allayed, Red was really going for it, asking for more and more dope. John took on the role of manservant as the other two giggled their way through bottles of pent-up youth. Sometimes they pointed at him when he made a cameo appearance in one of their remembered escapades. But at least it meant he was able to choose his own music without Red noticing. It soothed him to concentrate on some of his favourite lyrics. Then Red, becoming aware of the music, asked the question that would kill off any party.

'Have you got any Saw Doctors?'

John pissed himself laughing.

'No, we haven't,' he said. 'But I'm sure they're great ambassadors for the country.'

They all got uncontrollable giggles and then at eleven thirty Michelle tired very quickly and decided to go to bed. John went out to the hallway to order Red a taxi. When he came back, Red and Michelle were kissing each other. Michelle was having to control Red's *amour*. John stepped back into the hall, wanting to avoid a confrontation. He listened to Red repeating, 'Just a kiss, where's the harm? It's not like we haven't done it before.' Michelle gave him one last peck on the cheek and left him, giggling, unbalanced and with hiccups for company.

John re-entered the room announcing that the cab would be about twenty minutes. He listened to Red gabbling on about what a great girl Michelle was, how lucky they were. John was a little too out of it for small talk and his stomach too much of a queasy pit to focus on anything else. The only response he could manage was to say 'You'll be married soon yourself.'

'Indeed I will. I'm a settled man. You get sick of playing the field, don't you?' Red was slurring his words.

John was dreading having to get into one of those man-to-man chats. He prayed that the cab wouldn't be too long as the dope was swinging his moods. Red went on regardless.

'I'm a tit man myself.' He winked. 'But you know, once you've had your fair share of big-titted women, now I mean huge . . .' he demonstrated with his hands '. . . you do get bored. Like you touch them, you squeeze them, you can't even get your hands around them, you suck them, you look at them, and if you look close you see the veins because there's so much flesh . . . I like them fairly big, you know . . . but nice pert shaped ones, or even small, but big nipples, they're nice . . . now plum-shaped have their merits . . . What was my point?'

'You like tits.'

'Was it? Now I hope you don't mind me saying, but Michelle . . . her tits are dynamite.'

'Well they don't quite explode.'

Red giggled like a retarded child. He repeated again how lucky John was, and John took the opportunity to drop a little bombshell.

'I think you should know, myself and Michelle don't sleep together.'

Red tried to put on a concerned expression, failed, and mumbled, 'Are you'se going through a bad patch?'

'No . . . It's just not that kind of relationship.' John could hear a car coming up the driveway. 'Your cab's here.'

Red went to stand up but fell back into his chair. He tried a second time, using the arm rests for balance. He managed to get to his feet but John had to hold him to keep him steady. Stumbling, Red stood on Chrissie's tail: she screamed and no doubt would not make herself known for a couple of days. He was still apologising as they got outside. He gave John a big bear hug, the sweat pouring out of him. John could feel it clinging to his clothes.

'Thanks, John. It was a great night, you're a great friend . . .'

'But you're not going to kiss me on the lips.'

'Eh?'

'Nothing.' John was breathing out of his nose.

'Great guy, that's what you are. But you're fucking weird.' Red lunged into the cab.

John tapped the roof of the car. Before he sped off, the driver glanced at Red.

'Aaah, here, he's not going to be sick is he?'

Red butted in. 'No, no, I'm fine . . . are you a tit or an ass man?' and they were gone.

John was dazed, his stomach still churning, his head rattling. His whole body was mildly shaken. He found himself in Michelle's room. He'd forgotten how beautiful she was. Not a conventional beauty, but a face that creeps up on you, one where you become shocked by the devastation it could cause in you. She bewitched you with her face, and John wondered how he had been so blind. He went to cup her cheek. She awoke at the touch and smiled, which made her all the more radiant. John was turned on.

'You had a good time tonight, sweetheart. It was good to see you laugh.' He went to kiss her.

Her face took on an edge, and John became concerned.

'I don't want to beat around the bush . . .' she began.

John's anxiety went on to full alert. He was in no condition for any shocks.

'. . . But if you're going to have Red around in your life I think it's only fair you should know that I lost my virginity to him.'

The phone rang. John was losing control of his body. He looked at his watch: it had just gone midnight. Who could that be? The last thing he wanted to do was talk to anyone, but the ringing was beckoning him in spite of himself. He went to the phone and picked up the receiver, finding it hard even to muster a hello. His father's voice, naturally stern, sounded even more clipped than usual.

'I just thought you would like to know it was your mother's birthday today, and she went to bed crying when you didn't even bother to ring her.'

He hung up. John wanted to weep but that would have been too simple. His mind wanted to punish him: a burning ball went through his nervous system shooting up into his brain. A blackout would have been a relief but instead he was left with an overwhelming need for motion, to get fresh air, *I CAN'T FUCKING BREATHE*, anything to try and get away from his thoughts. Outside it had started to rain. *Good*, he thought, *a diversion*. No, it wasn't helping: he found himself jogging as the anxiety took hold, ebbing and flowing, ducking and diving away from his self. The padlocked door to darkness had been kicked open. *Hello madness*. He ran faster, his vision defective. *Please let me collapse, I don't care if I don't wake up, this is too much*. The darting gloom ran a second faster than he did, turning around to scare the shit out of him. There was no need for a *Boo*: words popped up at random: *unfit, sub-human, dismay, hate, madness. That's it you're going fucking mad.* Childhood nightmares were becoming stonethrows from reality: the straight-jacketed banging off padded walls, the slot on the door filled with his parents' eyes, the waving of official-looking forms, COMMITTED stamped upon them. Positive thoughts were quashed as they arose: parks, sunshine, ice cream. *Sorry pal, no can do, you've lost control, kill yourself, go on, kill yourself and you will fly.* Favourite songs, a nice bath, good friends, *you're all alone, nobody, nothing can help you. Think about it. MICHELLE FUCKED YOUR ENEMY. YOUR PARENTS DESPISE YOU. YOU KILLED YOUR OWN DOG . . . COME FLY WITH ME, COME FLY AWAY WITH ME.*

How do others cope? *This is everyone's state, they're just pretending to tolerate the whole sham, we're all going to lie down in disbelief and scream ourselves away, erode beyond silence.* Who is this talking to me? *Like you don't know? You know me well. I am the devil. Satan, Beelzebub, or, as I like to be known, The Prince of Darkness, that's nice, that title . . . I know you don't believe, and I can forgive that. Regardless of what you call me, I'll always be by your side; you are mine, and I'm coming to take you. It's not all bad down here ,you know. In fact I know somebody who's really looking forward to seeing you again. Isn't that right, PATRICK?*

But I'm only a little child. *You are a grown man and you deserve this and this is just the beginning. Boy, does it get worse.* Come on, pull yourself together, you've been through this before, you can handle it. *You're kidding yourself, you've never been in so deep.* As soon as he got home, John took four tranquillizers, came to a numbed calm, took off his drenched clothes and prepared to shake himself to sleep. Every time he closed his eyes horrific distorted monsters appeared, their faces belonging to those closest to him. Chrissie emerged out of nowhere and curled up beside him. He stroked her: she was his saviour. Tomorrow, he promised himself, he would go on the wagon.

Red slept like a baby.

CHAPTER 7

John filled up his diary in a crazed four-hour period. On the final full stop he slammed it shut, careless of corrections. Pushing away his problems, he opened Dominic's book. He found the most comfortable position in his reading chair, lit up a life-reducer and opened a bottle of water. Right then, let's see what Dominic has to say about the earth's inhabitants . . .

THE BLIND POET

James takes to the floor of the darkened space of the Kings Head downstairs room. Tuesday nights are set aside for poetry, and on these occasions the room is transformed into the Dungeon Club. Maybe twenty people are down there, all poets, assured or budding, all sweating profusely from nerves and lack of air conditioning. Outside it is the perfect climate, bright sunshine with a cooling breeze.

Five poets have read their work in progress. James is last. Five male and one female; all single; a bad ratio made all the more a long shot by the woman's refusal to identify with her womanhood. All of Jeanne's poems contain the word cunt. Her most memorable is the one where she calls all her household appliances cunts while referring to her vulva as an appliance. An example being:

You, you cretin,
you want to put your penis in my fridge freezer,
well nip over to my cunt and fix me
a cool drink first.

It's a very funny poem yet she sees no humour in it. She has become a bit of a joke to the other poets who refuse to look at the downside of the particular drums they beat themselves. They have all had furrow-browed discussions with her at some stage, engaging in chat in the hope of getting her into the sack, a tedious rigmarole which quickly stopped when she uttered the statement she always did when talking to open-gaped men – 'Do you want to fuck my brains out?' *A coy excitable* 'yes' *would fly back, to which she'd retort:* 'But then my brains would be smeared all over your penis and you would have me where you want me, a brainless plaything. Why don't you just fuck an empty head?' *She didn't get sent many flowers. The other five would gang up on her, safety in numbers saving them from embarrassment, not to mention that male trait of anguished hurt when they couldn't get what they wanted. The five males' poetic works consisted of digs at society, contemptuously throwing mud whenever possible. They all had their various causes, but if it was analyzed the main thrust of their work was about not being able to get laid. They each called it something different of course but then again that was their skill. They collectively hated elitism, and yet their constant mantra was* 'you just don't understand.'

James was centre stage. He had reams of notes with him but decided he only wanted to recite one line. James was everyone's favourite, because no one could resist his Leeds lilt. He played on this, and one of his most-requested poems was called 'When will someone with a Leeds accent get to read the News?' James was a powerful performer. His brown eyes matching his hair, he had an intensity that could be plugged in to at a second's notice, his expressive face bringing about a hospital of emotion which kept his audience on edge.

'Tonight I have a question. How soon . . .?'

The audience stared at his pause, half-wondering, was that it? Was that his week's work? The pause was unbearably long, but, like a natural performer, he knew exactly when to speak again.

'How soon . . . ' he repeated, heightening his build-up still further.

'How soon before your actual free range hen lays its egg with the bar-code already showing? Thank you.'

Gushing applause. Nobody really knew what he meant but they banked on it being profound. At the end of the night there was always an informal discussion: the other five asked him what it had been about. All James would offer was 'If I had to explain it there would be no need for poetry, we might as well meet up for a chat once a week instead.' 'Fair enough' was the sum of the concatenation of the conference. Every week they discussed the purpose of poetry in modern society, and every week they came to the same conclusion: that poetry is enlightenment, its questioning the norm; to try and find an understanding, to push forward ideas, to open a forum for debate, to bring people together.

Rolled-up cigarette butts and drained half-pint glasses filled the tables. The main light was switched on as the waitress began to ease the gentle souls away, shoo-shooing them out so she could prepare the room for the salsa classes the following night. Jeanne was first away, amplifying her enigma even further. James and Simon decided they could stretch to another half each and went upstairs to continue their discussion.

'Come on then, let's try and get a quiet corner away from the plebs.' As they upped the stairs they lowered their poetic souls, not wanting to associate themselves with others' perspectives. They saw a faded patterned carpet with years of alcoholic spillages and remnants of vomit wafting up into their nasal passages. Fags in their mouths helped to block out the smells. What they missed was the natural light shooting prisms down the stairs, battling against the darkness and winning. The big French windows acting like a colouring pot arcing beams as strong as lasers. Our heroes squinted, passing up on nature's free-for-all energies. The light was forcing the dust, dead skin and little bacterias downstairs out of harm's way. Space in the pub was so much in demand that James and Simon had to stand. The noise was too much for a proper discussion but enough of a din to stage a complaining session.

'These sad people drinking away their lives, shouting banality, dressing up for the privilege in their fancy clothes, that shirt, you could buy forty books with that. Look at them, these careless cordless-phone people, what understanding do

they have?' James was visibly upset with his surroundings.

'There's got to be a pay-back, but no, the fuckers have that covered as well with their sanitised version of the afterlife, these assholes, these good people . . . do you want to spend eternity with them? People you cross the road to avoid. My recurring nightmare is I'm constantly reborn into the wrong era, not the swinging sixties or the behind-the-door seventies or even the fucking re-issue eighties but the nineties, the nineties, the decade that hasn't even got an adjective; fucking post-feminist, pre-death X-xers, yesterday revivalists, recycled global villagers, advertising sloganistic intellectuals, opinioned verbatims, man, columnists are the new poets and a society without poets is no society.'

James had a pound in his pocket; did he have one more drink to vent his aggravation or feed his electricity meter? He walked outside and gave it to the group of six homeless people huddled by the door. Then he walked home. The one who had grabbed the coin was attacked by all the others, fists and old boots flying until James was out of sight. They had a last look to make sure he was gone and laughed amongst themselves. The one who had grabbed the pound went into the pub and gave the all clear; the rest of them took off their rags to reveal designer clothing and followed him in. Inside the pub the shouting stopped; the lights were dimmed to a more intriguing setting. Better music came on the juke box, seats appeared out of nowhere, everybody coupled up. Behind the bar the drinks were put away as there was no need for any chemical substances. Newcomers were greeted like old friends, the relaxed atmosphere producing broad natural smiles. Laughter was heard, and not the passing cackle on hearing a joke but the laughter of well-being. The room cleared of smoke and the air became golden fresh, the plastic flowers around the windows grew and their fragrance caressed the room. A swarm of bees hovered above offering honey instead of stings. Spiders webbed messages of love in corners, squirrels massaged backs and ants carried canapés. It seemed like a perfect utopia and in a way it was. The participants knew they could never reach perfection, because it didn't exist. If this was as close as they could come to it, then surely this was *perfection. They all understood this. They went home as one, each couple armed with one another; perfect crevices had formed on their bodies to accommodate their partners' limbs. Once home they made love, a silent ritual expressing what they knew with what they had been given.*

The six poets sat at home, missing each other, each of them hoping that they'd impress the rest of the group the following week. Jeanne was spray painting 'cunt' on to her hoover. She was thinking of getting into the visual arts. James sat in the dark hoping his teary inspiration might bring down the government.

John put down the book, marvelling at the story and letting its true meaning osmose itself within. Already, without him knowing why, it had helped, or more, encouraged him with his impending visit to his parents. He was really going to try to see the up-side of their life. Okay, it would involve a trip back to Treetown, which filled him with anguish, but he was more in control now that he had been prescribed a course of beta-blockers by his ever-giving doctor. The tablets stopped his heart from pounding. They were the ones that snooker players used to steady their nerves. They were good in the sense that they didn't tranquillize the brain, only the heart. On beta-blockers you could carry on as normal. Their only side-effect was that they made it impossible to fall in love. Or if you did, you wouldn't notice. The woman of your dreams could walk into a room and your heart would go *tick . . . tick . . . tick*.

Mondays were John's favourite day. It was his clear-out day, when he could shovel away the preceding week and look forward to what lay ahead. He would pay his bills, answer any correspondence and deal with any charity requests. On a Monday he was a soft touch. He gave money to the Aids Alliance Group and sent a donation to PETA, an animal welfare group who were presently campaigning against Gillette, accusing them of barbaric mistreatment of animals in the cause of giving people a smoother shave.

On a whim he wrote to Dominic Richards telling him when he was going to be in London and where he was staying in case there was any chance of meeting up. He felt like a twelve-year-old as he wrote gushingly about his enjoyment of Dominic's stories, trying not to sound like a Mark Chapman-type. He had only written to an idol once before, and that was Eric, the chubby bass player from the Bay City Rollers. Of course like everyone else he preferred Les the chubby singer, but he figured he had more of a chance of getting a reply from Eric. He had written saying that if he was ever in Dublin to be sure to pop in for a cup of tea. When the Rollers did play Dublin, he'd half expected to come in from school to find Eric strumming his bass while chatting with his mum in the kitchen. But after Eric failed to show he didn't hide his love for Les any more. In fact he'd nearly written to Eric again to tell him he didn't really like him anyway. The memory tickled him. He thought of the old footage of the screaming hordes of girls all shouting out for their favourite Roller. What sort of self-esteem could the ones who'd shouted for Derek have had? Derek, the even chubbier drummer. Derek who always wore the same inane grin wherever he went, his passport to the world. Looking back, it was clear that the grin was saying 'I can't believe my luck'. No doubt he would have gone down in the history books as the only teen idol whose eyebrows met in the middle, at least until the Gallaghers raised their ugly heads.

John decided to jog down to the village to post his letters. In school he'd done a lot of cross-country running. His scrawny bandy-kneed skin-and-bone body had been ideal. His PE teacher had said he had bags of potential and he'd won the school its first-ever trophy but like George Best before him, he'd let success go to his head. For him it hadn't been busty blondes and champagne breakfasts, but the odd fag behind the hedge. Now he wanted to run to rid himself of all the toxins he'd imbibed over the years. All kitted out he strolled out the front door promising to pace himself over the three-mile hike. But he hadn't really allowed for his seventeen-year lay-off and he was out of breath after five minutes, coughing out spittle that knotted itself and came out of his mouth like the magician's coloured handkerchief; it just kept coming and coming. At the same time he realised that jogging clothes may look okay if you see them brush past very quickly, but if you're walking at the same pace as the observers they get a full view of the hideousness of the get-up.

Safely back indoors, he changed into less colourful clothes. Michelle was up. It had been a tense week for both of them. They were polite and courteous to each other without ever really communicating. The deepest they'd been able to cut was 'Is anything the matter?' 'Nothing, everything's fine.' This stand-off was going on for longer than normal, but it was hard to pinpoint since it hadn't erupted into a row. They'd both been scared to bring up Michelle's earlier revelation and now they both knew they had left it too late to mention. It preyed on both their minds. Michelle was about to offload hers onto Dr Smiles with whom she had an appointment that afternoon. John mulled it over constantly, changing it from a piddling little part of her past which had nothing to do with him to being the most immovable wedge between them. Good weather was on the way and Michelle had started dressing for the season in light floral dresses, T-shirts and shorts. Spring suited Michelle. Her figure was at a peak and every time John looked at her and thought of Red's clammy hands fondling her it made him angry. The fact that she had been only fourteen made it worse. It was always the little girl that John sought in Michelle, the lost look of childhood which she still retained. When he met someone and fell in love he always wished he'd known her when they were children, regretting that they hadn't grown up together. When he thought of Red and Michelle together, he pictured Michelle as a teenager but saw Red as he was now. Then he had to stop thinking about it altogether because it was too unsettling. It wasn't the sex he objected to but the intimacy. The idea of Michelle, whom he truly loved, touching Red, the animal, the beast, the Neanderthal, made him question her whole character. He'd noticed from their little party that the two of them still had an attraction, a bond, but he couldn't even contemplate this: his mind just went into overdrive.

John had that typical male double standard when it came to sex. In previous relationships he had been unfaithful but he'd never seen it as anything worse than a lapse in concentration. A shag of relief without emotion, just letting the animal off the leash. Of course each time on the point of orgasm his head had spun with remorse and disgust, enabling him to treat his one-night stand with the utter contempt he'd shifted from himself. He had a warped morality of his own and would never have sex with a woman who was in a relationship. As was invariably the case with those brought up in a solely male domain, he'd never fully comprehended women. His mother being his only model, he expected his women to follow suit – hoover and nurse. His relationship with Michelle was a qualified success, with no messy sex to get in the way. It was beyond him that a woman could be unfaithful to her partners. She didn't have the excuse of being led by her penis. He couldn't believe that a woman might just want sex. No, if she slept with a man it could only be because she had strong feelings towards him. His baggage was severely weighed down by his first real love: not the pretend world of Peggy, the world which didn't exist, the world of the one perfect moment, but his first venture into the heart of a real person. He had failed miserably. She had run off with another. Well, not quite run off, more sat down and introduced her new man before slow-motioning away from him, locked in a tight embrace. To cope with the dismissal he had numbed his heart with alcohol, working beyond exhaustion levels until she had never really existed. He filed her away with Santa Claus, someone in whom he had once believed.

Michelle interrupted his thoughts with 'Are you ready?'

He looked at her and ached with the need to state a heartfelt 'I love you.' But he couldn't say it.

The car journey was muted. John wasn't playing games, he was simply deep in his own sphere. The Red House Painters offered a down beat. He had to concentrate on his driving which was difficult with the floaters that were impairing his vision, crashing into each other before his eyes. He wondered if he had purposely tried to destroy every relationship he had ever been in. Yes, he probably had, not out of malice but because he was emotionally crippled. He was grateful he had taken a beta-blocker, as these weren't his most calming minutes. He decided he'd have to ask Jodie, now happily married, a child on the way, where it had all gone wrong. They remained friendly and met up at least four times a year, but they'd never really discussed their love's demise.

He dropped Michelle off at the clinic, trying again in some way to communicate love and failing. It dawned on him when he was alone in the car that he was heading back to Treetown for the first time in ten years.

Dr Smiles ushered Michelle into the room with pleasantries and offers of tea. His polite concern was too similar to the atmosphere that had been festering at home over the last week. She couldn't help herself: she burst into tears. The doctor was surprised, but didn't say a word. He casually handed her a tissue.

'Myself and John are falling apart,' she blubbered. The doctor remained silent, letting her tell him whatever she had to in her own time. His own marriage was on the verge of collapse and he wanted to steer the afternoon away from too many painful associations.

'He doesn't talk to me,' she pleaded. 'He looks at me as if I'm in the way, he leaves the room when I enter.' There was a long pause while Michelle gathered her waywards.

'Red came around for dinner and as you know they've seen a lot of each other lately. . . Look, the thing is, well, I thought if they were going to be friends he should know that I lost my virginity to him. I didn't want it coming out as drunken talk . . . I don't know why I told him. It just felt right, we don't keep secrets. But he's been very cold since, I don't know why, it's not like we have sex . . . you know me and John have never had sex.'

The doctor nodded.

'Maybe it's me . . . lately I've been . . . oh, I don't know . . . the middle ground between where I am and where I dream of being. I want to be a woman again, platonic love isn't enough . . . and maybe . . . I would like children.'

She hesitated for a second, and again not getting any reply, she went on.

'I know that's a turnaround but I know that not wanting them was a reaction against my own upbringing . . . I'm not a bad person, am I? . . . I'm ready for more responsibility in my life. John doesn't see that, he lets me get on with it, as if I'm a piece of furniture . . . There's so many things I want to do before I die, but I've been just lying there in wait . . . Maybe that's why I told him, just pure and simply to gauge his reaction, to get a reaction. I feel unlovable. . . I want to be cherished, to be noticed . . . Look, if the truth be told I have feelings for Red . . . no, no, not Red; well, yes, Red but not necessarily Red –' she took a deep breath '– do you know what I mean? It could be anyone, anyone who is affectionate to me . . . I don't even fancy him. Maybe I do, Christ I haven't had sex for three years . . . Look, are you going to say anything?'

'You're doing fine.' Dr Smiles picked up his pen. 'What piece of furniture do you think he sees you as?'

John was pleased that the sun was still shining as he approached the new by-pass which linked Treetown with the rest of civilisation. He'd half-expected a dark cloud to have settled on the place. As he drove on to the Treetown road he saw that the green fields of his youth were gone and the area was now a burial ground for cheap and cheerful box houses. Its atmosphere was that of a seaside town out of season. His hands tingled and he took a firmer grip on the steering wheel. He drove past the dilapidated shopping centre and watched the dead-end gangs of young teens jumping over the cul-de-sacs looking for adventure where there wasn't any to be found. He pulled up at his parents' house which had remained the same, at least on the ouside. The whole of Treetown looked as if it could do with a lick of paint. His father's Escort was in the drive, parked slightly lop-sided. No doubt his father had driven home drunk the night before. John got out of the car, grasping a huge bouquet of assorted roses with a simple note saying 'Sorry'. Inside the envelope was a cheque for a thousand pounds. As he approached the patio door, the front door opened. His mother, beaming: a few missing teeth, but overall a pleasing-looking face. She took the flowers and immediately went to put them in some water. John made his way to the sitting room affecting tiredness in the hope that they wouldn't expect too much from him. As he settled himself on the sofa his father appeared, tea towel in hand, wiping away suds, an impish grin on his face, the nearest he got to a full smile. He went to shake John's hand. John put his hand out with a sarcastic 'You know me, actually. We're related.' It was cruel of him as he knew his father wasn't good with company and never knew what to do at any sort of social gathering. His mother came in with a cup of tea and kept repeating how gorgeous the flowers were. John asked her if she had opened the card. She hadn't, and went back out to the kitchen to fetch it

'Oh,' she gushed when she saw his cheque. 'You shouldn't have, you shouldn't have.'

'It's the least I could do, Mum. It was terrible of me forgetting your birthday. There's no excuse, all I can say is that I've had a lot on.'

'You forget mine every year,' his father chipped in.

'Yeah, but as you keep telling us Dad, you don't believe in birthdays.'

They established an equilibrium: John got more comfortable on the sofa; his parents stared at him more intently, plying him with prosaical questions. He tried his best but he couldn't muster any enthusiasm for them.

'Business is fine, house is fine, Michelle is fine; Chrissie's doing well, she's already grown.'

He felt nauseous, and was all the more unsettled because he didn't know what was causing it. The various smells that wafted around the house, though innocent enough, brought back his claustrophobic past. He shifted weight from one knee to the other, unable to concentrate on anything else. His mother launched into her local news bulletin about people John did not know. He tried to show interest by adding his own questions, but she was content to talk to herself, steaming off on a train of thought, taking no passengers. His father said that he'd got a pasta dish in for him and went to the freezer to show him. He was under the illusion that all pasta dishes were vegetarian, and when he showed John the ham and mushroom tagliatelli, John laughed out loud at his ignorance. His mother joined in, calling her husband a buffoon, and this led on to three examples of other stupid things he'd done lately. His father took these jibes in good humour because like John he knew that this was one of the few ways the family could share a moment. The television was turned on for the News and the soap operas that followed on, keeping the small talk down to the ad breaks. John was getting restless and every time he looked at his mother's smiling face, overjoyed that her son was in her company, his already laden heart sank deeper. He wanted to love her. He wanted to hold her, talk shit to her, white-lie her into the unchartable happiness he knew he was capable of giving her. But he couldn't. His lack of commitment to all those close to him upset him. Even to himself, happiness was rebuked by a part of him always silently reflecting 'you can't'. The predictability of his emotions was cutting off his lifeline.

Then his mind was torn asunder and he couldn't get an idea out of his head that was coming at him like a bullet. What if he was allergic to his parents, and he was always going to feel this way whenever he was near them? He suggested very calmly that he should go out for a walk to check out his old haunts. His mother said that she'd fix him eggs and chips when he came back. He left the house and wondered whether his parents sighed the same sigh of relief that he did. Did they think 'Thank God that waste of space has gone out for a while, he's so boring and he's no idea what it's like to be one of our generation. Ignorance, that's his problem, and if he asks me one of those stock questions once more I'll brain him, I need to have a bath.' He hoped they did.

John slipped into the cutting wind which was Treetown's oldest resident. Some of the buildings shielded him and pushed the breeze on to detours around the area. Coiffured hair was pointless in Treetown, which explained why there'd never been a fancy hairdressers in the locale. He took the same route he had as a paperboy: new constructions had shot up, ugly grey cemented rectangles which all came in under budget, a community centre and a school replacing the old pre-fabs. The area had matured with him, except that he'd fared better. He only had the odd grey hair, compared to the kaleidoscope of grey that was dimming his vision. He remembered exploring the area for the first time with his brother, trooping out with their cowboy outfits. He was seven and Paul was eight. There they were in their wild west, plenty of mounds and crevices to pretend with, watching each other's backs, thinking that this was the real start to their lives. They had their settlement, no more staying with grumpy Granny or kind aunties, a chance to start anew, to really build on their personalities. Walking along the estates now he still felt alien; he was still waiting for his life to begin. He thought of his brother again and their first new friend, Tony, an affable soul who was just as keen as they were to have cronies to explore with. They'd become a holy trinity, often spending upwards of sixteen hours a day together. Together they'd been invincible – until they'd met one of the earlier settlers, Declan, who wasn't too keen on strangers. He was older and due respect, that is until they'd discovered that he stuttered. The Trinity didn't make fun of him openly but they couldn't help their sniggers. Of course they tried to hide it but Declan noticed and his face had flushed with rage.

'I'm going to fucking ki-ki-ki-ki . . .'

They knew what was coming next and prayed that he wouldn't be able to finish his sentence, at the same time trying to help him along.

'Ki-ki-ki-kill . . .'

The tension was unbearable as all of them stood in pre-fight stance. John's legs wobbled because Declan was pointing at him. He knew he was going to get hit, even if the other two managed to save him soon after. He couldn't take it any more.

'Kill me, you're going to bloody kill me, that's what you're trying to say, isn't it?'

Declan punched John hard on the side of the head. It didn't really hurt but down he went, crying. Paul stepped in; he was only slightly smaller than Declan.

'Leave him alone!'

Bang, side of the head, down Paul went to join the other cry-baby. Tony had no option but to protect his new friends but before he managed a word he got it smack on the nose. Blood everywhere, he started to wail. The blood and tears mingled on his face frightened the other two. Their soaked faces dripped to form a puddle of solidarity. Their fear quickly turned it to ice. Declan cracked this open with his malice before going home, unable to believe his luck, stuttering 'L-let that be a lesson to you.'

That was the closest the three boys ever were, united in embarrassed defeat. When school started John had been separated from his crying comrades, being a year younger. His first day in class the teacher announced, 'We have a new boy,' and he was shepherded in, shy beyond recognition, his whole body blushing.

'This is John Palmer. Say "hello, John".'

'Hnn.'

John looked around at the thirty assorted boys and noticed the one at the front was sticking his tongue out. He was flummoxed. If the swots are like that, he thought, what are the ones skulking at the back like. He crunched his shoulders up, taking the weight off his head, as he went searching for the one empty desk. He remained like that for seven years.

Michelle had talked for forty-five minutes without interruption. Dr Smiles, with his calculated flippancy, was coaxing a much more aggressive session out of her than usual. It was old ground, but the doctor was aware that she went into greater detail with each recital. She would rarely talk of her wilderness years in London, when she'd been forced onto the street, and this was understandable; but the doctor always prompted her to tell him about those days because he believed she had blocked out certain truths. His approach was working well today, so much so that he was shocked when she gave him a harrowing account of a knife-point rape. Before, she had always attributed this to one of the other girls but this time she admitted that she herself had been through the ordeal. She was hoping that by confronting this trauma she might unburden herself of her imbalance, as if it was the final piece of the jig-saw. Still Dr Smiles was silent. No one event was the key to her problem, but he was pleased that her very acknowledgement of the episode meant that the feeling of self-hatred which frequently follows such an assault was fading.

Michelle was telling him how she had met John.

'I was operating out of one of those badly wallpapered one-bedroom flats you find around Soho. We had to keep on switching addresses as undercover cops were continually finding and fining us. Myself and two of the other girls used to meet for a drink every night in a pub called the Dog and Duck. We'd get vodka-ed up to numb what was to follow. One night I noticed a man staring at me. His face looked vaguely familiar. I assumed it was an old customer, but when he kept staring it began to unnerve me. The other girls noticed and told him to stop. Well, they said, "Fuck off, we're on a break." I remember John going extremely red and apologising. He asked could he buy us a drink and then eyeballed me, saying I looked like a girl he used to know, called Michelle. The other girls started needling him, saying he didn't have to be coy; just put the money on the table, that there was no need to chat us up. They knew me as Trish, and just thought he was a shy punter.

'I still couldn't place him. I was doing a lot of speed and poppers at the time and my head was in a permanent fog. John noticed my accent and asked me where I was from. I lied at first, but when he mentioned Treetown I just started sobbing. I was inconsolable. I'd been living in denial and it all came flooding out.

'He stood there not knowing what to do. It suddenly dawned on me who he was and it seemed so obvious, he hadn't changed at all. He said he had to go, and left the phone number of the hotel where he was staying. He asked me if I wanted to have dinner. The girls laughed, as this was the expression we used if a punter left us a large tip.

'I figured he couldn't get out of there fast enough once he had sussed what I'd become. It would have been hard to take up his offer. I had the mentality of a blow-up doll at the time and it was for the best . . . Well, you know it was impossible to pretend to be . . . human. To do normal things . . . It was for the best not to enter into it. It was too much. You hear about prostitutes who earn enough money and then stop, but I've never come across one. You get sucked in. The money isn't that good and the drugs start to take their toll.

'I threw away his number. I decided to go home and take the rest of my life off. I saw no way out; I just swallowed what pills I had and laid down. I woke up two days later in hospital with John by my side. He'd gone back to the pub. One of the girls happened to be there. He got my address, he had to pay twenty quid for it. Hearts of gold those girls. John found me, saved me and took me home.'

'Michelle, I've been seeing you for many years now . . . how come you never told me you tried to kill yourself before?'

Michelle didn't know what to say.

'I didn't want to worry you.'

'Let me ask you this . . . do you feel there's a cycle evolving?'

'I know what you're getting at. And to be fair, I don't really know. I hope not. I don't want to go that low again . . . but it has crossed my mind to get John to save me all over again. We were happy then. Or at least occupied.'

'I think we should leave it there for today. But I suggest you come twice a week for the foreseeable . . . And I've one question. It might seem an odd one, but do you always tell me the truth, Michelle?'

'Sometimes.'

The doctor closed his file and showed Michelle to the door. Then he rang his own shrink and booked himself an appointment.

John found himself inside the Treetown shopping centre. It was closing time and there were few people around, but those that were gave an impression of bustle, since there was an urgency about their shopping. He peered in at Red's unit, past the huge 'Opening Soon' sign sprayed on the window. There was no stock to see, only empty display cabinets. A couple of fitters were putting the finishing touches to them. It looked like a thrift shop: the wood was cheap and of course the cabinets were painted red. There was a tap on John's shoulder accompanied by a 'Boo!'

'That probably took a year off your life,' said Simon O'Donnell, laughing his laugh. John leant against the window, trying to gather his composure, muttering 'bastard' in a friendly tone.

'Do you fancy a snifter? You look like you could do with one.' Simon didn't wait for an answer as he locked his arm in John's and led him to his local, Cromwell's Head. In the two-minute walk, Simon took three calls on his mobile, ending each conversation with 'you're giving me cancer, gotta go.' Off the phone he went into raptures over the latest reports that overuse of mobile phones was being linked to cancer. 'I'm a hundred a day man myself, I'm fucked.'

Inside the pub Simon ordered two whiskeys. John didn't bother to correct him despite the fact that he couldn't bear the stuff. He asked for water and filled the glass to the brim to dilute the taste. Simon drank his straight.

'Hey, that pal of yours is a bit of an eraserhead . . . I tried to give him some invaluables but he doesn't want to know.'

He ordered two more drinks, not noticing John hadn't touched his.

'I hope he knows what he's doing, 'cos sports has never worked here. The only sports the kids around here are interested in are steroids. I'd say he'll do an Australian within six months.'

'What?'

'Go down under.'

'Really? Here, Simon what about that protection racket, have they been in?'

'No, they're a class act . . . scumbags. What they do is they come in on the opening day, always wear suits, and it's a word in your shell-like . . . They don't even give a warning, but if they're thrown out, the shop knows all about it soon after.'

'Can you not do anything about it?'

'No. They're Sid Vicious, you just don't mess with them. I wouldn't mind, but they're all kids, fifteen-year-olds . . . the parents do the more dangerous racketeering – and you don't mess with the railway children, if you know what I mean.'

'You've lost me again, Simon.'

'Connections everywhere.' Simon finished off his drink. 'I don't know, there's too much violence on the telly, maybe a sports shop will do the area some good.'

'Are you going to tell Red any of this?'

'Three monkeys, pal.' Simon touched the side of his nose. 'I'm out of here, good luck,' and he was gone.

John stared at his drinks before his eyes wandered around the pub. He'd never come in here in his youth and now he remembered why. It was an auld fellows' pub. There were four of them now scattered in corners who wouldn't look out of place on the Aran Islands. He thought of the night ahead of him with his parents. He stared at his drinks again and downed them both in one. The task left his face contorting the faces of the old men.

Red and Peter had positioned themselves in a quiet enclave of the Treetown Inn. Red was still preoccupied by the grand opening planned for two weeks' time. Peter was cautiously excited by the venture.

'Who to get to open it?' wondered Red. 'Who would they come out to see?'

'Red, it's Treetown. They come out to see the binmen, for Christ's sake.'

'I want to start with a bang.'

'Get the IRA to do the opening then, or better still the gas board.'

'Yeah, yeah. Very funny. I want it to become the shop that things can happen in . . . what about George Best?'

'Why stop there? Why don't you get Pele?'

'Stop acting the bollox, Peter. We gotta think seriously. This could be our way out. If this goes well we could start a chain of shops, become big business . . We could be set up for life.'

'Maybe you should concentrate on getting some stock for this one first.'

'That's all in hand, I've got two suppliers battling for exclusive rights. I'm juggling between the two. One of them is willing to throw in one of those pressing machines – you know, to print names on the back of jerseys – for free.'

'What about John? Does he have any showbiz connections?'

'He's all mouth, he is. Anyway he hasn't the first idea about sports, the wimp. I think he's a little unstable, actually.'

'What do you mean?'

'He's a bit of a boozer. Really knocks the stuff back. He's always fidgeting. Himself and Michelle have a very strange relationship . . . They don't even have sex you know. What sort of relationship is that? She's way too good for him. He's a loser. Always was, always will be.' Red drained his pint.

'He seems to be doing okay from where I'm sitting.'

'He's just got the rub of the green, hasn't he? He's jammy . . . There's no brains behind it, just pure luck.'

'So when are we going to meet your elusive fiancée?'

'Soon.'

'You haven't rung her since you got back.'

'I've been busy. Anyway Mum would go spare if I rocketed her phone bill, and the time zones make it awkward.'

'It just seems strange . . . Why all the mystery? You never talk about her, what's she like?'

'Look, she's an absolute queen . . . You'll meet her soon enough.'

'Why did you come back in such a hurry?'

'Why all the fucking questions?' Red was getting visibly annoyed. 'We're supposed to be relaxing. Anyway, you know why. To see Mum, to spend some time with her.'

'But you've hardly spent any time with her.'

'Ah, come on now . . . don't start.'

'That's you all over, avoiding your problems . . . You

know I think we should start making arrangements for the funeral.'

'Now call me old-fashioned, but aren't funerals for dead people?'

'It's only a matter of time.'

'She hasn't got any worse.'

'She hasn't got any better, either.'

'She could stay that way for ages.'

'You don't see it, do you? Your coming back, your starting a business . . . none of it has improved her condition. Does that not tell you she's on her last legs.'

'Do you want another?'

John had whiled away a couple of hours nodding at his parents in between bland comedy shows on the television. Now he had the sitting-room to himself. They'd decided to go for a drink at the Treetown Inn, which meant that his parents had to get all dolled up. His father would put on one of his three suits. He insisted on looking dapper even if he was only popping down to the newsagent. He had his little ritual of trying on six or seven ties, never really happy with his decision. A splash of aftershave and a rudimentary comb of the few remaining hairs and he was ready. His mother would try on several different oufits, each time catwalking down to John to ask his opinion, ending up with an assortment from each ensemble. By the time she left the house she'd be wearing a composite of her wardrobe.

John dreaded the pub. He was sure to bump into people who'd sat beside him in school; sisters of older brothers, ex-football-team mates, girls who'd snubbed his youthful features and now spent all their time trying to reshape their bodies after five pregnancies, parents of old friends; all eager to toast his success and welcome back one of their own. It was nine o'clock when they got there and the bar was stuffed but they managed to scramble together three seats. The waitress was straight over; two pints of Guinness and a vodka and red were ordered. They milled down the first drink, each anxious to steady the nerves with which all three were struggling. It took his mother two drinks to send her on her merry way, John five and his father six. The parade of the friendly neighbourhood greeting committee was steady and polite. Left to their own devices the family slipped into automatic anecdotal mode. His mother had ten tales to tell about John's youth of which she never tired. It was always the same ones: Do you remember the time he put on that dress, gave cheek to the priest, started smoking and hiding his fags in a gully? The time he went camping but came home scared, won his first race, crashed the car, got bitten by the dog, lost his front tooth, bashed his brother with her expensive antique kettle and, of course, had his first girlfriend. Now and then his father would interrupt with 'I don't remember that.'

Red spotted them and came over with a round of drinks. He was charm personified as he invited them all to the grand opening. John's father insisted that Red should call him Pat and the two of them rapidly bonded as the older man listened to Red's big plans for sports in the area. Pat thought he was an expert in all sport-related talk and kept reminding Red about their common link of being great ball players in their day.

John, feeling drunk, juggled his attention between his mother and Peter, both of whom were being ignored. He also kept an eye on the waitress, who was becoming prettier by the pint. His mother went from merry to maudlin, never quite managing to get drunk. Peter stayed the same, never animating a conversation. John liked Peter, or at least felt sympathy towards him. He wondered whether Red had bullied him as well. Peter seemed to resent all the attention his brother was getting. What riled him more than anything was the number of people who came and commiserated with Red about his mother's condition. Meanwhile Red had got bored of Pat and his habit of asking the same questions over and over when he was drunk. He tried to change the subject on to John.

'You must be very proud of the boy, he's done well.'

Pat began his proud father speech. 'He's the brains in the family . . .'

Red, still in his public relations mode, agreed. 'He's a clever fella alright.'

John's mother was about to launch into anecdote number five when Peter interrupted them for the first time that night.

'That's odd.' His voice was louder than normal and all eyes fell on him. 'Because Red was only saying earlier on that he thought John was stupid and it was pure luck that got him where he is. Isn't that right, Red?'

Red blushed and tried a little damage limitation.

'You'll have to excuse my brother, he doesn't get out of the house much.'

Peter got up and left, leaving them with, 'Yes he's

right, I'd better get back there now. Goodnight.'

The four remaining didn't know where to look. Red apologised for Peter, blaming the pressures of their mother's illness for his outburst. John remained silent, enjoying watching Red squirm, his eyes giving away nothing of his mood. Red compensated with endless chat. Yes, thought John, this was beautiful; this was the prettiest sight he had come upon in a long time. Red having to confront himself. *Oh, I'll have to see more of this, this is practically addictive.* He smiled a little smile, and it could have been his imagination but Red looked frightened.

Yes, he thought, this will do nicely.

CHAPTER 8

'You're a gas ticket you are.' Michelle was being sarcastic. John had packed and was ready to leave for the airport. The taxi was waiting outside.

'Michelle, can you stop staring at me like we've never met before? It unnerves me.'

She continued to fix her eyes on him, locking him into her vision. When he ignored her she picked up an empty plastic bottle and threw it at him. It wasn't to hurt him physically but to show her disapproval.

'Look, I'll be back by the end of the week. Maybe we can talk then. But this is pathetic, we can't have the big discussion as I'm going out the door.'

'I don't want you to go. I need you here. What if I get sick?'

John was losing his temper.

'Oh for fuck's sake, Michelle, just stop it will you. I'll ring you when I arrive.'

He grabbed his bag and didn't look behind. He jumped into the back of the cab and exhaled heavily, breathing away his problems. Leaving Ireland seemed to take a giant weight off his shoulders. Being able to go over to civilised London and become a stranger in a strange land even for a week was exactly what he needed. It would allow him the chance to clear his head of all responsibilities and catch up on his life. Michelle was no doubt crying into her pillow at this moment and he surprised himself because he really didn't give a fuck.

'It's yourself, isn't it?'

Oh shit, he had got the chatty driver. They'd once got into a spirited conversation and now, every time, the driver wanted to continue where they'd left off.

'Off to London is it?' he queried, checking his mirror for a reaction. John simply nodded, hoping this might stop the rot.

'Taking some time off away from the Dublin gangsters, are we? They're running the fucking city, honest to God this place is going to the dogs. I remember a time when you could walk the city at night and the most you'd see was a couple of stabbings.'

Another non-committal snort from John.

'I only took this job because I live by the airport. Handy for the holliers as well. Noisy as fuck though . . . I have to pop in on the missus when I drop you, I'm in the doghouse at the mo.'

The fact that John had not replied to the five-pronged

attack and had even taken out a book did not stop the blabbering.

'I didn't get home last night, I've got a bit of spare in Cabra and we got carried away, you know what it's like. She's got an arse you could park a caravan up. I'd leave the missus, only for the kids.'

Out of politeness John asked how many kids he had.

'Wha'? No, I haven't got any kids, me spare has, can't stand the fuckers meself.'

John gave in. 'Well, there's more to life than a nice arse you know.'

'Oh, she's got great tits as well.' The cabbie was pleased with his little joke. He was on a roll. 'So what takes you to London? Are you over to plant a bomb or is it an abortion you're after. . . ha ha.'

'Business trip.'

'And what line are you in?'

'Antiques.'

'I'll give you the missus for a tenner. She's saggin' a bit but with a polish and a rub down you'd get a fair price for her.'

John was left with no option but to smile the fake smile and let out an elongated 'yeaah.'

'Any pleasure while you're over there?'

'I'll take in a soccer match.'

'Who do you follow?'

'Arsenal.'

'Fucking shite, who are they playing?'

'United.'

'Now there's a team.'

'Who do you support yourself?'

'Bohs.'

'Do you not support any English teams?'

'Yes I do, the Republic of Ireland.' They both laughed.

'And why do you support Arsenal?'

'I guess I like fucking shite.'

The conversation petered out after the taxi driver had used up his week's quota of chat. Still hustling for activity he got on his mobile and ordered flowers for his wife and a smaller bunch for the woman with the great arse.

At the airport John decided to upgrade to first class. He didn't want to take the chance of hearing another rendition of somebody else's life. He picked up some cigarettes in the Duty Free and headed for the bar where he joined other revellers bidding goodbye to their last pint of authentic Guinness. He dreaded flying. At least, he thought, it would be better to crash in first class. They'd have softer cushions on impact. He was scruffily dressed and the ageing Aer Lingus air hostess was openly perturbed to see him take his seat in the second row. The need to have the row to himself was not essential. Dominic's book close up to his face acted as a partition, hinting that he wasn't open for discourse. He sensed a body storing luggage over his head but didn't avert his gaze. The body sat down beside him, his seat rising slightly as the other seat was occupied. It was someone light at least. One of the hostesses was handing out complimentary newspapers. The upgrade had cost him sixty pounds: John reckoned he might as well take one since it was costing him around a fiver. It would also give him the chance to glimpse his neighbour.

She was pretty, with short, bobbed brown hair, the eyes giving an air of knowing abandonment. Her overall look was that of the perpetual woman in a girl's body; John's type. When she spoke it was in a slightly husky middle-England accent, the voice continually questioning, regardless of the situation. John was intrigued, but for the moment he preferred to concentrate on his fear of flying. The plane started to push for position on the runway. John's heart kept its pace thanks to the beta-blockers but his hands clenched up as he indented the arm rest. He started deep-breathing as the plane got airborne, swaying with it as if he was in control of the joystick.

'You're not a flyer either.'

John kept staring at the dining fold.

'No.'

He hoped she wasn't going to impress him with tales of near-crashes which was how people usually tried to comfort those in his predicament.

'I hate it myself, and my father's a pilot.'

'Yeah.' He couldn't enter into any sort of conversation. In his mind he dismissed her as a posh Daddy's girl. He assumed she had never paid for anything in her life.

'I'm dying for a fag,' was her next gambit. When she got no response, she apologised, 'I'm sorry, I'm gabbling on, it's the nerves. I'll leave you be.'

'No, no, I'm sorry . . .' He introduced himself. 'John. I'd offer my hand but half the water in my body is seeping through them at the moment.'

'Tara,' she smiled.

The drinks trolley arrived. Tara ordered a double vodka straight. John, who hadn't planned to drink, asked for a red wine.

'Were you in Dublin for a holiday?'

'It seemed to work out that way . . . I teach art to over-privileged twelve-year-olds. I attended a conference trying to pull all the EC countries into what they call a tangible work structure. It was supposed to be followed by two days of think-tanking which turned out to be a pub crawl.'

John gazed into her eyes, completely entranced, his fear of flying disappearing fast. She finished her drink and excused herself and made her way to the toilet. John flicked through the airline magazine, taking none of it in, wishing it was crammed with details about Tara. She was other-worldly and it made him curse that he hadn't seen more of the planet. Yes, he'd escaped from Treetown, only to snare himself into the confines of Blessington. There was more to life than the moping faces that stared at him in the mirror. Tara had that lust for life which he admired but could never imitate. Suddenly he was distracted by a commotion on the plane. An alarm went off and he went into automatic panic. He saw Tara being forced out of the toilet where she had been caught smoking and he knew he was in love.

Her father had a lot more sway in the world of aviation than she'd mentioned and she got away with an on-the-spot fine. John spent the rest of the journey trying to determine whether or not she was single without seeming to come on to her. Surely someone of such beauty and razzamatazz would have parades running after her. She had no rings on, so he slipped off his own and shoved it into his breast pocket. An invitation to a small gathering she was having in her flat in Hampstead that night offered a glimmer of romance. John clutched at it. When they parted at the airport arrivals, he wanted to kiss her on the lips, but he didn't get the chance as they'd both started chain-smoking the second they touched the ground. A peck on both cheeks was the order of the day. She smiled a conspiratorial smile, her eyes closing a fraction, emphasising the shape of her face. John wished he had a camera. He pictured that face all the way to the city centre. He wanted to see it on billboards; this was a justifiable size. It annoyed him that he hadn't memorised every minute feature: his identikit memory kept narrowing her chin in to a sharp triangle.

His London associate, Philip Andrews, had booked him a room at the Groucho Club, telling him that he'd get a kick out of it. John thought it must have been a mistake as he alighted outside what appeared to be nothing more than a drinking den which bore the same name. He approached the reception area with a hesitant step.

'Have you got a room booked for Palmer?'

'John Palmer – yes, sir, if you would sign here. And we have a message for you.'

It couldn't be Tara, could it? Maybe she was just as keen on him . . . a little deduction and he realised it had to be from Michelle. It irked him that he'd been catapulted back to that level. It was only five hours since he'd seen her last but it might as well have been five months. He took the note and decided to read it in private. He was escorted up to his room and apologised to the porter for having no English money, a lie he decided to tell. The room was a poky affair: a sizeable bed, a tiny television which he turned on immediately, a standard dresser and wardrobe and, of course, the existential trouser press. He sat on the bed and studied his message. He had to read it twice before it sank in. It was from Dominic Richards. He would be in London at lunchtime on Sunday and would love to meet. For John this was a dream come true, but now it was relegated to second place with the advent of Tara. He quickly unpacked, making the room more homely, shoving all his clothes into one drawer, except for his Paul Smith suit which had cost him a fortune and demanded more respect. He'd only worn the suit once. Tonight it would get its second outing. As he carefully placed it in the wardrobe, he felt the rattle of the beta-blockers in his pocket. He went to the bathroom to get some water when an urge came over him and he chucked the pills down the toilet and flushed them away. He felt emancipated. He knew he was jumping the gun, but if this was the real thing with Tara, he wanted to live the experience to the full.

He lay on the bed, grabbed the spare pillow and curled up to her. He missed her beyond reason, and duck feathers snapped under his passion.

He was awoken by Philip Andrews, who was waiting downstairs in the bar, eager to party. John said he'd be down in two shakes. He planned to concoct tiredness to enable himself to sneak off to his Hampstead rendezvous. Still, he enjoyed Philip's company. It would give him a good opportunity to sip a few Dutch courages before he saw the ringless one again. He stopped himself dead in front of the mirror and saw a fool staring back at him. He needed to talk aloud.

'Cop yourself on John, this is a woman who sat beside you on a plane. She invited you to the party out of politeness, nothing more, nothing less. She probably has a boyfriend anyway.'

The phone rang again, startling him. He picked up the receiver.

'I'm coming, I'm coming.'

'You're eager, missing me already.' It was her voice, telepathically diminishing his dolour. He swooned into the phone and could only mumble excitement. In between small-talk he took the details down again, lit a cigarette, left a big ash trail on it, paced as much as the cable would allow and wished he had taped their first telephone conversation. When he asked why she rang, she said she just felt like it.

'That's good enough for me.' He was aware that he was talking for the sake of it. 'See you around ten' was exchanged at least eight times and her voice was gone.

John smiled with untouchable joy. Downstairs he found Philip sitting with two women. *Ah fuck, he's gone and set us up with prostitutes* was his first reaction.

'John!' Philip gathered him into a bear-hug. 'This is Sheena and . . .'

'Jessica,' Jessica answered.

'Pleased to meet you,' John managed as Philip whisked him into his corner.

'Right pair of crackers,' Philip winked.

'Are they hookers?'

'What? Have we met? They work in the office, and Jessie there has a thing for Irish guys.'

'Yeah, what's that? The pox?'

'That's just charming, John.'

'Ah, look, I'm sorry. I'm a bit whacked.'

'Yeah, that hour flight really takes it out of you.'

'It's been a bit frantic on the home front just lately.'

'And how is the lovely Bella?'

'Michelle? Yeah, she's fine.'

'Michelle, of course. I'm sorry, I always have trouble with names. I get these little systems together. I thought your . . .' He lowered his voice and looked around '. . . wife, Beatles song, Michelle my belle, bella, sorry I'm so stupid.' With this Philip spotted somebody he knew. He introduced John to his friend but then went on to ignore him for ten minutes. John smiled over at the girls. They were both stunners in that pure sex way, legs, lips and tits, full-bodied shag machines. Normally he'd be only too pleased to spend a raucous night out with the two bubblies but now that he had his new-found love he felt it would be beneath him. Philip sat back down.

'What do you think of the place then?'

'It's alright.' John was non-committal.

'It's alright? This is celeb central, the cream drink in here.' Philip rubber-necked for celebrities. 'That guy over there is one of the highest paid writers in the country.'

'What's he done?'

'Novels, but he mainly does food columns now.' He added out of the side of his mouth, 'A bit of a drug head.'

'Is he any good?'

'Wonderful capacity.'

'I meant at writing.'

'I don't read books. When would I get the time? He's well respected, uses a lot of big words . . . Hey, see that table over there? . . . Couple of Blurs, a Pulp and a taxidermist.'

Philip went on for over an hour relentlessly naming names. John was elsewhere. The good-looking women that brushed past him didn't even warrant a second look. Normally he would fall in love with at least three of them. He'd never do anything about it, but tonight he was actively sneering at them and their strutting. At nine-thirty he called it a night, his excuse being that he wanted to be on top of things for tomorrow, when they had two warehouse auctions to attend. Upstairs, his heart thumping, he changed into his suit. He darted past reception, taking on the personality of a teenager sneaking out of his parents' house in the middle of the night. In the cab he was once again burdened with excitement. His suit was uncomfortable and he kept doing up and then undoing the buttons of his jacket to find the best look. He passed the time watching Londoners scurrying about in the dark. It struck him that London was an incredibly well lit city. There was activity around each bend; flashing lights and zappy signs. The black cab was a novelty to him and he enjoyed the unique purring sound of its engine. He even got a thrill from the meter ticking away his money. The cabbie didn't say much and John wondered whether it was because of his Irish accent.

He reached his destination and told the driver to make it a round tenner. He saw lights and shadows coming from the second floor of the purpose-built apartment block. A split second of scepticism, and then his body started to walk towards the party regardless.

John wasn't really one for parties. He usually ended up in the quietest corner, getting blotto. The door to the flat was open and there were five sheepish types wearing serious we-need-cocaine expressions by the stairwell. Whooping and a hollering and an early Bee Gees album was coming from the main party area. John couldn't spot Tara anywhere and some of the guests were giving him strange looks.

'You must be John.'

He turned around to be smiled at by a docile blonde covered head to toe in PVC. John wondered which distinguishing characteristic made him so easily recognizable.

'Come on, we'll find Tara for you.' She put her arm around John's waist, her hand caressing his ass on the way around. John needed a drink. They found Tara in the kitchen, a joint in her mouth, struggling to open a bottle of wine. She was being helped by two guys who looked like they were big in the City but whose postures hinted they'd never done a day's work in their lives. John felt embarrassingly out of place, as if he'd wandered on to the set of *Friends*. Tara was prodded in John's direction. She put down the bottle and launched herself at him, arms flapping towards him, encircling his neck and expecting him to balance her. He was left with no option but to place his hands around her waist. She went to kiss him, forgetting she still had a joint in her mouth, the ashes sparking over his jacket, leaving two little burn holes. Tara grabbed a wet towel and rubbed at the damage which left the impression that a very tall person had pissed on him. He took off the jacket at Tara's insistence and she suggested that they should put it in her bedroom.

The blonde stopped necking one of the City boys to pipe up with, 'Tara, remember safe sex, check his bank balance first' before she went on to snog the other one. It was all happening too fast for John. He didn't like these people; he had come across the wannabe version in Dublin. A bottom-slapping society set based on inherited wealth, they went to the same schools, the same universities and ended up in the same jobs. They all hung out together, ultimately fucking each other in a pass-the-parcel manner. An incestuous bunch of clever people who unwittingly led a primordial existence, they'd invited John along to the fringes of their gatherings as nothing more than an oddity in whom they were vaguely interested. John was aware of this but had always believed in the individual as opposed to the group. His dislike probably stemmed from his resentment at being rejected by such a shower and the fool he had been for trying to infiltrate their ranks. He was worried that he was about to be kicked in the balls again but for now he was happy enough to have them tickled by Tara in her lair. All his instincts told him to leave, but he was smitten, a stab through the heart his only means of exit.

Tara became even more divine to him as they explored each other's bodies. He wanted to gift-wrap her and take her home in a box. Tara was kissing his face, holding it back, smiling and kissing again in a Woody-Woodpecker fashion. All John could contemplate was 'I've found the right person. It is possible, all those years of non-compromise have paid off.' He thought about all those sad fuckers who say they're in love, frightened to deal with the car-crash of emotion. *No, no you're not in love; come into this room, here is love, feel this, this is the real thing. You've been drinking Pepsi all this time, you fools. Observe, stay there in the corner, don't get in the way, keep quiet but watch us kiss. I know you've seen better but that's not the point. Christ, even her breath smells, and I'm sure mine does as well. Normally her bad breath would be enough to stop the affair there and then. A lifetime of halitosis, no thank you. But no . . . that's part of her personality, that's an integral part of her.*

Are you starting to understand?

They undressed each other and there may have been some passion-killing time involving tugging, unzipping and unclipping but it wasn't noted. There, naked, were two skinny people. Tara with her little boy's body except for her triangle of pubic hair and long-distance-runner breasts: alongside her knelt John with his little boy's body, age adding wayward nipple hair and the makings of a pot belly. Not a developed muscle in sight. They interlocked, and hey presto, two perfect bodies.

Is it starting to make sense? Let the lovemaking commence. It was a gentle session, a bit of rough discounted by the fragility of their bodies. There was no point in risking broken bones. John's task was to give pleasure, his own orgasm being nothing more than a pit stop. They settled into a position side by side, John taking control, grasping her bottom to deepen his motion. He felt the wetness as she embarked on a series of tennis-player grunts, not full-blown Nordic grunts but ones of the *enfant terrible* variety. Slowly building a rhythm. They were lost in trance when John was brought to his senses. At first he dismissed it, but as she orgasmed her whole body odour changed. Unsettled and arcane, its smell swelled, searching for its purpose. *That's what love must smell like.* This is the fragrance of love, and love likes to hang out with the garbage. They stayed in position as they silently lullabyed each other to sleep. The group of hapless real-love-seekers took notes and sneaked out of John's consciousness.

The perfect couple awoke in the same positions, too early for hangovers. The tenderness was still there and they drifted seamlessly from conversation to quick morning fuck. This time on the point of her orgasm John was bracing himself for the sudden smell of love. When it didn't come he was both relieved and disappointed to find the magic replaced with the sound of the rain banging against the window, its drumming the ideal accompaniment to her groaning. He remembered the Garbage song 'Only Happy When it Rains'. A little more textural caressing and it was time for him to put on his business hat. He asked for a cab number but she offered to give him a lift. They stopped off at a petrol station to fill the tank up. John went to get newpapers and soft drinks. He was part of a couple, a two into one, and cursed the last thirty years of his life. Tara dropped him off at the Groucho, arranging to meet him again at six that night. They shared each other's bad breath once more and parted, palms sliding over one another.

John had half an hour before Philip was due and he became downcast at being dumped back into reality without any cushioning. He lay on the bed, slowly dissolving into himself once again. He thought of those people who walk out on their families and disappear without trace. He understood their pain, their selfishness, their ability to admit that their lives had become one big mistake. A bravery which ultimately became a cowardice, all under the guise of popping out for a bottle of milk. Or maybe it's just that milk has that effect on certain types.

He wanted a bath, but he didn't want to wash Tara away. He stared at his reflection in the mirror just to have a peek at the lucky sod. His eyes had come to life and he winked at himself. He noticed the burns on the pocket of his Paul Smith suit. The little burns of love which he would treasure. He was also aware that he was turning into a sap.

Philip was down at reception knocking back a glass of Resolve. On seeing John he rose to his feet and greeted him, 'You just missed Sting.'

'That's a pity, we've so much to catch up on.'

'The bloke hasn't got any hair.'

John was bursting to tell Philip about Tara but he was afraid that he'd downgrade the whole experience.

'You left me in a right pickle last night,' complained Philip, tossing his head.

'What, with the two hookers?'

'I told you, they work at head office. I had to wine and dine them all night.'

'I'm sure your wife appreciated that.'

'You know me, John. I always put the job first.'

'Sheena's blow job? Or Jessica's?'

'I'm a gentleman, John, I don't kiss and tell. Suffice to

say that Sheena's hobby is playing the saxophone.' Philip nudged him.

They spent the day in different spheres, John urging on six o'clock, Philip eyeing up every woman they came in contact with. At the warehouse sale John bought twenty broken Helter Skelter double seats from a run-down funfair. It worked out well, he got them dirt cheap, intending to do them up and pass them off as garden furniture. From the second auction he bought fifty workable traffic lights and six authentic red phone boxes.

Philip had managed to procure him two tickets for the Arsenal-United game that night. Philip had contacts in every trade and always came up trumps when it came to freebies. His job with John was basically to take care of him on his visits and arrange for the shipping of any goods he bought. Philip wanted to take him out on the town after the game but John insisted he had to meet up with a cousin. He wouldn't take no for an answer and eventually John was forced to tell him the truth.

'Look Philip, I've got a date.'

'Why didn't you say? You kept that one a bit close to your chest. Is it one of the staff?'

'Someone I met on the plane, actually.'

'Jesus, you're a fast worker . . . Did you join the mile-high club?'

'Have you seen the toilets on Aer Lingus? . . . Anyway, it's not like that.'

'Sure.'

'It isn't.'

'Yeah . . . Well we've got nothing on tomorrow, so

keep all day Friday and all night free for me . . . Now is there anything else I can do for you?'

'Well . . . Do you have any contacts in the private detective business?'

'Bella hasn't been cheating on you, has she?'

'No, nothing like that. I just want to do a security check on someone. Do you reckon you can help me?'

'Doddle, what's the name?'

'Alan Bulger, better known as Red. I have all the relevant details written down here.' John handed Philip a small brown envelope. 'Cheers, Philip.'

'No problem. You know he doesn't even leave his room, does it all on the Net these days.'

'See you Friday.' John got out of the car.

'I think that was Patsy What's-her-face going in. Hurry up and you might catch something off her.'

John laughed and found himself in his room having bought a bouquet of flowers. He was not a romantic, and the idea of flowers or holding hands, in fact any form of public affection, didn't come near his antenna of thought. Now he was gazing at the different colours, smelling the individual scents, thinking this was a wonderful way to display love. His mother had always doted on the flowers he had bought her. He understood the process; the three or four days that the flowers would stand proud before they slowly started to die, a little back-breaking wilt, tired at having the pressure of human emotions to cater for but willing themselves alive, drinking to sustain one more day's glory; the inevitable fade until the whole bunch admitted defeat, the only consolation being that they knew they had done their job. Dead, they were buried with the trash.

The idea of giving flowers to terminally ill patients in hospitals and how they watched them bloom and wither and then disappear, knowing this would be the way they would go too, disturbed him. This rant was dark enough to warrant him putting his flowers in a glass of water, giving them that extra little help.

He went to lie on the bed but the thought wouldn't go away. In three or four days these flowers would be dead. He looked at the bunch again and this time he didn't see the beauty, he saw the slowing decay. He pictured Tony Curtis as he was now, an old man, and then as he had been in the sixties, possibly the most beautiful man in the world. In a flash, he knew what he had to do: not to dismiss beauty but to soak up as much of it as he could. He sat up a little, waiting, biding his time, looking at the football tickets. Arsenal could do them tonight, he reckoned. They always rose to the big occasion; it was when they played a team like Derby County that they failed to do themselves justice. It was as if the players resented such non-events, believing that it was an insult to make them play against such tripe. Their chameleon tendencies had cost them many a championship.

Tara rang.

'Come and get me.'

He was intoxicated by her voice.

'I'll be straight down. In the meantime, can you rough yourself up a bit because if you're as beautiful as you were this morning, I'll explode.'

'You're a sweetie.'

John grabbed his denim jacket and picked up the flowers which dripped onto his trousers, hurrying down to where Tara sat cross-legged in reception. There was that smile again. John speeded up his pace and thrust the flowers towards her.

'Do you like them?' He led her to the door.

'They are the most fantastic flowers I have ever been given.'

'Good. Now I want you to study them, feel them, cherish them. Take everything you can from them. Tell me when they have become an indelible part of your life.'

They found themselves in Soho Square. Tara embraced the flowers in every way she could, enjoying the foolplay. Excited, she said, 'I'm ready. They're part of me now.'

'Good.' John took the flowers from her and stopped a passer-by. 'Excuse me sir, I'm not weird or anything but do you think these flowers are beautiful?'

The middle-aged man was a little embarrassed and shrugged.

'Would you like them?'

Tara looked puzzled. The man noticed her frown. 'Have you two had a row?'

'*Au contraire.*'

'Why don't you give them to her?'

'Because, my dear friend, she has already soaked up their beauty, and now I feel it is your turn to do so.'

'Well, okay then.'

The man was unsure what to do. John handed over the flowers.

'There is one condition.' They both looked towards John. 'You can have them only until you have got everything you can from them. But then you must give them away also . . . with the same instructions.'

'Okay then.'

The man took the flowers and they watched as he strode down Frith Street, smiling and sniffing. John grinned at Tara. She jumped on him, legs akimbo, and started kissing his face. John held on to her. She nibbled on his ear and said, 'I love you.' John held back tears. He'd assumed he was beyond such spontaneity.

'Tara, do you like football?'

'You read my mind.'

'Well close your eyes.'

'No, you close yours.'

John covered his eyes with his hands.

'You can open them now.'

He did as he was told and Tara was holding out two football tickets. 'We're going to see Crystal Palace against Grimsby.'

John was in a state of disbelief. *Crystal Palace v Grimsby?* He was about to show Tara his own superior tickets when she confessed, 'I've supported Palace all my life. I haven't missed a home game in two years.'

John accepted his fate.

'Do you want to see someone else have happiness thrust upon them?'

She nodded as if hypnotised. Two young homeless men were huddled in sleeping bags in a nearby doorway. John approached them.

'Excuse me, where are you from?'

'You're not from the social, are you?' one said in a heavy scouse accent.

'No. You're from Liverpool?' He pointed to the other. 'And you?'

'Manchester.'

John couldn't believe his luck.

'Well, I have a little present for you.'

He handed the Mancunian his football tickets. The boy took them and looked at them for a moment and then handed them back.

'No ta, I'm a City fan.'

'You can sell them if you want.'

The Liverpudlian joined in. 'Yeah, they're going to believe us aren't they? I've got one of those faces that just says counterfeit.'

John gave them a tenner and spotted an Arsenal jersey-wearer walking on the other side of the street. They dashed across and gave him the tickets. Himself and Tara witnessed a gaping mouth; one big enough to stuff a bowl of fruit into. They were thanked at least twenty times as they ambled hand in hand in the direction of South London. John felt as if he was in one of Dominic's stories.

An eager mix of Palace fans beavered around Selhurst Park, the floodlights spraying light over the neighbourhood. A family atmosphere prevailed. Smiles and resigned frowns mixed it with tattooed faces and twelve-laced Doc Marten boots. Tara filled John in on the club's history. Every season Palace were either involved in a relegation dog-fight or a promotion push, with internal turmoil at least every third year. John flicked through the programme notes and recognised only one footballer – Ray Houghton, a Scot who was a folk hero in Ireland after declaring for the country and then having the audacity to score against England in a vital European Championship game.

Under the lights the Palace colours of red and blue made for a dazzling display which you couldn't help but get excited about. A meagre crowd of twelve thousand spread their legs in the roomy stadium, and about four hundred travelling Grimsby fans did their best to create a mood. As the game kicked off Tara grabbed John's hand and started shouting 'Red and Blue Army' and the old Dave Clark Five song, 'Glad All Over'. 'You say that you love me, all of the time,' she sang. John joined in half-heartedly, surprising himself that he was chanting and more so that he was doing it in a South London accent.

The game was one of huffing and puffing, pacey runs and misplaced tackles, broken bicycle kicks with the occasional flurry of bad passing. John wondered how the Arsenal were doing. He had been to see them twelve times over the last seven years and the football was in a different league, both in terms of the quality of play and support. The biggest difference between the clubs was that Arsenal fans went full of expectancy, while Palace fans seemed grateful for a shot on target. The Arsenal crowd had greater volume, but John found himself enjoying the Palace fans. He put it down to the company he was keeping but recognised a humour in the crowd which was sadly moving away from football. Even when they were barracking the opposition fans with taunts of 'No-where, Grimsby are going no-where,' it was done with affection. Tara knew all the chants and the camaraderie was special: John had been invited into her family home. The Palace fans had chants he had never heard before. When the home team had a corner, a section of the crowd would shout 'Dodgy keep-er, dod-gy keep-er' in the hope of putting him off his stride. Tonight they had changed the chant of 'You only sing when you are winning' to a customised Grimsby version which went 'You only sing when you are fishing', which was just as well as there wasn't much happening on the field.

The game ended nil-nil and the crowd left in a whisper. John overheard one fan complaining to another, 'That's the last time I am going to see those cunts, they were fucking shite.'

'But you've got a season ticket.'

'Harry, I'm just letting off steam. Of course I'll never miss a game. I'm just saying they are shite.'

John decided there and then that he'd always keep an eye out for Crystal Palace. As an Arsenal fan he'd never been able to fathom how you could support a team like Palace unless you were a local but now he'd drunk from the same cup and witnessed the spirit which surrounds the smaller clubs. When the numbers aren't there, the individual fan's passion is intensified. He forgot all about the Arsenal game until they went into a local boozer and saw the televised result – Arsenal 4, Manchester United 3. A classic. They showed Ian Wright's hat-trick, much to the dismay of Palace fans in the pub who kept shouting 'Judas' at the screen each time he scored. It took John a while before he remembered that Ian Wright used to play for Crystal Palace. When she saw the report Tara covered his face in kisses, full of pretend apologies.

'I'm sorry John, I'm sorry. I promise when we get back I'll give you a blow job.'

John, who never liked public talk of sex, assured her, 'That won't be necessary.'

The barman, who was listening in, chanced his arm with 'I'm an Arsenal fan too you know, love.'

They took a bottle of the house's finest red up to John's room. The fact that they both loathed champagne inspired the inevitable discussion of their respective likes and dislikes. Tara lay on John's lap and splashed out her family history. Hand-me-down to look down upon, middle child, sandwiched between two sisters; one long-term boyfriend, a six-year stretch, the rows turning to blows, from clever bastard to evil bastard, pushy to pushing his luck. John held her tighter. He started kissing her neck and before they knew it they were having their first not-under-the-sheets fuck. A flurry and a scurry and the bits of clothing that came off went back on. In the grand tradition of Irish men through the ages John asked about contraception after the sexual act.

'Are you on the pill?'

'You'd know all about it if I was.'

John threw her a look.

'I'd grow fangs and horns and green stuff would be coming out of my mouth.'

John reflected for a moment on the prospect of Tara becoming pregnant. He had never wanted kids but he'd been mellowing of late. Doting on Tara, it would make sense with her; to bring up a child in a house of love.

'What are you thinking?' Tara asked.

'Oh, just about you, O spirited one, and how well you'd look with a baby in your belly.'

'Don't get any ideas, I'm using a cap.'

'Oh, right,' he said, a little disappointed and not having a clue what the cap actually was. 'How often do you use the cap?' hoping to gain vital information without giving the game away.

'Whenever I can.'

'Were you using one last night?'

Tara, amused by his line of questioning, twigged that he didn't know what it was.

'Did you not see me swallow it?' She was trying to keep in a laugh.

'Oh, right.'

Tara burst out laughing and stuck two fingers up her vagina and pulled it out.

'This, my man of the world, is the cap, an industrial-rubber, lubricated in spermicide and dripping with your hot, salty cum.'

'And they let you teach kids?' John was disgusted. She threw it at him playfully. John reacted as if she'd tossed him a dead rat and ran into the bathroom, refusing to come out until she had put it away. Tara, in fits of giggles, started banging on the bathroom door, hearing protracted little retches from the other side, when the phone rang. John picked up the receiver in the bathroom.

'Why haven't you rung?' It was Michelle.

Tara was still banging away at the door as John tried to change his mood.

'I've been very busy.'

'You said you'd ring when you arrived. I was worried.'

'No, I'm fine. It's just been non-stop since I got here.

Philip arranged a lot more than I expected.'

'What's all the banging?'

'It's just room service. Hang on a tic.'

John opened the door and shushed Tara who still had the cap in her hand. She was miffed at having to curtail their shenanigans, but resignedly went to the bed and switched on the television.

John turned his attention back to the phone.

'Right, where were we?'

'You were saying you were too busy to call me.'

'Yeah, that's right. And how's everything at home?'

'Fine.'

A long pause followed which John didn't have the energy to fill. Michelle eventually broke the silence.

'Is that it?'

'Well, I don't want to bore you with work details. But look, I'll be back on Sunday night.'

'Maybe I won't be here by then.'

'Look Michelle, it's a bit late at night to be playing games. I'm getting sick of this . . . Just do what you want.'

'I'm sorry, I'm sorry.' Michelle was crying. 'It's just that I miss you. It's very lonely here. And I had one of my turns.'

John, who had been dealing with these turns for nearly four years, was close to blowing-up point.

'Why don't you invite one of your friends over? A bit of company would do you good.'

'Like who?'

'I don't know . . . your sister, your folks.'

'How about Red?'

'Anyone you feel like . . . Listen, I've got to go . . . my

food's getting cold. Take care. I'll try and speak to you tomorrow.'

'I love you.'

'Yeah, okay. Speak to you tomorrow.'

John hung up. He knew it wasn't an oversight that he hadn't returned Michelle's declaration. It didn't worry him that his omission would cause her a restless night. The fact of the matter was that he didn't love her. He didn't even like her much at this moment and the way that things were going it would remain that way. He sat on the toilet contemplating his lot. Michelle's next plan of action would be to try and make him jealous. It always was. He started to imagine what she had up her sleeve but quickly stopped himself. He banged his forehead lightly, muttering to himself, 'Get her out of your mind. You're worse than she is, playing along with her pettiness.' He slapped his thighs and went back in to Tara, jumping on her and snuggling up to her back. She was dozing and he followed suit, clearing his head of all thoughts of Michelle and resting it on the shoulder of his way forward. He was just arriving at the land of Nod when he was interrupted.

'John? John?'

'Yeah?'

'When did you realise you loved me?'

Staying in the same position he answered, 'First sight.'

'Really?'

'Well, first sight of your soul, when you set off the smoke alarm. What about you?'

'When you took off your wedding ring.'

'Do you want to talk about it?'

'Only if you do.'

'All I'll say is, I'm not a grubby man looking for a bit of away-from-home action.'

'Was that her on the phone?'

'Yeah. She's sick. She always has been. I guess I've played the nurse for too long.'

'Did you ever love her?'

'I loved what I was able to do for her. That's as far as it went . . . This doesn't affect us, does it?'

'No.'

John eased in closer. He'd forgotten what a discussion was like. With Michelle there was only chat and argument. Some time in the dark of the morning he rose, drenched with the night sweats. This pleased him, ridding himself of more of his poisoned past.

John awoke to the noise of a phone ringing. The sound confused him since it wasn't coming from his telephone. Then he saw Tara reach for her bag and take out a mobile. She took the call in the bathroom and John dozed off again, to be woken some time later when a breakfast tray was shoved into his face. Double portions of egg, toast, Weetabix and orange juice.

'Thanks, Tara, but I couldn't touch a thing.'

'I'll hear none of it. You'll need all of your strength today because we'll be doing the most strenuous exercise known to the human race. Yes, you've guessed it. We're going shopping.'

John looked at her with raised eyebrows.

'You didn't think I was going to forget about burning your jacket. It's pay-back time.'

She spooned some scrambled eggs into his mouth.

They had a lustful fuck in the power shower and were soon on the way to Covent Garden.

John tended to buy his clothes in bulk, three pairs of jeans there, four shirts here, and always when the shops happened to be about him. He'd never consciously been on a clothes-shopping expedition. His wardrobe, when opened, resembled a black hole; a mass of dark colours, of which grey was the most sparkling. His day-to-day clothes were perfect for gatecrashing funerals. Tara was leading him by the hand into the land of designer garments, in shops where jazzy funk was piped through the speakers, subliminally telling you to dress hip, and you could tell the prices by the amount of stock on show. The less-is-more factor was the key. The shop assistants, or fashion advisers as they preferred to be known, took pains to wear distinctive clothes but all of them had that same short haircut. With their nipple rings and tongue studs, they gave the impression of hooked carp.

John was shuffled from one store to the next, one bag heavier each time. He dreaded having to wear the colourful clothes that Tara was stockpiling for him. If he wore them all together, he would look like a combination of all the European flags. He'd always gone for plain clothes. He didn't like to stand out. On the occasional flight of fancy, a stylish jacket would catch his eye but regardless of how it suited him, he always looked like a pimp. Today, John lost his liberty as he became Tara's Barbie doll.

He decided to put his foot down when Tara began to go weak at the knees over a pair of leather pants. He explained to her that he was not, and had no intention of, joining a heavy metal band. The camp fashion adviser, seeing 'sucker' on John's forehead, eyed the trews salaciously. He was drooling about how wonderful these particular trousers were. He had a pair himself and the amount of sweat they caused was a heavenly part of their charm. Catching John's disapproving look, he tried a defensive tack, claiming, 'Yes, you're probably right, they are a little adventurous for you. There's a Marks and Spencer's down the road and they've got a sale on anoraks at the moment.' Down off his soap-box, he seized the trousers and returned them to the rack in an almighty huff. As he got back behind his counter, he was close to tears. John didn't know whether to laugh or pat his back, but his continual glaring forced them back onto the street. They laughed about steering clear of London's gay clubs tonight to be on the safe side.

Over a cup of coffee, Tara went through her checklist.

'Right. We've got two pairs of socks, a pair of jockeys, shoes, trousers, three shirts and the jacket, which I insist on paying for.'

John was relieved that they'd finished, when Tara went into a state of panic.

'A hat! We've got to get you a hat.'

'You can fuck right off, Tara.'

'Look John, I know what I'm doing. I know exactly what I want you to look like.'

'Wouldn't it have been easier to just hire out one of the Village People?'

Tara pointed at him. 'No hat, no cap.'

'What do you mean?'

'I want you dressed perfectly tonight so that I can

undress you. I want to take off all your new expensive clothes one by one and then give you the best fuck you've ever had.'

John astounded himself as an erection tightened his jeans.

'Jesus, Tara, will you stop that, you're getting me going.'

As soon as he said it, he knew he shouldn't have done because Tara put her hand under the table and started stroking the outline of his penis. John shifted away slightly and whispered, 'Stop it, will you, or I'll come in my pants.'

'Come on,' she said. 'Let's do it in the toilet.'

John couldn't believe it. Surely this only happened in movies and only then if Mickey Rourke was starring. John was more your Jimmy Stewart – kiss and fadeout. Tara ushered him into the Ladies, saying it was less smelly in there. She pulled him into the cubicle and started undoing his zip. She cupped his penis in her hands and was gently rubbing it while teasing out 'Somebody's pleased to see me.' John was indicating to her that there was somebody in the next cubicle, at the same time hoping she wouldn't stop because he was incredibly turned on. This little scene was going to amount to five years' worth of masturbatory fantasy. He questioned her sanity when he looked down to find her using his penis as a microphone. She was crooning the Bee Gees' 'I've Just Got To Get A Message To You' into it. John was unbearably tense and moments away from lift-off. The second she put his penis in her mouth, he came. He eased her head closer with his hands and watched her beautiful eyes which were fully concentrated. There was even a hint of that smile. He couldn't help but groan with the relief and thought God was looking down on him when the next door toilet started to flush in unison. He wanted to show his love for her and the only way that seemed appropriate was to lift her face up to his and kiss her full on the lips, but there was no way he was tasting his own cum. His morning's breakfast was restless at the very notion. *This is what Meatloaf must have meant in that song – 'I'll do anything for love but I won't do that.'* He kissed her on the cheek instead. There followed that awkward moment which came after public sex: the feeling of knowing you've done something unusual but now it was over, it's time to rejoin the crowd. John tried to ease them back into the day.

'So how much did all that clobber set me back?'

'About two grand.'

'God, that's more than the sum total I've spent on clothes to date.'

'Ah, stop complaining. It puts value on the price of your body.'

'What do you want to do now?'

'A funfair, and then a hat.'

'Fair enough, boss.'

They ended up at one of those London travelling funfairs, which had made its home in Finsbury Park for the week. Tara led John eagerly, swinging their arms in excitement. John was slightly embarrassed attending a fair and wished he had a child with him to use as an excuse. They mingled in with a ready-made bunch of working-class young families, gangs of teenagers strutting their stuff and the hard man who played the boxing machine, addicted to the noise it made whenever he scored a direct hit. Pop hits of yestermonth blared out, conspiring to create a buzz. People were embracing the distorted makeshift ambience. Tara wouldn't go on any of the fast rides herself because they made her nervous but she practically forced John onto the waltzer. He sat in the three-seater on his own feeling very self-conscious with Tara egging him on. As the machine started up she waved at him, bouncing with little hops of joy. One of the operators spotted this and started spinning John faster. Every forty seconds or so he would be plunged toward Tara and despite his reservations he was enjoying himself. The other operator joined his mate and they concentrated on John, spinning him to within a fraction of an inch of a funfair fatality. As others around him screamed with false hysteria, John was busy wondering whether the safety regulations were being adhered to. As the ride stopped, Tara came to his rescue, hugging him back to stability. The two operators were chatting her up to no avail. John teased her.

'You could be in there, you know. Take one of them home and while you're shagging, you could put his jeans in the wash. And of course the big advantage to going out with someone from a funfair is that you get to meet their parents straight away.'

'Dodgems,' said Tara, and within a moment she had them waiting in the queue. John explained that in Ireland they called them bumper cars.

'There lies the big difference in the two countries' cultures. You think the purpose is to avoid. We see it as a constant collision.'

'We'll see.'

They took a car each and Tara bumped John as soon as they were motoring, which was pointless as she hadn't amassed any speed. John sped off with Tara in hot pursuit. He swerved away from other drivers, building up his momentum. Tara was slowed by the fact that one of the operators was standing on the back of her car, giving her patronising instructions while helping her steer. John was going as fast as he could and was steering towards a head-on collision with Tara. She threw one hand up to her face in mock fright. John waited until he was centimetres away before he changed direction, shouting 'Love you.' This became his little routine. Speed, head-to-head, swerve and 'Love you.'

Next they tried the ghost train, which even kids were scoffing at, but Tara insisted on screaming every time a skeleton or patch of darkness appeared. They got off with Tara's nails imprinted on John's arm. Finished with the rides, they decided to try the skill stalls, knocking the cans off with the cork gun, throwing a hoop over the bottle, until they came to the Football Crazy stall. With four darts you had to score less than thirty; 'no doubles or trebles and no complete misses and definitely no two in a bed', which was the extent of the peddler's patter. John was shit at darts and usually scored under thirty anyhow. He decided to give it a whirl because one of the prizes was a Crystal Palace cap. Tara agreed that if he won the prize it would be counted as his new hat. This added a little more pressure to the game. It was a pound a go and after twenty quid's worth, John's frustration was beginning to mount. On the twenty-fifth go, the woman behind the stall gave him the hat out of sympathy and because she liked his accent. John put it on with a strange sense of dented pride. He felt he didn't deserve to wear it and tried to take it off but Tara was having none of it. Her mobile phone rang. On saying 'Hello,' she wandered off on her own. It was a brief conversation. When she came back she looked drained.

'Listen, John.' She put her arm around his waist. 'Something's come up. Will you be able to make your own way back?'

'Sure, yeah. What's up?'

'It's nothing really. I just have to sort something out.'

'We're still on for tonight, yeah?' His hopes were fading.

'Of course we are. I've got the whole thing planned out. Look, I'm sorry about this.'

'Do you want to tell me about it?'

'Come on, I'll give you a lift to a mini-cab office.'

She drove faster than normal. She had nothing to say and John didn't want to force conversation. He couldn't help wondering what the problem was. He knew it was not his place to ask but having shared everything for the last couple of days he figured he had a warped right. He tried to dismiss it. Tara's face was stern and preoccupied. Then she winced and sniffed the air.

'Do you smell burning rubber?'

'It's probably your cap.'

She was not amused and within minutes had dropped him off, laden with shopping. A cursory kiss and 'See you around seven' and she zoomed off; no smile, no wave, no look back.

John was back in his room at five thirty. There was a message waiting from Michelle: 'Ring straight away. I have some great news.'

John started mentally preparing himself to return her call. He was gripped with Tara's sudden disappearance. He looked at the bundle of designer bags spread on the bed and the thought of putting his new clothes on lifted him a little. He was feeling sleepy and switched on the television. *Neighbours* lit up in front of him. He gazed at the full lives and started to doze off. The signature tune and the phone woke him. He was having a disturbing dream about Chrissie clawing into him tighter and tighter, screaming at him all the while as he tried to loosen her grip. Awake his hand was sore and numb where he'd been lying on it. It was a real effort picking up the receiver.

'John, why haven't you rung me?'

'I was having a nap. So what's your good news?'

'I can't tell you on the phone. Can you fly back tonight?'

'Michelle, what are you playing at?' John raised his voice. 'You know that's not possible.'

'But I want to tell you my good news.'

'Tell me, then.'

'I can't tell you over the phone, it's too important.'

'Well it's going to have to fucking wait then, isn't it.'

Michelle started crying, infuriating John still more.

'You don't care,' she sobbed, 'you just don't care.'

'Michelle, would you ever cop yourself on. I'm very happy for you and I'll see you on Sunday and you can tell me then.'

There was silence on the other end. John filled it. 'I can't talk to you when you're like this.'

More silence.

'I'll tell you what. I'll ring Red and ask him to go for a drink with me, he can keep me company.'

'Do what you want, Michelle.'

She hung up.

John held on to the phone for thirty seconds in disbelief. Then he dismissed the whole incident. He clapped his hands, shouting 'Right!' to re-energise himself for the night ahead. He showered and put on his new clothes and was ready on the dot of seven. At five past, he raided the mini-bar and sat on the bed, cocking his eye at a quiz show, worrying whether Tara was going to turn up while half answering the questions. At half past seven, he was on his third miniature bottle of red wine and had an overwhelming sense of being mutton dressed as designer mutton. At a quarter to eight the phone rang. Tara was downstairs. All the anger of his long wait dissipated. As he locked the door behind him he strutted like one who had been paroled from his cell, his loved one outside to greet him. When he got down to reception, Tara was on her mobile. When she saw him she put it away and gave him a quick non-contacting kiss on the lips.

'Aren't we the dandiest gent in London.' She touched the felt of his collar.

'You're not so bad yourself.' She was wearing the same clothes she'd had on earlier. 'Where are we off to?'

'I've booked us a table at Mezzo.'

They walked to the restaurant, keeping their arms

apart. The wine had blunted John's hunger and Tara was acting very matter-of-fact. The place was jammed and they had to eat within breathing space of another couple. John ordered the house red as they were being seated, and scanning the menu was peeved to see only one vegetarian meal on offer. He dealt with his disgruntlement in the only way he knew, by being sarcastic to the waitress.

Tara ordered a steak underdone, John's least favourite sight in the world. The wine took the edge off his worries. He wanted to question Tara about this afternoon but didn't want it to spoil the evening. Wherever she'd been this afternoon, she was still there now. After the meal, he put his hand on hers. She flinched slightly but gave him a dainty squeeze. Then she took him on to a scuzzy club off Oxford Street. It didn't seem her type of place and John's inebriated state was bombarding him with questions. *'Why are we in this dump? Why doesn't she take me to her normal haunts? Where are all her friends? Is she embarrassed by me?'* The club didn't sell wine and John was forced onto tins of Red Stripe. He needed to go to the toilet and he was scared that Tara wouldn't be there when he got back. In the toilet an impeccably dressed wide boy was selling Ecstasy tablets with neither subtlety nor grace. At first John took no notice, but then he thought that might be just the ticket, a love enhancer. He asked for two. The dealer offered him the midnight special, two Es and two acid tabs for twenty-five notes. To get rid of him, John hurriedly agreed the sale.

Tara was seated where he had left her, wispily sipping from her can. John suggested they try to find somewhere less grim. He told her about the Ecstasy but she dismissed it out of hand. She said she was tired and they should go back to his hotel. John was surprised. He'd expected her to want to go home alone. He jumped at the chance, his earlier paranoia coaxing itself away.

Back at the Groucho the bar was heaving. They toddled up the stairs, John the worse for wear. As soon as she entered the room, Tara stripped off all her clothes and dived beneath the sheets. John was slurring out compliments while struggling with his own attire. He slid in beside her and started kissing her back and her neck but she didn't respond. John had half an erection and tried to place Tara's hand on it. She half-heartedly played with it for a couple of seconds before she returned to her original position. John, getting more and more turned on, pressed himself against her. She lay there listlessly. He gave up hope and turned onto his back. He didn't want to belittle himself or the love he felt for her any longer. He hoped he was better than that. He turned once more and gave her the tenderest kiss on the back by way of apology. He put himself in sleeping position, allowing her plenty of space. He focused on her back, feeling euphoric about being able to breathe the same air as she did. He drifted off, projecting that in his dying moment, the last sight he would love to see on this earth was Tara.

The phone woke him in the morning. It was seven o'clock. He snatched at it, putting on his 'I've been up for hours' voice. It was Philip, brimming with life downstairs. John articulated as best he could that he'd slept in and would need half an hour. It was only when

Philip asked, 'Is she still up there?' that he realised he was alone. He put down the phone, hoping she was in the bathroom. But he could sense otherwise. His eyes scoured the room until he saw the note on top of the television. It read: 'I'm really sorry. Goodbye.' John studied it for at least ten minutes, trying to come to the least painful conclusion. His body had clearly read it properly the first time because it jittered and pulsed. His brain sympathised, but knew that there was an air of finality about it. He needed a beta-blocker fast. Already he was nostalgic for yesterday.

CHAPTER 9

John got into Philip's car, trying very hard to appear normal. This ordeal put him even more on edge. The smell of air freshener was a slap in the face to his empty stomach. He pressed back onto the headrest, turning slightly away from Philip. The gesture was deliberate, but also necessary, because the strong sun was flashing blindness through the windscreen. Philip could tell straight away that something was up and had the good grace to keep conversation down to a minimum. John couldn't remain still, continually shifting his position as his brain insisted on tumbling over events. Hot flushes unnerved him to the extent that he had to open his window and practically stick his whole head out. Philip was a fast driver. He had just got his licence back after a six-month ban for speeding. They turned on to the Hammersmith Flyover doing sixty-nine miles per hour. John could barely catch his breath, which was just what he needed because he was brewing up a limbic storm. He lit up a cigarette which acted as a starting gun for his hangover. He looked at the high-rise blocks to his left and pondered the lack of opportunities that were afforded to the occupants. All of a sudden his own trifling problems were put into perspective. Yes, his worries were much more important. He remembered his mother's one piece of advice which she gave him whenever he'd been depressed as a boy. It had obviously been passed down as a kind of family heirloom. 'If you went into a field with all your problems and then looked at everyone else's problems, you would always come back with your own problems intact.' *That's all very well mother dearest, you sad deluded sentimentalist, but maybe it's best to avoid that particular field.*

As a child he had loved the idea of living in a high-rise building. They were a novelty in Ireland but he knew that it was really the lift that held his fascination, the innocent idea of accelerating skyward with gravity being outdone by machinery. Twenty years of sub-living later, the thought of the lift petrified him. The idea of stepping into it, if it was working that is, made him shudder. Having to share it with the battered wife, the alcoholic husband, the junkie teen, the toddler learning his ABCs with graffiti and a spray can, and the tramp leaving pools of rancid piss as his calling card. It worried him that he was turning into a Tory.

How could you do this to me, Tara? The merry dance, the

garden path, the beaten track . . . I thought it was bricks and mortar; saplings, little apples. The trauma destroys or builds you. I will be strong. I will show you. I have willpower. I will get over this. You are nothing. A butterfly flaps its wings in China and you don't love me any more. Your karma better find a good hiding place. I am not your whipping boy. Accept your faith, young man, and the body will follow. I will leave you be. We'll leave it there, you piece of shit. How could you do this to another? See, I'm already over you. I've put myself in the third person. You can't hurt me, you left me in smithereens. Parts of my heart have fallen down to my toes. I lift my leg and hear the rattle.

It's for the best. You did me a favour. You simply changed your mind. You saved yourself months of forced fun, of unprecedented pretence, of shallow sex. I'm an arsehole. Excuse me, I can't take your call, I've got the rest of my life to get on with. Well don't worry, my angel, I will not call. I took the hint. I saw the fingerprints on the sledgehammer. I will leave you be, and we will bump into each other when we are in our seventies and we will be badly made up as in one of those span-the-ages BBC dramas, and we will look at each other. I will have a moustache, and you'll be a fraction smaller. You will ask me if I want a blow job and we will cry and we will curse the waste our lives have become and we will take it from where we left off and we will make love, a love so intense that it would make able-bodied people puke, and we will take comfort in that and then a week later you will change your mind again and I will laugh out of despair.

Yes, you did the right thing. You had my long-term feelings in mind and I am strong. My brain is flexing its muscles. I just wanted to be able to say goodbye. Did you want me to see you as a cruel, heartless witch? Did you think that would make it easier on me? Did you? Well, you're a fool then because you've become a cruel, heartless witch who I still love.

It's for the best. Get it into your head John, it's for the best. Leave it. Que sera, sera. *I will not ring you. I will forget you. I'll keep my dignity. I will crawl back down my hole and ring bells when I venture out. I will sit on my comfortable chair in my sitting room, alone but relaxed, in a position that is not good for my back. But hey, I'll be living for today and I will watch the postman quicken his pace as he goes by my house. He will snigger and his sack will be filled to bursting point with mail for others.*

Enough self-pitying. I am better than you and that's the last voluntary thought I will have about you. I will wait for the next stage of evolution. Now, my life, where were we?

'Philip, can I borrow your mobile? Tara, it's John, can you ring me on this number please . . .'

John went about his business, picking up items of stock from dusty warehouses, but his real day consisted of waiting for that call. After he'd left his third anguished self-hating message, Philip felt the need to offer a vocal shoulder.

'John, leave it. She doesn't want to know. I'm no expert on women but no amount of calls are going to change her mind. I hate seeing a mate going through this.'

John knew that Philip was stating the obvious, and it needed to be said. Later he would thank him for trying. But for now a 'Mind-your-own-fucking-business' was his response. Philip sighed. John fumed in silence as they went back to their respective corners, despairing that he had nobody in the world to talk to. Michelle was out of the picture, the relationship on its last legs. He knew she was on the point of doing something extreme, and maybe he was too. It was time to have a clear-out. He had outlived his life. The only thing he missed from home was his music: other people venting their emotions at the end of doomed affairs; all alone, all thinking they were expressing the inexpressible. He could think of no greater joy than slowly getting drunk, dancing with the singer's words, moving to music that moved him, gyrating to sounds which didn't lend themselves to dancing and all in the comfort of his own room. Yes, that's when he was happiest, in a sing-along-to-pain session.

Philip pulled up outside the Groucho. John didn't know what to do. He needed time alone but he didn't want to be alone during it. He expected Philip to utter a quick goodbye and zoom away. Instead he got a life-reaffirming order.

'Right, what you and me are going to do is get more pissed than we have ever been. We will get so drunk that we're going to apologise to the barman before we start, and the night won't be considered a success unless we get barred.'

'You're on, give me ten minutes. You get the booze in.' They shook hands on it.

John checked at reception for messages. There were three. His brain crashed. There were too many possibilities to consider. He had to tear them open on the spot: all of them were from Michelle. He crunched them into a ball and threw them in the bin. As usual he missed, denting the drama by having to walk across and place the ball of responsibilities into the bin by hand.

Two hours later, Philip and John were well on the way to kidney failure, giggling like children in the Groucho bar. Their loudness was granting them plenty of space in their immediate vicinity.

'See Philip, you might see it as a little love affair, nothing more, nothing less. But, and this is a big but, she danced for me . . . you know, danced; uninhibited dancing. I'm not saying we had a bop together, but she stood in front of me and moved . . . everything. Now you can stick your Giant's Causeway . . . your . . . uh . . . that big rock in America . . . your fucking poxy Big Ben. This was a sight . . . It was just . . .' he tried to emphasise with his hands ' . . . fucking amazing. I've never felt more alive in my life. It was the coming together of intellect and soul, an explosion of—'

'So, she was a bit of a mover then . . . ?'

'You don't get it, do you, Philip?'

'No.'

Philip tried to look concerned. They stared at each other.

'It doesn't matter.'

They couldn't stop laughing. John hadn't laughed like this in years and he was savouring it, the more so because he was the butt of the joke: he was laughing at himself. People around them caught the infectious laughter and it might have been the exaggeration of thirty percent proof but he thought the whole bar was in an unbridled fit of giggles. People were laughing at different things. It would calm down to a breathless snort before a full throttle from someone would get the room going again, rising to a crescendo when every now and then a hand would be raised in a helpless 'stop' gesture. New people would walk in and walk out just as quickly, thinking they had gatecrashed a private party. John saw it as a spontaneous show of solidarity for those who had had their hearts broken. All of them rattled their legs. Eventually the laughter turned to yawns as energy levels hit all-time lows. The crushing equation that every high must be paid for with a low was lost on no one. The group divided, back to their own lives, little conversational naps keeping the tone to a murmur. But the acknowledgement of that special moment remained. Their eyes told the tale. There would be no need to stay in touch.

'Philip, do us a favour will you? Ring Michelle for me.'

'What do you want me to say?'

'Just that I'm sorry I haven't been in touch, but I've been reaching for the stars.'

'You haven't even spoken to one of them.'

'Not those kind of stars.'

'Anyway, I'm not saying that. How about you've been waylaid at the warehouse and you'll ring her tomorrow.'

'Alright.'

'But I'll have to go outside. They don't let you use your mobiles in here. It's a classy joint.'

Philip straightened his jacket and walked the way he figured classy people walked. John's three minutes alone brought Tara to mind, the same points ferris-wheeling the futility of his position. Philip had said all the things that blokes say to other blokes who are in this situation: common sense with emotion swept under the carpet.

Philip was back.

'Everything alright?' John asked eagerly.

'She's fine. A bit drunk. She has that Red over. Is that the man you asked me to do the check on?'

John nodded.

'I should have that for you tomorrow, by the way.'

'Great. And she wasn't in a foul mood?'

'She wasn't letting on. I got the impression he was in the room with her. She probably couldn't talk. And anyway, she was hardly going to take it out on me.'

Philip nudged John in the ribs and pointed at the corner with his eyes and head. There sat Johnny Depp, wearing the expression he always wore: 'Don't fuck with me unless you want to fuck me.'

They drank for another hour, never reaching the giddy heights of before. Even though it was still only half past ten, John decided to call it a night. He gave Philip a huge hug, and every part of the grip was heartfelt.

Upstairs he fell onto his bed, confused by the fact that he felt compelled to ring Michelle. With Red there and the state she was in, the fact that she was drunk and the knowledge that she was bound to do something to try and upset him didn't bode well. He knew his mind was addled but as usual certain unwelcome thoughts wouldn't leave him alone. He rang his number and his worst fears were confirmed when the answer machine came on. He hung up without leaving a message. He sat up on the bed feeling completely sober. All the negative vibes that had been swelling up inside him focused onto Red.

'That's it, Red,' he said out loud. 'You're fucking dead.'

His own state of mind was scaring him and he knew he was capable of anything. *Think about it, think it through. That doesn't mean anything. Don't be too hasty. She's probably just asleep . . .*

Red and Michelle were kissing on the couch when the phone rang. Michelle made an attempt to get it but Red prevented her, tightening his embrace. He pulled her bra down over her tits, freeing them but leaving her uncomfortable. Michelle moaned 'No,' meshed in with pleasurable groans which gave mixed signals and it didn't really matter because Red had no intention of stopping. He groped at her breasts, squeezing them into the shape of his cupped hands. Her left nipple was rock solid so Red started tonguing the right one, then rotating from one to the other until he was achieving double erection of the nipples. He felt an unwanted hair on the left one which displeased him and he bit it off. Michelle was grabbing the back of his head and drawing him towards her. Red, bored with the altitude, shoved his hands inside her jeans, undoing the top button. He struggled, but managed to get two fingers up her vagina while stroking the region with his spares. She was turned on and aching to feel Red's penis inside her. Red, feeling pleased with himself, stopped his manoeuvring to take off both their jeans and underwear, ripping Michelle's knickers in the process. Michelle couldn't take her eyes off his penis which was bigger than she remembered. Red, done with skinny-dipping, went down on her, burying his face into her vagina and slurping as if he was drinking coconut milk from a shell.

He squirmed his body around, leaving her no option but to swell her cheeks with his penis. It was slightly banana-shaped and she couldn't take all of it in before it hit the back of her throat. He thrust it in and out of her mouth making her gag at first but she soon got used to the rhythm and she smelt the faint aroma of patchouli oil from it. His balls were drooping into her eyes, taking off layers of make-up. It was too much for her and she was banging her arms against the side of the settee, but Red's weight pinned her down. She felt a momentary compulsion to bite his penis off but instead she sucked it harder, exhaling noisily through her nose. Red continued lapping juices from her which were running as if on tap. He was very drunk and was mindful that he wouldn't be able to come until he fucked her. He got up and carried her into the bedroom. She knew she shouldn't be doing this but she had lost control. Red threw her on to the bed and she expected him to penetrate her straight away, but then suddenly she felt his whole fist ramming up inside her. He was pushing very hard, trying to get that extra inch. She was frightened and shocked and although it wasn't a pleasurable experience, she didn't want him to stop.

'You like that, don't you?'

She half nodded. He pushed again and she recoiled.

'You like feeling big things inside you. You can't wait for me to fuck you, can you? Because you know it is going to be the best fuck you ever had.' Red spat the word 'fuck' as if he'd never said it before. 'Shall we fuck then, my little whore? You don't know what you've been missing, do you?'

With little elegance, Red turned her over and started

angling himself behind her.

'For God's sake Red, use a condom, it isn't safe.'

He turned her head forcefully.

'Look at it. What harm can he do you? He's a nice fella. I call him Sunny.'

'I think it's best you use a condom.'

'I'm telling you Michelle, it will be okay. Come on, you don't put a hat on when it's sunny.'

He was inside her. She felt a mix of intense pleasure and anxiety.

'No, stop it, oh God, no.'

She tried to get him out of her but he held her hips with his arms, giving her no leverage. He started pushing harder, quick stop-starty bangs inside her, slowly building up a rhythm. Michelle orgasmed, which brought about total confusion. She stopped struggling and resigned herself to this rape. Little sobs accompanied her groans and she was already blaming herself for this predicament.

Red was boasting, 'I haven't even started yet. I learnt some tricks in America – I'm going to fuck you all night.'

He wrapped a hand around her stomach with his penis still inside her and using his free hand, he grabbed a cigarette and lit it. He kept on bragging as he casually smoked the cigarette, occasionally deep-thrusting inside her. Once he had finished the cigarette, he put it out and started pounding into her. Michelle was sore and dry and full of hate. She tried to take her mind off the action of what was happening, remembering how sweet Red had been earlier on: reminiscing about their little escapades, whispering sweet nothings into her ear and gently caressing her hair. He'd bought her flowers and chocolates and now he was behind her, hurting her, all the while mantra-ing, 'Oh baby that feels good. We must make this a regular thing.'

The phone rang. It was very late. Michelle snatched at it. The voice at the other end of the line was as full of panic as she was.

'Is Alan there?'

Michelle handed the phone to Red.

'It's for you.'

It amazed her that he was still fucking her and he hadn't missed a beat. Then suddenly he stopped.

'Peter, what's up?' he said.

'Are you sitting down?' asked his brother's voice.

'Sort of.'

'It's Mum. She's . . . dead.'

'Oh no . . . When?'

'In the last half hour.'

Red muttered, 'Thanks,' for want of anything better to say, and then hung up. He eased himself onto his back, his eyes beginning to swell. Michelle cried harder, his pain being so paramount. She didn't know what to do. She looked at him, his hands covering his face, heavy shuddering dry tears seeping through. He resorted to the foetal position, an oversized baby. She felt tremendous pity for him, and yet she couldn't bring herself to help him, because the most overwhelming sight was that of his still-erect penis.

CHAPTER 10

'Long time no see, Johnny Boy. Get in the car.'

Jimmy looked manic and John was frightened to eye-contact him. John's legs started to quiver as Jimmy put the car in automatic lock mode.

'You've been avoiding me then, Little Johnny.'

'I've just been busy . . . Family problems.'

'Are you not going to ask where I've been?' Jimmy put his foot down hard on the accelerator, the rev counter going ballistic.

'I've been enjoying the hospitality in Mountjoy, haven't I? With anal eaters, kill for fun-ers and drip-droppers, lovely company to keep, wouldn't ya say? Got busted with half a kilo of horse.' He took his eye off the road for prolonged stares at John. 'Very convenient for the cops, wasn't it?' He lightened his tone. 'It was as if,' he smiled, 'they knew.'

'Hold on a second there, Jimmy. You're not suggesting . . .'

'I'm always open for a suggestion, Johnny. It's good business practice.'

'Where are we going?' Panicking, John swayed from side to side in motion with the car. In doorways tramps appeared, primal screaming their future shocks.

'Let's see where the car takes us. It'll be like a magical mystery tour. Did you like them when you were a kid, Johnny? . . . Your parents now, they must call you Johnny too, how are they? Give them a ring.' Jimmy took out his mobile phone and dialled John's parents' number. He held the phone out towards John, and the operator's voice could be clearly heard: 'I'm sorry, this number doesn't exist.'

'Hey,' John protested, shifting in his seat. 'What's going on, Jimmy?' Jimmy mimicked him.

'How's Michelle, lovely girl, she gets lonely doesn't she? We should call her too.' Again Jimmy dialled the number and handed the phone to John. Red answered, 'What do you want?'

'Is Michelle there?'

'Is that you, Johnny? Listen, she doesn't want to see you any more. I'm living here now, don't even think about showing your face, you're a fucking disgrace.'

He hung up. Sweat was pouring down John's face, his forehead was a sponge.

'It's not your day, is it boy? You don't look too well, there's only one place for you.' Jimmy pulled up outside a hospital emergency ward. John tried to open the car door to no avail. Diamond Dave appeared at the window, his teeth fang-like. John, petrified, shouted, 'What's going on here, Jimmy? Stop fucking about, I don't know anything about your drug dealings. What are we doing here?'

Jimmy took a small pistol from his breast pocket and shot John twice, once in each knee. He opened the door and bundled him out on to the pavement. The noise from the pistol surprised John because it sounded like a dull knock, where he expected a loud bang. He came to his senses and it took him a couple of seconds before he realised that he was having a nightmare. A porter knocked again on the door of his room, jolting him awake. An envelope was squeezed under the door and his body was trembling. John didn't recall many of his dreams but the ones that he did stayed with him a long time. They tended to creep up on him in instants of dormancy, leaving him side-stepping the rational. He pulled open the curtain hoping daylight might rescue him, his balance shaky as he grabbed the parcel. He climbed back on to the bed, lighting a cigarette which made him queasy and as he pulled on the fag he had problems breathing. He got up once more, the movement unsettling phlegm, and wedged open the window. He could only prise it open an inch: hotels didn't like suicide statistics.

Soho wafted into the room, the staleness of the night before smeared onto him. Dead cum and fresh bread, boozy morning farts and discarded doner kebabs; broken hearts and failed chat-up lines clung to him. The demeanour of normality was called for. The sensation of stickiness had him running the bath, the tiny tub filling in less than a minute, the steam making him light-headed. He squeezed the little bottle of foam bath and grabbed his miniature soap packet and dipped a foot in. For a second it seemed the right temperature, until his brain registered the searing pain of heat. He tried to stick his hand in to unplug a couple of inches but the pain was too much. He laid back on his bed naked and decided to masturbate. The Groucho Club had kindly laid on a small tube of body lotion to avoid the manic friction of jerk *au naturel.* He palmed a glob and started to flag-pole his penis. He thought of Tara which had a debilitating effect. Wanking off pretending to shag a woman who has rejected you was not an ideal aphrodisiac. Michelle sprang to mind, drooping his already flaccid member; her image brought too many questions with it. He quickly tried to picture anyone he had come into contact with in the last month; fast-flash sexy scenarios: three-in-a-beds, fucking in stables, on the decks of ships, doggy fashion in confessional boxes, blow-jobs while driving Formula One cars; different nationalities, golden showers and gang-bangs. None of them was any use. Nothing could arouse him and he felt a complete failure. He couldn't even have sex with himself.

He looked at the breakfast menu. At least his stomach was aroused. A form for overseas members of the Groucho Club fell to the floor. Yes, he thought, he could become a flaccid member of the Groucho. He had a quick in-and-out bath and ordered a boiled egg from room service. Getting dressed, he saw his bundle of new clothes and contemplated binning the lot, but he resisted for now and put on his ordinary suit of armour. Sitting down on the bed he noticed the package. He picked it up and opened it. Philip had come up trumps: a two-page dossier on Red. It was very thorough. Schools attended, minor shoplifting offences, the standard fare of a growing boy. He turned the page and his eye focused on the word 'fugitive'. The word was the same size as the others but it jumped out at him as if it was twice as big and in bold print. It seemed that Red had got into a mêlée in a Boston bar with another Irish immigrant, one Pat O'Keefe. The brawl had resulted in a stabbing, for which Red had been arrested, but had jumped bail before the case had come to trial. The bail money had been put up by Mary Beth Delaware, who was now being held for questioning.

John was blown away. That was the name of Red's fiancée. What was he up to? At first he was puzzled; then it all started falling into place. A couple of phone calls would verify the details. But was it possible that Red could be that evil? *Fuck, Michelle, is she okay? She hasn't rung.* How to pass this day. Tara was still breathing down his neck. *Jesus where is the air in this city?* The bright Saturday morning had just been christened by a downpour. Thunder belly-ached from the sky, lightning flashed to inspire the demented and an odious smell was bad-egging its way into every orifice.

Red, can't get over it. And you thought you'd get away with it. I don't think so. Every negative thought that he had harvested about him was justified now. *Ah, Tara, why did you fucking leave me? You might as well fly a blimp over London with your name on it. Back with the batterer no doubt, rather take a hammering than spend time with me. Cheers, on your side sister, and Michelle, poor predictable Michelle. If only I could recast my life.*

A knock came on the door, emptying him of thought. A grumpy porter with an old war medal pinned to his chest positioned the forty-five-minute-old boiled egg in a tip-friendly place. *Even the extras are pathetic in my life. The strangest thing is that I don't even have the lead in my own life. It's time for my action scene.*

He dialled his home number. Michelle's tense 'hello' came through the miles of tele-communications wires. John decided to waste no more time.

'Have you got anything to tell me?'

Silence.

'Well?'

'Red's mother died last night.'

'While you were fucking him?' John shocked himself with his own question.

'How did you know?'

Even though John had embarked on this line of questioning, her reply floored him. He wanted to ask more probing questions but he couldn't handle detail.

'Michelle, you're a real dead loss,' he told her, keeping up his air of upper-handed knowingness. He hung up, giving her just enough rope. Impulsively he rang Red's number. Red answered on the first ring. 'Yeah?' he said, his voice subdued.

'Red, it's John here.'

'Hi.'

'Listen, I'm really sorry to hear about your mother. I just want you to know that I come back tomorrow, and if there is anything I can do . . . I know it sounds like a cliché, but I mean it, you're a good pal Red, and I really want to help.'

'Thanks, John. That means a lot.'

Michelle stared at the phone as if the piece of machinery was going to give her answers. It started taking on strange shapes in front of her. In a crisis she resorted to the role of her mother and frantically started to clean the house from top to bottom. Each room took on connotations of her parents' relationship: kitchen – rows over money; sitting room – Dad's power play; bedroom – rough and tumble; kids' room – would you ever make something of your lives; and spare room – the all-too-much room, a refuge of sorts, a cell to protect you from your nearest and dearest. Chrissie stayed out of sight, annoyed that the hoovering was interrupting her twenty-three-hour nap.

Michelle wanted to talk to her mother, wanted to be held and comforted, to be bailed out, to be told everything was going to be alright, but she'd known since the first time she'd kept a secret from her that the generation gap had widened and it wasn't possible just to slip back in. She thought of her younger sister, Gillian, only two years between them. They'd been so close growing up and now they were barely on speaking terms. Why had she shut everybody out? A tiredness seemed to come over her when she was with other people: she would try to be sociable but fail.

When she approached the bedroom the linen was scattered on the floor. A shudder went up her back as she gathered up the bundle. She turned her head away from the stained sheets as she put them in the wash. She used almost half a box of powder and set the programme on to the industrial cycle. She was still saddle sore from the night before and even though she had showered earlier, now she wanted a bath. She looked at the deep suds washing Red's escaped sperm and odours away when she spotted Chrissie in the wash. She could see her little mouth opening but could not hear her. She turned off the programme and tried to prise the door open. It wouldn't budge. She desperately scanned the kitchen for a heavy object and grabbed a Buddha-shaped bronze bookmark. The row of cookery books it was supporting fell to the floor, the impact making her turn around, losing valuable seconds. She started viciously butting the washing machine door with the Buddha, but the tough plastic wouldn't crack. She could see that Chrissie was still breathing in her own underwater adventure. She tried the door again, and this time it opened, gushing soapy water onto the floor, Chrissie surfing the wave. Getting to her feet, she scarpered, desperate to get out of this mad house.

Red and Peter sat on the sofa, every ten minutes refusing tea alternately from their motherly aunt and a concerned neighbour. The two women pottered about with pained expressions. The men, who were treated as boys for the mourning period, were eager to turn the television on but dared not do so in case it appeared disrespectful. Peter had wanted his mother laid out in her room but Red insisted that she should be taken to the funeral parlour. Two mousy-grimaced little men prepared her for her journey. Peter assisted them. Red, who'd refused to look at his mother since her death, went out for a walk. The mice tried to ease Peter's pain with their mournalese. Aunt Mary had taken the reins of the situation. She had come to visit once a week since it first became apparent her sister was dying. She had done the same with her own mother and now the role was officially hers. The caring neighbour annoyed her and she subtly tried to oust her, finally telling her, 'Look, this is a family matter, so if you wouldn't mind . . .' in order to drive her back to her own brood. Red found it spooky that their aunt slept in their mother's bed. They were of a similar build and she smoothed herself into the hollow her sister's body had left. Red had never got on with his Aunt and he expected her to take him to task for his absence over the years. A wonderful Saturday night was looming.

The three of them sat for dinner at the kitchen table. Mary had made them standard fare of sausage, potato, mushrooms and peas. A lifetime of cooking experience bypassed, she had shrivelled the peas to a punched-in half size which was like eating bubble-wrap. The mushrooms died screaming in own-brand cooking oil, the potatoes had hard burnt corners, their foul taste not appreciated until after at least four bites. The sausages looked presentable enough until mid-bite when the little gristly white bone inside them made its presence known.

Red's stomach was somersaulting. He pushed his plate away protesting his lack of appetite. He knew he could get away with it under the circumstances, though his belly groaned with hunger and he was already planning sneaky little snack attacks for later on. Peter suffered in silence, frowning and nibbling. Aunt Mary sliced more butter onto her plate unaware that anything was amiss. It's amazing what a lifetime of tolerance will allow.

After dinner, Aunt Mary decided on a cup of tea. Red made it, bemoaning the fact that it would probaby keep her up for another couple of hours. Peter went for the bottle of whiskey which was kept under the sink. It had been in the house since Christmas. They purchased one every year in case any visitors turned up, and of course it remained unopened throughout the festive season. Mary, a teetotaller all her life, assumed that anyone who drank whiskey must be an alcoholic, and tried to convey her disapproval with one all-encompassing frown. Peter didn't look her way, still coming to terms with his loss. Red's state of denial infuriated him. He wanted to share his grief with his brother but Red refused to tilt his emotions either way. Aunt Mary's omnipresent calmness wasn't helping, frightening soulful yearnings away, leaving a state of superficiality bearing down heavily on the pretend family.

Red began washing up, using it as his 'do not trespass' sign to keep him from any real connection. As he scraped away the detastified food he kept muttering to himself, 'doom, gloom and mushrooms.' He found this funny and had to stifle giggles. Peter was knocking back the whiskey, finding the silence unbearable. Aunt Mary half-sipped her tea, making that annoying 'aahh' sound as she swallowed. Peter stared at Red still at the sink and thought of a beautiful poem that Seamus Heaney had written about his mother's death.

'Red,' he began, 'have you ever come across that

poem, *Clearances*? I think it might help you to come to terms—'

Aunt Mary butted in. 'Poems now is it, how can they help? Sitting on their arses all day writing down their pretty little words, never doing an honest day's work in their lives.'

She reminded Peter of the worst points of his own mother when she was at full strength. They had similar eyes and, eerily, the exact same facial expression as if they'd been caught by the wind in the middle of an old wives' tale. At that juncture Peter concluded that his mother was better off dead.

'Your mother never had time for those poem writers. She used to say they were no better than the tinkers . . . At least they had the honesty to put the begging bowl out, they had no illusions.' For the next half hour she ranted like a prize bigot with neither brother listening or even pretending to. Red took refuge in officialdom.

'What time is the funeral on Tuesday?'

Aunt Mary was in her element now. 'The Mass is at seven Monday night. The funeral Mass is at ten o'clock Tuesday morning, followed by the burial and the wake, and we'll go along to the funeral parlour tomorrow to pay our final respects.'

'I'm not going tomorrow night,' said Red. 'I want to remember her as she was.'

The other two tutted their objections. Red braced himself for the outpouring of simmering rage he knew was coming. The rattle of the lid was building up a steady rhythm, steam pressure punctuating the beats. Aunt Mary seethed like she cooked, her boiling point ignored until there was nothing there except what had to be, no turning back. Red was growing impatient. *Come on you stupid old cunt, give it your best shot . . .*

'Remember her like she was? And what way was that, Alan? 'Cos you didn't really know her, did you?'

Red was prepared for this but the fact that the missile came from Peter had him quickly thinking on his feet, a host of answers considered and rejected. An arrogant silence was all that Peter perceived. Red knew that Peter wanted a confrontation, but he felt jittery as if drunk and he wanted to hold Peter and cry together and say to him 'please, Peter, this is my way of dealing with it.' *Come on Aunt Mary, referee this properly. I don't want to get hurt, say something useful for once you old hag, look he's drinking more whiskey, there's a demon rising*. Red started crying, tears of fear, repulsion, acceptance, torment and overwhelmingly of grief. He hoped the tears would bring sympathy his way.

'There's no point in crying now, it's too late,' said Peter. 'You're a fucking idiot.'

'There's no need for the language, Peter,' Aunt Mary admonished him, trying to bring the evening back to a formal calm. Peter was having none of it.

'It's him, she doted on him and he never showed her any love, swanning in and out . . . And what did I get, huh? I got to clean her piss-soaked sheets.' He pointed at Red with disdain. 'What can you mourn? You didn't know the woman, she died when you left here.'

Red still wouldn't rise to the bait. His muted response was creating a tension which Mary deemed proper and necessary. Slithers of rain splashed on to the window and the lack of air in the room pillared them into statuesque poses. They were characters in a standard

Irish play: no eye contact, precise movements; no connections but a heavy hint of crisis. Peter, caught up in his gloom, lost the energy to fight his brother. Aunt Mary was comfortable in the mire. This was a holiday from her own treachery, an awayday to take on the role of a glow-in-the-dark saint for which she expected to be rewarded at the pearly gates. Red, unaccustomed to death, didn't appreciate its etiquette. He wanted to play music, turn on the television, live a little, fuck a woman. A bunch of kids knocked on the door and ran away, the wreath that Mary had put on it too much of a temptation for them. Red, starving, daydreamed about the Italian chipper, his appetite supplying the details. Whenever they closed the shop they would put up a sign, 'closed due to death in the family', as if that was the only valid reason for forcing Treetown's population to forego their spot-causing feast. It wasn't a great advertisement for their chips, either. He scanned the newspaper which again brought disapproving looks from the other two. He looked up the TV listings page and spotted that *Naked Gun* was starting in half an hour. Would Mum really mind if he watched it or did she want them to show respect by being dead a couple of days themselves? He decided to break the tension.

'Are you coming to the opening of the sports shop, Aunty Mary?'

It came out a little too up and he tried to bring it down again midway through the sentence, never quite capturing the right balance.

'When is that, dear?'

'Wednesday.'

Peter found another burst of indignant energy.

'Surely you're going to postpone it for the time being?'

Red shrugged.

'No. I'm sure it's what Mum would have wanted.'

'Oh yes, that was her dying request. *Make sure Red sells a load of golf balls the day after my funeral*. You really take the biscuit, you do. I can't bear to be in the same room as you.'

Peter snatched up his bottle and headed for his room. Red turned to Mary.

'What can I do?' he pleaded. 'It's bound to affect him more. He saw a lot more of her, it's more of a loss to him. It hits us in different ways.'

Aunt Mary had never liked Red. She'd intended to reproach him for his neglect of his mother but she couldn't do it when all she could see in front of her was a little boy. She bid him goodnight. Red went into the sitting room and turned on the film at a low volume and chuckled the night away, eating crisps and sugar sandwiches.

John had spent the day walking around Charing Cross Road and Covent Garden. When it got too crowded he ducked into a side street. He found an old man's pub in the midst of all the youthful trendiness. He ordered a pint of Guinness from the Irish barman, who poured it with the proper care and reverence, even shaping a shamrock on its head but it still tasted shit. John eavesdropped on an old man leaning against the counter. He had one of those huge West of Ireland heads with a fine thatch of hair and broken veins protruding from his cheeks. There was froth on his lips as he asked the barman for a lend of a black tie. This simple request saddened John who saw a man in his seventies hardened by death, drinking to another corpse, biding his time, making his living with the pennies he amassed for his thoughts. John sipped his Guinness. He got up to go, leaving his glass three-quarters full, nodding farewell to the barman who was clearly disappointed that the Guinness hadn't met with his approval. John wanted colour and vitality. Down one of his side routes he came across a tiny premises above which a big sign read 'The Problematic Shop'. Intrigued he went in. On display were a tartan scarf, an African spear, a dusty bottle of wine and an old cavalry uniform.

'Are these for sale?' he asked.

'No, sir,' a pretty bookish woman in her thirties replied before going back to her book.

'What actually is for sale?'

She put down her book again and smiled at him. 'Anything you want.'

John was puzzled. 'What do you mean?'

'If you want something which is hard to get, we will do our utmost to get it for you. These items you see around you were all requested and found. They're just waiting to be collected.'

'Wow, what a great idea. What's your success rate?'

'About eighty percent. I have a network of people who all have their own specialities.'

'Could you get me a video copy of *The Tin Drum*?'

'I can give it a whirl. It's not available from normal video stockists?'

'I could never find it.'

'Is cost a problem?'

'No.'

'And just out of curiosity, what is so special about *The Tin Drum*?'

'It's my wife's favourite film. Apparently I remind her of the little boy refusing to grow up and all that.'

'We'll try extra hard then,' she promised him, giving him the sweetest smile.

John was tempted to ask her out for coffee but didn't in case he fell for her. She took his details, blank cheque, message to go with the gift, and they parted. That's how life should be, a spark and away, thought John. As if to contradict himself he found himself back in the café where he and Tara had shared their bodily fluids. He tried to pretend it was a coincidence but an internal homing device was at play. A desperate heart being deviant of the mind. He supped his watery tea and read the *Independent* cover to cover. The sun and the setting brought out the overdressed people. John observed them Filofaxing their lives. Happy couples passed the café, walking the half pace of lovers, teasing John with a glimpse of their bliss. He didn't resent them – he just couldn't figure out how they did it. The surmountable-problem carriers, the settle-for-what-we've-got people, the mirage-becomes-reality brigade all making it work; unless a giant conspiracy was at play and this was our maker's twisted joke, watching the wrenched pain caused by his grand illusion. *Nah – I just haven't found the right person. Or if I did it was at the wrong time or I was wrong for them at the right time or maybe I'm just an ugly cunt.* Chemistry . . . there must be a mathematical equation that can be bought but you only find it via word of mouth. A steady stream of single people balanced his playful paranoia. These were his people, the ones who knew love was basically tolerance or loneliness. He imagined having relationships with them, having to go through the ordeal of getting to know someone while impersonating a different person. Coming out of one's shell until the time was right to go back for hibernation, only this time trying to stuff your new love in there with you until the inevitable 'I need my own space, man' crushes the initial love. You peek your head out and make a decision: do I go out into that scary cold world or stay where I am.

Tired of intellectualising, John started looking at breasts, a fascination he still held dear. Three cheers for the bra-makers and their tricks. Men never tire of looking at tits: the possibilities were endless. Even as a child sunbathing with his family in the back garden he couldn't resist taking a quick glance at his mother's mammaries. It wasn't a sexual curiosity; it was more scientific, another particular shape to study. He was sure that's what scientists did all day down in the lab. They put pictures of naked ladies under the microscope, working out new theories on gravity and shape. He laughed to himself but the illusory scenario had him walking into a newsagents to purchase a pornography magazine for the first time in his life. Outside the shop he spotted a guy wearing an identical jacket to the one that Tara had bought him. It didn't suit him either. Had he been duped into buying one too? Then he spotted another. Tara must be paid a commission to sell these jackets at all costs. That was her real job, putting guys under her spell until they became so transfixed that she could dress them. All the men who passed him looked uncomfortable in their clothes. All of them dressed to their lady's taste, a tagging system to make it easier for her to pick out her man in the crowd.

Michelle left lots of little treats around the house for Chrissie as peace offerings. She sat down to her first cup of tea of the day having found a photo album in the attic during her clearout. She flicked through it, her way of mentally packing her bags. The pictures were from their honeymoon in Reykjavik; no laying towels on the beach for these two newlyweds. John had wanted to go to Iceland because he believed it didn't get dark during the summer and he liked the idea of constant daylight. Michelle wasn't sold on the idea but eventually she relented. She remembered John's stupid argument: 'And think about it honey, we won't need one of those cameras with a built-in flash.'

It had ended up being a week with the bleak. The Icelanders were incredibly similar to the Irish, morose joker drinkers. The pub culture had just arrived on the island and the inhabitants were embracing it wholeheartedly. The ride from the airport had them scanning for any signs of civilisation. All they could see for miles were the moon-crater surfaces, constantly cast in a different light by the ever dependable changing weather. In the photos they both looked suitably glum beside natural hot springs, volcanic hills, wooden houses, and friendly locals who insisted on having their picture taken with them. The Icelanders had an affinity with the Irish which no one had bothered to tell the Irish about.

In all the photographs Michelle could see a distance in John's eyes which she hadn't been aware of at the time. She turned the pages trying to find a picture where there was physical contact between them. They had shared the same bed for the first three nights but when John began to have problems sleeping because of the constant light they opted for separate beds. He was an irritable holiday companion who'd been more interested in the locals than in talking to her. He was only tender when drunk. All the photos pointed to inevitable doom. Two dead-eyed people along for the ride. But that first night he'd held her close and she'd been safe and loved and he'd stroked her hair, ballooning his whole body around hers, his warm breath heating her neck before it had rushed through her whole body bringing a state of near-levitation. She awoke in the morning having succumbed to the sweetest dreams to find John curled up tightly on the other side of the bed, finely balanced on the edge. From that moment on he was courteous and nice but never a cuddler. Ever since he'd been inching away. Some of the photos had faded, a claylike brown smudging on to the dark features making it feel an even longer time ago. Michelle put the album away and put on Jan Garbarek and the Hillard Ensemble's *Officialdom* to put music to her pain.

John flushed away the tissue which a sperm bank would have paid good money for and washed his hand. He'd relieved himself with a little help from Isabella from Ipswich and Bernice from Basingstoke, who particularly liked to be taken from behind by greasy bikers with her husband watching. John didn't like pornography. He didn't agree with it, and he hated the idea that the stories were written by sad old men who left little to the imagination because they themselves had no imagination. He knew that these magazines helped unbalanced types to see women even more as sexual objects but on the other hand they made him horny as hell. In fact he masturbated twice, the first time being so intense that the sperm flew as if shot from a fire extinguisher, the process over in seconds. He was nearly put off his second wank when he happened upon the readers' wives page. Never mind putting him off porn: this page put him off the whole idea of marriage itself. Still flicking he came across a story which had some nonsense about a hotel receptionist who had access to the bridal suite, nudge nudge, wink wink, and by the end of the paragraph there's six of them sucking and fucking, smearing and fingering. He didn't manage to get to the end but he thought about getting Philip to book him in there on his next trip.

Happily rid of his sperm count he showered and got ready to go out. By chance he had noticed that one of his favourite singers, Mark Eizel from The American Music Club, was playing in town that night. Red and Michelle kept flickering into his consciousness but he had decided to let that fester, promising himself that he'd deal with it on touch down in Dublin. He arrived at the Bloomsbury Theatre at nine fifty-five, in time to catch the opening of the show without having to stand around outside looking like a spare. He'd never been to a gig on his own before but he felt that this was a suitable occasion, since nearly all Eizel's songs were to do with being alone. The theatre looked a shabby mess from the outside, taking on the appearance of a public swimming pool, but inside it was wonderful, comfortable seats and good eye lines. Before the show John overheard two fanatics talking about the previous night's performance. Eizel had played for only forty-five minutes, and he'd been pissed and incoherent, spitting and vomiting throughout the set. They wondered if he was on the verge of suicide.

As if that had been a buzzword the band ambled on. Eizel went straight to the keyboards and started hitting the low notes, singing some lyrics about which of his nightmares he'd change if he had to live his life all over again. John knew he was in for a treat. For over two hours the singer stumbled over beautiful melodies about failed relationships, constantly raising the spirits of his congregation. If only Mass could be like this. This was the church of the unloved. It made you want to forsake sex for higher planes. Sex is a pleasure but not a communication and the audience understood this. Nobody wanted to leave and yet they were also itching to get away to validate the experience. Complete, they could enjoy it more. It would be part of their lives. Eizel's sharing of pain gave them hope. The only sadness was the knowledge that nobody bought his records. He engendered feelings of brotherly love and yet as the concert ended you wanted to riot in gymnasiums and garden centres, smash up DIY shops, set fire to all the West End cinemas which were showing action movies; round up all the complacent people and aim a gun which shoots out anxiety pellets; make actors in Lloyd Webber musicals admit to terrible deeds in front of their wholesome audiences; replace their parents with Ricki and Oprah and make them discuss endless piddle; take away their tabloids and make them read books; give them cake. John settled instead for buying a T-shirt and a comfortable sleep.

Red sat with Peter and Aunt Mary in the second row of Treetown's modern church. The boys wore suits and accepted sympathetic nods from others attending the ten o'clock Mass. Aunt Mary wore a smart black dress with a bee-net hat and veil. The church was built like a prison with its high walls and pebble-dashed courtyard surrounding the founding stone which the Archbishop of Dublin had blessed. The inside was fully adorned with religious artefacts but to the redemption-seekers it still felt as if they were simply sitting inside a big room. Twenty-five rows on either side of the aisle were fitted with gym-type benches making both standing and kneeling a relief. Babies let out occasional screams while mothers rocked and hushed them. Gangs of teens stifled yawns and continued the dream of last night's sleep, all the time showing off to the opposite sex, and men breathed alcoholic fumes into air which was already having trouble dealing with their body odours. The altar boys sweet-walked the priest to the altar, where, taking up his rightful place, he went onto automatic pilot. Cantankerous old near-priest people shoved plates at the parishioners to help feed their habits, and Red was bored shitless.

His mother's death preyed on his mind, of course. He remembered the time she tried to break up a fight between him and Peter. She was chopping onions when the bout started and during her refereeing had managed to stick the knife into her own hand, a tiny cut which was deep enough to see the white of the bone. The thought of the endless cups of sweet tea she made him gulp down as a cure for everything from bruises to chickenpox produced a rueful smile. It came to the part of the Mass where peace was offered to those beside you and Red shook hands with the entire row. The priest banged on about loss and a better place, but nobody was listening, until he mentioned Mrs Bulger by name, when the gathering bucked up and showed their respect by looking towards the three mourners. Red didn't like the attention and couldn't help crying. Peter, anticipating that their mother's death was eventually sinking in, shouldered Red. Aunt Mary was crying too. Red went for the full monty: dramatically he got up and left the building in full view of his future customers. As he reached the door he put a five-pound note in the box and lit a candle. Peter went after him as the priest began to offer communion. This was the hangover-sufferers' opportunity to ditch out also, missing the priest's summing up and the second collection round.

Outside, Peter tried to comfort him.

'Do you want to talk about it, Red?'

Red played along, knowing it would get him off his back.

'Not yet, Peter. Not yet.'

Red arrived home, proud of his master stroke. His little scene would have them all flocking to his shop. He went to the kitchen table with every gossip-mongering tabloid he could carry. Aunt Mary had a joint of beef roasting in the oven and the smell of it flooded his senses. If there'd been football on the television it would have been a perfect day. The aroma of sizzling beef was up there with petrol on Red's list of favourite smells. It teased him with delicate hints of the meal to come, wafting into his hunger, causing his belly to rumble with anticipation. Red was happy and he didn't feel bad about it either. He turned on the radio to hear some tunes, tapping his fingers on the table in between turning the pages of the newspaper. Three flies and a flapping moth were flying Red Devil-ish stunts around him. The moth found the lampshade, noisily banging its body weight over and over against the sides. Red rolled up his paper and strolled over to the lamp and rattled it. The panicking moth slapped harder against the shade before making a dash for freedom. It settled on the white kitchen door thinking it had camouflaged itself. Red took aim. *Whack! Skinned it.* The moth lost some of its undercarriage, fell to the ground in shock and struggled to get mobile. Dana came out of her slumber and clawed it. Too old to take her proper place on the food chain, she still had the instinct for the kill. She bit at it, while the moth, sensing its life was over, made one last supreme effort for survival. Finally Dana squashed it with her paw, just like somebody putting a cigarette out with their foot. Red crouched down to get a closer look at the moth's insides and the reality of death stared back at him. A deranged rush engulfed him, dizzy vision pushing away his surroundings. Voices became distorted and the radio seemed to be playing at twice its normal speed. His mother's death hit him just as his head bounced off the tiled floor. It settled on a white square, a perfect fit.

'Shall we have a drink?' John asked of Dominic, conscious of his nerves and talking for the sake of it.

Dominic declined his offer. 'It's a bit early for me.'

John glanced at his watch, having to tug at his shirt sleeve twice. It was five past one. He only half caught the end of Dominic's joke, '. . . I don't intend to get into heavy drinking until I'm in my fifties.'

It was too late to laugh spontaneously and to do so now would only make him look slow. But he didn't want to be rude and he wished he could start again. He ordered a glass of white wine for himself while Dominic opted for sparkling water. John's hands were clammy and blotched and he excused himself and went to the toilet. He washed his hands and noticed a dark hair coming out of one of his nostrils. He yanked it out with his fingers which made his eyes water. Three other hairs came along for the ride. He looked at them, disgusted. They were long enough to use as strings for a violin. This vain extraction made him aware of other shortcomings in his general grooming. Uneven and unwanted sideburns; tufts of shaving-escapee hair; a long eyebrow strand doing a detour up to the forehead, the others arranging to meet up and mingle in no-man's-land; the fluffy minute hairs which had settled onto his ears . . . Yes, he was definitely having a bad hair day. The bags under his eyes gave the impression he was wearing trendy sunglasses. The nose was taking its shape as if spending a lifetime pressed up against a window. The cheeks resembled camels' humps and his Adam's apple protruded like a shuttlecock bobbing from side to side. He almost barked at his own reflection. He felt confused that he hadn't noticed these blemishes before. This was what he'd expected Dominic to look like: a geeky pale skinny hippy type; but he was a smartly-dressed, healthy-looking forty-something. He started preparing his conversation hoping it wouldn't come over as pre-rehearsed. He dried his hands on the towel to find them sweating again.

When he got back to the table he tried to explain.

'Sorry I took so long, I . . .' The rest of the sentence tailed off and he quickly changed tack. 'This is very hard for me, because I'm such a big fan. Your stories mean so much to me.'

'Thanks very much. But they are only stories.'

'I must say that story you wrote about the blind man who gets his sight back to find that his wife was astonishingly beautiful was a stroke of genius.'

'Thanks very much. Yeah, I enjoyed writing that.'

'And he left her because he felt it was pity rather than love that she'd shown him all their lives?' John's eyes were pleading for assurance.

'Yes . . .'

John stopped listening, too busy sighing with relief.

'. . . But it was more that he rejected happiness because he couldn't come to terms with what he had been missing all those years. He'd never conceived of such beauty, and her remaining would have been a constant reminder.'

'And do you think he did the right thing?'

Dominic looked through John. 'He did the only thing he could do.'

'So essentially it was about balance and moderation?'

'The whole collection's to do with balance, that's why it was called *Trapezing through Dubai*.'

John was lost.

'As in the other side of the world. I like the metaphor of falling into the sky.'

Feeling suitably stupid, John continued, 'And the new collection? I feel a sense of going for goals where even inactions result in actions.'

'To a certain extent, yes. But the wider picture is that existence will happen regardless . . . It's a matter of facing up to your life and staying at a tangent with fate.'

John nodded knowingly, adoring the way Dominic was articulating himself, having grasped the basics but feeling the need to analyse it later.

'Are you working on anything new?'

'Yeah, I've been looking at the word "impossible". This might sound ridiculous, but I've never liked that word. And when I studied it, I split it up to make a two-word statement, "I'm possible". I'm trying to write a range of stories looking at hopeless situations and putting hope in there. It's like solving a puzzle.'

'Have you written any yet?'

'One.' Dominic went to his briefcase. 'Which I'm going to let you have a sneak preview of.'

John was ecstatic. This was backstage at the Point, the Vatican's inner sanctum, watching an athlete take steroids. He wanted to kiss Dominic hard on the lips as he was handed a large brown envelope.

'It's very short.'

'I'll read it on the plane.' He hugged it under his arm. The rest of the conversation was an anti-climax. What use was Christmas once you'd been given your presents? Their respective roles made conversation restricted. They found out many things about each other, but no secrets. John could hardly believe how normal Dominic was: married with two children, barely venturing outside his village. He did all his travelling in his head.

Dominic shook hands informally with John, thanking him for lunch, wondering if all his readers were as nutty, already regretting giving John his home number. John watched him go, instantly regretting meeting his hero. He still worshipped his words, but he'd hoped they would have been more like-minded. And yet, in a way it made his writing more special still, knowing that Dominic himself was so ordinary.

John got to his room just as the maid was leaving it, a bundle of sheets heaved to her bosom. He gave her a friendly nod which she dismissed with a frown. *Charming,* he thought, trying to make sense of the anti-gesture. The answer lay on his bed where he'd left the porno mag open at the centre spread. He was embarrassed, even though he didn't care what strangers thought. He had one final flick through the magazine. It was amazing how repulsive some of the girls' poses were when you weren't turned on. These young nubiles shoving their gussets in your face, by-lining it with how hot they were for you. Then John had one of those moments of clarity where you simply refuse to believe your own eyes. The shock had him quickly closing the magazine while he prepared himself to take a proper look. He wanted to give it his full concentration. He made himself a cup of tea and lit himself a cigarette while waiting to have a cigarette. He took a sup of the tea and it tasted like hotel tea always did, a bland gritty taste and never hot enough. It was something to do with the little kettles not boiling fully or perhaps the shape of those white half-cups.

He lay back on the bed, allowing the pillows to support his back, and picked up the magazine. Forever the innocent he started on page one, building up to the showdown. He came to the page he'd stopped at before and there with her arse poking up over the chaise longue was Sally from Swansea. In the first pose she looked as if she was searching for loose change. The photo-story showed her in white suspenders, black stilettos and cutesy pullover. It amounted to a gradual strip, teasing the reader with her vulva before trying to take her knickers off by the side. Fully naked she looked like a drunkard who couldn't quite make it onto the chair. There she was on the edge of it, falling off, climbing on, head peeking over the top. The words that accompanied the piece began: 'It's amazing what a girl with no tits has to do to get a guy's attention.' Then they went on to extol the virtues of pussy. Sally was quoted as saying, 'Tits, they're just a stop-off on the way.' Her various facial expressions consisted of passion, contentment, satisfaction, willingness and a general lust but there was no mistaking that smile. It was Tara. John could practically smell her; he checked to see if the page was scratch-and-sniff.

He didn't know if this latest twist was a help or a

hindrance to his cause. The world was certainly a smaller place. It was another kick in the face for his self-esteem: *rejected by a slut, what's her fucking game? It surely wasn't for money, was it simply doing the undo-able, smoking on a plane, appearing naked in magazines? That girl needs a new hobby and who the hell did I meet, Sally, Tara? Maybe she has one of those faces that you can pull off to reveal itself. If it was, no doubt it would be Red fucking with my head a little more. At least now there's a context to the week, no more dreaming, a definite non-runner. Hi Mum this is the love of my life she has a tremendous-looking cunt, check out page sixty-nine of this month's* Little 'Uns.

He rolled the magazine up and threw it into the wastepaper basket. The grand gesture, putting her where she belonged. Of course he missed, and made a mental note not to make that particular gesture again. Thinking positively, at least his new clothes had no more nasty connotations. He decided to wear his new jacket back to Ireland, back to the mess, the limbering fiasco lit on a short fuse. He didn't know why, but he was looking forward to the confrontation; he wanted to tackle it head on.

Michelle was knee-deep in traffic on the Swords Road; Sunday traffic caught up by the police cordon while a blanketed dead person was lifted into an ambulance. The victim's car had blocked both lanes. It was bullet-riddled and couldn't be moved until it had been completely checked over. Michelle was worried about getting through the makeshift thoroughfare the police were allowing the traffic to edge towards. She only had a provisional licence and wasn't a competent or confident driver. This was her first time alone in the car but she wanted to surprise John, to catch him unawares, make herself useful. The radio cut off Phil Collins mid-song to bring a report of the killing. There's something positive in every situation. A suspected tit-for-tat gang murder was the slant of the report. An eyewitness was being interviewed, and Michelle could see him there by the side of the road on his mobile phone.

'It's pandemonium down here. I'm a little shook up meself. We were just driving along, you know, I'm supposed to be going on my holliers to Portugal, but me nerves are shattered, maybe I could stay for an extra week . . . Anyway, we were just driving along, you know, fair pace when this lunatic started weaving in and out of the lanes. We thought it was joyriders, but then, and I'm not joking, the window opened and the fella in the passenger seat opened fire with a – I'm telling you – a machine gun, just round after round after round, it was like something out of Bugsy Malone, only these weren't kids, oh no. Anyway, the car swerved and it was bang, bang, bang one car into another. Then the killers sped off breaking speed limits and everything, they had an Audi, terrific acceleration but not very durable regardless of what they say about German cars. Anyway everybody got out of their cars—'

'And what could you see?'

'. . . The main lights, bumper and bonnet were wrecked, there goes my fucking no-claims bonus—'

Abruptly he was cut off, the presenter apologising for the robustness of the language. Michelle could see him looking confused, mouthing 'Hello?' repeatedly into his phone. She found it hard to laugh after such carnage.

Her imagination ran away with itself and it was obvious to her that the murdered man had been trying to flee the country: that was the only reason they would have done such a deed on one of the busiest roads. The officials were rapidly losing control over criminals whose activities were becoming increasingly bare-faced. Soon they would hold the whole country to ransom. A far cry from their youth when stolen bicycles still got reported in the newspapers. Michelle hit a pothole and momentarily lost control of the steering wheel, leaving her shaky and dazed and stuck in the wrong gear.

John browsed through the bargain bin in the Our Price shop at Heathrow. He was always on the hunt for CDs to replace the albums of his youth. His shoulder bag was cutting into his shoulder. The hot sticky air and the idea of flying had sweat pouring from his forehead and armpits. The extra layer of clothes he had on owing to the abundance of luggage wasn't helping. He shuffled towards the departure lounge, a *Dexy's Greatest Hits* plus four bonus tracks heavier. As he approached the X-ray machine he started fidgeting for the loose change, lighter and keys which always set the blasted metal detector off. His heart stopped as he fingered his breast pocket and felt the outline of the four tabs he had completely forgotten about. All his energies transfixed themselves onto his eyes which filled with terror, guilt and blood. It was bad enough when he was innocent. At best he resembled a junkie doing cold turkey on a bad day. He would always try to walk through security desperately trying to look preoccupied but he might as well have had a syringe hanging from his arm for all the good it did him. He'd have a struggle to do the same while carrying class As. He tried to control the signals he was putting out but his body was play-acting, seeking revenge for the copious amounts of drugs it had had to endure in its prime. His body was going to grass him up. His head was giving signs of losing the battle.

Make a run for it. Shut up. *Don't tell me to shut up, oops there go the legs, wobbly wobbly jelly. 'Excuse me sir, can you empty your pockets.' No, you're alright . . . Oh, you're fucked now. Look at your hands, a dead giveaway, they're moving like you're playing on an imaginary pinball machine and you're not exactly a bloody wizard, are you? Roger Daltry, he did drugs, didn't he . . . You're through. You did it, thank God, do a lap of honour, go through all the security checks. Hang on, don't get carried away. It wasn't going to be their biggest haul, was it? Not exactly the ten o'clock news. 'Customs at Heathrow seized two Ecstasy tablets and two dots of acid, they're taking the rest of the year off.'* Okay okay, now shut the fuck up.

John dreaded to think of the facial expressions he'd pulled to get him through. His body was aftershocking as he held onto the conveyor belt of the escalator, all his strength sapped away. He downed two pints of Guinness and chain-smoked five cigarettes in twenty minutes, punishing his body for letting him down so badly. On the plane he napped for five minutes, waking up for the take-off. This time he had the two seats to himself; porno stars obviously rested on a Sunday. Once he'd refused the steamed vegetarian delight that was offered he took out Dominic's latest story. He was now fully awake, the aroma of the food acting as smelling salts.

He began to read.

'I hate that man, I hate his guts. I'd like to fillet him, cause him unbearable pain. I'd like to squash his head, hear the crack of the skull, watch the pus, poke out his eye, pick it up in my hand, look him straight in the eye and say leave me alone, but the fucker won't go away.'

'And you told him this?'

'I don't like confrontation.'

'What does he want?'

'That's it . . . I don't know. It's either to punish me or himself.'

'I don't follow.'

'He comes around to my house once a week, on a Tuesday, it's like clockwork. He knows I don't like him. But he insists on telling me every detail of his life, even though all he says is lies.'

'What do you mean?'

'This is the weird thing. I get a letter from him on a Monday. He uses a pseudonym and it's always written in the third person and the letter is always full of nasty deeds he's done.'

'That guy needs serious help.'

'Tell me about it! The strange thing is, I think I prefer the bad guy, because he doesn't bug the shit out of me. Anyway he sits there and he talks about, you know, his hopes for the future, his love for his parents . . . total drivel. Then I bring up the letter and he goes quiet and then he admits to his misgivings and he always says the same thing. 'Do you think that's a bad thing?' And I say yes, it's a terrible thing and

then he stares at me with a crushed look on his face and just waits until I say I can understand where he's coming from, and that's it. Then he smiles, gets up and leaves, thanking me.'

'You've taken on the mantle of priest to his sinner.'

'Yeah . . . But why?'

'Because he knows you hate him. If you can forgive him it appeases everything. You're justifying his badness, you're his accomplice.'

'That's nonsense. He thinks he's above me in every way, so why does he need me?'

'He thinks you hold the key. And because that's what he thinks, you do.'

'And what do you suggest I do?'

'Simply tell him that you despise him and all he stands for, make him face up to himself. I guarantee you'll never see him again.'

John was engulfed in the story. There was a tension coming from the small of his back. He ordered a red wine from the hostess, refusing to look at the page until he'd swigged at least half of it. He didn't want to read on.

'What if he goes nuts and does something stupid?'

'Are you frightened of him?'

'I'm frightened of what he is capable of. Wouldn't you be?'

'Well, it's all hypothetical for me. I'm removed from the situation, he can't touch me.'

'But aren't you frightened of the unknown?'

'We're only frightened of the unknown of the known.'

'I get jumpy thinking about it.'

'It would be a good exercise for you, facing up to your own self, your own fears. You've made yourself part of his game . . . now it's up to you to change the rules.'

'But then I'd be entering into a certain pact, debasing myself, lowering myself to his level, manipulating the situation.'

'Do you want to remain in this loop?'

'What if he's waiting for the confrontation, it's all part of his plan?'

'Do you think he's that intelligent?'

'No . . . but what if it's me, what if the confrontation is all a part of my own subconscious plan?'

'That's the risk, my dear friend. Calculated, yes. But wouldn't it be great to know?'

'I'm happy coasting along.'

'No, you're not. It's taking up all your energies. And if I know you at all, you're enjoying this sense of purpose.'

'Right. I'm going to go for it. I'll confront.'

John was unbearably claustrophobic and wished he was wearing a shirt that he could loosen. He snatched at his wine, knocking it onto the page. The hand-written words spread. He wiped the wine away frantically which smudged the ink into different directions, turning the rest of the story into an ink-blot. John was furious with himself. The piece disturbed him. It was almost as if Dominic was aware of his situation. He had always related to Dominic's stories, but never so directly. He trusted him, and all the words were pointing towards a direct confrontation. *I'll confront, I'll reach for the stars.* The poet's inaction brought hopeless depression; life was about doing undo-able things. What was it that Dominic had said? Things will happen regardless, face up to them and you will have the advantage of being one step ahead of your fate. *Fuck it, the time is now. Alright Red let's do it, it's time you faced the music.* Thank you Dominic, thank you.

The stewardess interrupted him. 'Would you like another drink, sir?'

'No. I'll be needing a clear head.'

CHAPTER 11

John's flight landed on time. He watched the hurried scurrying off the plane to be at vantage points for the fifteen-minute wait at the baggage carousel. John's luggage was the first on to the conveyor belt. He wasn't worried about Irish customs as it didn't exist any more; the most he would encounter was one man dozing over a paperback. All the same he didn't like having acid on his person because of the dreadful experience he'd had on it in his teens. He'd only taken it once and now he understood why The Grateful Dead had such an apt name. Through the electronic doors he could see the motley crew of the individual welcoming committees visually casting him aside, craning their necks in case they missed a moment of their loved ones' homecomings. As he wheeled his way towards the taxi rank, he thought he heard his name. He ignored it, but it came again, this time a little louder. He turned around and spotted Michelle half-waving at him. She stood her ground, waiting to be beckoned forward. John waved back and she came towards him with a ridiculous step and a half pace, as if she was attempting the run-up to a triple jump. John watched her, making her even more self-conscious, her vulnerable face reminding him why he craved for her. She stopped two feet away, folding her arms and then dropping them to her sides.

'Come here to me,' John half-smiled.

Michelle practically cannoned into him. He pecked her on the cheek and gave her a hug. The blood rushed back to her face. John, trying not to give her a false impression, brought the scene back to the mundane.

'Did you come in a cab?'

'No, I drove,' said Michelle, trying to sound normal.

'Yeah!'

She was pleased with herself. An innocent smile rounded her face, as if leaving a flat surface on her head where it could be patted. It was a beautiful moment; but then John remembered that she'd fucked Red. It was almost as if she'd registered his thought. She took control of his baggage trolley with a 'Better get you home.'

London was instantly forgotten as Michelle's perfume made John aware of his situation and all its implications. He half-slept in the car, juddering with Michelle's to-and-fro driving. They passed the scene of the crime, but the bullet-riddled car was gone and traffic was back to normal. It was as if nothing had ever happened. Michelle turned on the radio to make sure that her head wasn't playing tricks on her. On the News a crime expert was analysing the latest criminal outrage. It was coming to light that this was a case of mistaken identity. An innocent man had been murdered, his only mistake to be in the wrong place at the wrong time driving a black 95D reg Volvo. The tinted glass had been his most costly accessory: a major player in the gang war drove an identical car. The report ended with the usual comment from a cynical Garda spokesman: 'Even though we know those responsible it's unlikely we'll be able to bring the culprits to justice.'

John switched the radio off. It annoyed him that the media ran these short-lived cycles of news. The papers would be full of it tomorrow and then the Sundays would comment on the event before it went down into the vault of statistics. Christ, minor incidents in soap operas stayed with you longer. At the same time he was fascinated by home-grown violence and its recent acceleration. The media had given the gangsters personalities which had the effect of lessening their deadly deeds and gave the criminals an incentive to do more outlandish heists, gaining their immorality through folklore. *They should put plaques up where there's been a murder, a constant reminder of our lack of morals. We treat these occasions as if they were flies, waving a hand of discontent at them, trusting them to go away.* Steam was puffing out of him and every so often he squeezed Michelle's hand, letting her know she wasn't the cause of his anger.

At home they eased back into the sweet sourness of their relationship. Michelle waited for the discussion to take place, yet although she was prepared for it, she had no answers. John sat on his favourite bench in the garden reading the papers, trying to catch up on what had happened while he'd been away. The pile of post that was waiting for him was of the discarding variety. Michelle kept looming into the corner of his vision. He threw the odd smile her way. He had fully intended to interrogate her, had brought a higher-wattage light bulb with him for the proceedings, but now he felt there was no point. He had to look forward, he would need all his energies for the slaughter to come. In all likelihood he wouldn't see Michelle after this episode, and it was better that she was not aware of this.

The series of plans formulating in his head had him napping in the garden. He woke up feeling refreshed and ready. He went to his study. The possibilities were endless. The freedom of not feeling responsible for his actions made him light-headed and for the first time in his entirety he didn't need anything or anybody. This in itself was a revelation. Up to now his existence had been one of dipping into a crowd and desperately trying to go with the flow. The childhood nightmares of short-haired bespectacled white-coat-wearers assessing the fragility of his brain, the presence of his parents' signatures allowing them to do whatever they had to to make him normal, didn't frighten him any more. He had wasted his life assuming the identity of those around him, never becoming himself. Any notion of change had been stamped out. All those words to the wise believed. *No man is an island,* indeed. Think about it. The saying is there because some men think they are islands, and if that's what they think they are, that's what they'll become.

It was time for the farewells.

'Hello, Mum. How are you?'

'Oh, hello, son. When did you get back?'

He heard his mother light a cigarette, suck on it hard and cough. She obviously wanted the conversation to last at least the length of the cigarette. The predictability of her chat drove John to the point of hanging up but tonight he wanted to give her happiness.

'Mum, I was wondering . . . What was I like as a child?'

She lit another cigarette and launched into anecdotal mode.

'No Mum, not what did I do . . . What was I like?'

'You were a very happy child, always singing and joking and larking about.'

He stopped listening. His mother's selective memory was short-changing him and she'd clearly mistaken the family upbringing for that of *The Waltons*.

'Goodnight, John-boy.'

'Goodnight, Mum.'

Bath time for the mountain boy. John endlessly tried to get the water just right. Bathing was an important pleasure and he had fitted the biggest antique tub he could find into his house. He wanted to immerse himself fully into water. He always used bubble bath, to avoid having to look at his skinny body. If he was uptight he could barely stay in the bath, but if relaxed the water would be cold before he noticed. He'd let his body take the pressure of the hot water, become comfortable with it before his head was dunked under. Emerging, he'd pop his ears via his nose. He would read magazines to take his mind off the little pains his back would give him. When he'd finished his ritual he would grab the soap and give himself a gentle all-over rub, then he would sponge all the hard skin away. It was always about new beginnings, ridding himself of toxins, dirt, personas. It was time to stop worshipping false gods.

Another reason the bath sessions took so long was because he didn't like to dry himself. He would rather drip dry onto the bathroom floor. A towel around his waist, he would poke a stick into his ear, rummage around the wax and watch it trying to flush itself away over the following couple of days. Naked but for wet patches he would choose his underwear. Tonight he was visiting Jodie so it called for his favourite boxers, not in the chance of a for-old-times-sake shag but for the general confidence it gave him. He had two pairs of over-sized boxers which he despised, but refused to throw out. His crucifix in moments of self-hatred. Cleansed and clothed, it irriated him that he needed to fart.

The drive along Sandeycove Road during twilight made for a special occasion as if he was driving into night itself. The Dublin combo A House ranted in tune, singing snippets of regret and despair which John cradled as his own. Although this was John's home town he felt like a worthless tourist, the more so because all around him other people relaxed into their environment, taking their rightful place in the community. John had known from an early age that his mind was slightly out of kilter. He'd noticed it first in the cinema where he'd watched the James Bond films. He preferred Roger Moore; weird or what? But where he felt truly alone was when the bad guy came on the scene with his plans to blow up the earth and live in an underworld surrounded only by his own beautiful people. Bond, with eyebrows raised and racy music egging him on, would try and stop the baddie, encouraged by the cheers of the audience. John would silently side with the bad guy and sneer at the smallmindedness of those around him. He too wanted to live with the beautiful people. He recognised the Nazi connotations of such a plan but he also understood the bad guy's need to be left to his own devices. It was always like this: even when watching television he wanted to live on the *Knots Landing* cul-de-sac, away from danger, emotion and Frank Spencer. Closer to home the only luxury he wanted for his own house was a moat.

He thought of Jodie and wondered. Jodie had come into his life at a trade fair party in Edinburgh. She was half seeing one of his rival dealers but they were going through a rough patch and she'd attended the party on her own, her big brown eyes looking for introductions. She hovered in the hallway beside the telephone as if she was waiting for a call. John fell in love instantly and was surprised to find Jodie knew so much about him. They slowly got drunk together, his hand discreetly pushing hair from her face, the action lasting longer each time. He walked her to her hotel hand in hand, not the way lovers do, more like children who were frightened of getting lost. They arranged to meet the following day in the Botanical Gardens. They'd strolled along the shrubbery, taking each other in; they had tea and went to an art exhibition because that's what intelligent adults did. They sat on the park bench nudging closer, discussing their love lives, helping to wipe the past away. The slate was clean. They kissed awkwardly and necessarily and arranged to meet back in Dublin.

They saw each other on and off for two years. They had sex, which didn't work or matter, but regardless of how they tried they couldn't get past the doting stage. In his heart John knew they could never be a couple. She didn't deserve him as he didn't deserve her. If truth be told he loved her too much. She was his dream girl. The cynical lost romantic in him knew that the rigours of day-to-day life would destroy that love. Of course she didn't see it that way, and slowly she drifted back to her dealer who was ripening into a better bet. Married now, with a child on the way, she seemed happy, and was content to give that impression to those not close enough. John had kept in regular contact with her. Initially they fooled themselves that the relationship would remain strong but the visits became more infrequent and the conversations more distant, a gradual seamless disintegration. It was mainly down to lunch visits now, the baby in belly to ward off any past passions. Strangers they encountered assumed they were a young family and John enjoyed this pretence, knowing as he pampered her that Jodie was also sucked into their imaginary life.

He got to see her at night about four times a year; a

film, a meal, a band or a teeny weeny bit of alcohol. Nothing too impulsive, and John would always chaperone her home in good time and in one piece, her husband Derek taking the place of the father-figure during their little innocent dates. These liaisons always ended too soon for John. He longed for them to bring about a connection, for the click to be heard and heeded. Poor, poor Jodie; there had been moments of absolute perfection when all was in its rightful place, but John would dismiss this, selfishly waiting for the next relationship without working on this one. He was aware of this, but he thought that he would one day chance upon the essence of true love. The grand lie was always just around the corner. He knew now it was unlikely, but if he stopped searching it would make a mockery of his life, total.

He pulled up outside her house, the home she seemed happy in, with its tidy happy-seeming garden. Tonight he was going to go full circle and take her to St Stephen's Green. They would finally finish their walk. He beeped the horn and she came out straight away. She was dressed up in a slinky black dress that dropped at the knee. Derek gave him a cursory wave. John reciprocated, but he never got out of the car; he was always scared to contemplate the fact that Jodie might tell her husband everything. She kissed John on the cheek, surprised that he didn't make eye contact with her.

'Where are you taking me tonight, John?'

'Tonight I thought we'd talk.'

'We always talk.'

'Yeah, we go and see something, we catch up, we

have a drink and then reminisce about our former glories . . . '

Jodie looked blank.

'. . . It leaves me unfulfilled, so tonight I thought we'd talk.'

'John, we've been through this so many times.' She sounded resigned.

'No, no, this isn't about that, it's not me trying to impress you in the hope that you'll come to your senses and run away with me. But . . .' he looked at her for the first time '. . . I want to know you, and I want to know what went wrong with us.'

'Ah, come on, I get that at home. This is my night out.'

'Jesus, Jodie, do you know how insulting that is to me? I'm a distraction for you . . .'

Jodie tried to reassure him. 'You know I love you. I look forward to being with you, you're different.'

'I don't want to be different. I'm sick of being this circus act. I don't want monologues, I want dialogues.'

'And what are we going to do? Get pissed so you can get maudlin and self-pitying?'

John cut in. 'I'm off the drink . . . I thought we could go for a walk in the park.We can get a McDonald's.'

'Great, I got all dressed up for a McDonald's.'

'Alright, Burger King then.'

John stopped at a drive-thru. Jodie, like him a confirmed vegetarian, had fries, bean burger and shake. John only had the shake and fries. He kept conversation to a minimum, giving Jodie time to get used to the situation. The fries gave him the energy boost he needed.

The car parked up, they started the walk and talk. He knew there was no point in asking her straight out where it had all gone wrong. In his experience this only led to beating around the bush. He took her hand, and she went along with it slightly against her will.

'Were we different people back then, Jodie?' he began.

'No, but I think we're more rounded now, more complete.'

'You mean we don't step out of line any more?'

'Well, there does come a time when you just have to grow up.'

'You say that like it's a good thing.'

'Sometimes you're impossible, John. Any good thing that comes your way you throw it away, and any bad situation you hold on to for dear life. It's as if you won't allow yourself happiness. Take a day off, will you, you're not seventeen any more.'

'Jodie, can't you see I'd love to be able to accept the norm? If I could only twist the control dial over a fraction, I'm sure I'd be okay.'

'I don't think you'll ever find love, and that's a pity and a waste.'

'A waste? No, surely not. Without the unlovables your so-called normal society wouldn't have a Top Twenty chart or any books or paintings . . . you'd have no culture whatsoever. Lack of love fuels all that. What do you want? A world of inane grinners?'

'That's another little difference between us. I'm happy with my lot, but you have to see everything globally as if your life was more important . . . What is it you want, John?'

'I want you to ring me when I ring you, not put me on a list of chores you have to deal with. I want truth, not excuses. I want you to love me.'

He looked at her pleadingly. Her eyes darted around his face.

'I do love you . . . but I've got a different set of priorities now. Time hasn't stood still. Things move on. But you know, I do love you.'

'No you don't. I want that do or die intense love.'

'Ah, John, we're a bit old for that.'

'Now if we're talking about differences, yes, I would agree I digress too much into my youth, but Christ, you're really embracing old age with a vengeance.'

'I feel you have something on your mind which you're not telling me.'

'Possibly. But I haven't told myself yet, either.'

John led them to a bench where they sat hand in hand.

'Do you tell Derek everything?'

'No, of course I don't.'

'Why not?'

'Because it wouldn't be right.' She took her hand away.

'But who do you tell your secrets to?'

'I haven't got secrets.'

'But that's like saying you won't admit them to yourself.'

'No it isn't.' She was getting visibly irritated.

'You look very beautiful tonight, Jodie.'

She wore her hair short now but he couldn't resist brushing the hair of yesteryear away from her face. The gesture endeared him to her.

'I remember that day in the park,' she began.

John went to hush her. 'I said no "I remember" conversations.'

'No, no, let me, it's a question. You said to me that once you knew everything about me we would be together for the rest of our lives.'

'Yeah, and what's your point?'

She looked straight into his eyes. 'Why did you stop asking questions?'

John was uncomfortable with the affection and started to bite his fingernails.

'I think what I meant by that was not that I wanted to know everything about you, but that I was able to tell you everything about me. And there came a time when I knew I couldn't and I gently pushed you away from me, out of harm's way.'

'And do you regret that?'

'Every day.'

John had to put his hand up to his eyes to brush away the tears that were trying to make an impromptu appearance. Jodie hugged him.

'You're not going to ring me any more, are you?'

'No, Jodie, I'm not.'

'Is there a reason?'

'I don't know. I expect so. Probably more bad shit coming my way . . . gotta get rid of the good stuff, give it room.'

'If ever . . .'

'I know.' He stopped her with a gesture. 'Come on, I'll give you a lift home.'

'No . . . if I remember correctly, we parted in the park in Edinburgh that day. Let's do this properly.'

They kissed passionately and parted. They didn't say good-bye.

Monday morning found Red putting the final touches to his fully stocked sports shop. The suppliers had come up trumps and the signwriters were painting his name on the front. He had installed a video screen in the window with the idea of showing continuous Irish sporting glories in the hope of shepherding punters over to his fifty square feet. He walked around his premises and felt grown up. He stamped his foot on the ground, a futile gesture to test the strength of the floor, his floor. Everything was in place: he wanted to jump up and down, but he had to keep his true feelings under wraps. He was still hazy from the fainting and felt an overwhelming need to do something for his mother. A show of love to express his slow of love, but as was his tendency he put it to the back of his mind. He was relieved that he only had the two signwriters to contend with just now. The constant flow of well-wishers offering their condolences, not knowing quite what to say, made him jumpy. He would cast them aside, avoiding eye contact, looking in and around their faces, waiting for the hand which he would shake with a terse 'thanks'. This would be quickly followed by the 'good luck with the opening' to which he'd express his appreciation with a slightly wide eyed 'cheers'. The other shopkeepers kept their distance, gossiping about his hard heart in the café as they blocked their own arteries with their full Irish breakfasts.

Gillian came into the shop to gape. Red was a little tense, not knowing whether she knew about him and

Michelle. She didn't let on if she did but nevertheless he ushered her out of the shop as politely as he could, feigning mountains of paperwork. He hadn't given Michelle a second thought, putting the incident down to a drunken shag. His penis budged with the memory. It was a great fuck and he wondered whether she had enjoyed it as much. He hoped when things were less deranged they could arrange another session.

The painters came in with an 'all done.' Red stepped outside to admire their handiwork: the Red-worded, 'Red's Sporting Emporium'. Red watched passers-by looking up and smiling, swelling his sense of pride. He tipped the boys. They cleared up their bits and pieces and disappeared. Red stayed on his spot feeling ten foot tall. He assumed this was what it was like to stand on the winner's podium at the Olympics. A life's hard graft had paid off and now he wanted to soak in its achievement.

Simon O'Donnell tapped him on the shoulder. Red left his fantasy and prepared himself to accept another condolence.

'Should be a big hit with the dyslexic members of the community, your shop,' said Simon. Red was puzzled. 'There's only one "u" in emporium.'

'What?' Red looked up at his sign again. Sure enough, there it was: Red's Sporting Empourium.

'Those stupid money-grabbing cunts!'

'Relax would you, look on the positive side . . . you got an extra letter for free.'

Simon's phone rang and he was off.

Michelle sat in the kitchen stroking Chrissie who was focusing on a black spot on the wall. John had locked himself into his study with his solicitor. It was the first time a door had been locked in the house. He had even had the cheek to ask her to find the key. Another day chasing light for her. Her life had amounted to getting up, sitting down on various chairs until it was time to lie down again. The only difference between this and being put in a home was that here she had to feed herself and she saw her family less. This constant doing nothing clouded her head, bringing on waves of tiredness resulting in much-needed naps throughout the day. She had become nothing but a lump of matter which was best avoided. Purely out of boredom she was eating more than usual and she imagined the extra weight was going straight on to her bottom. It wasn't; she had a metabolism which shed all food. The mainstay of her thought was nostalgia, and today she was obsessed with Little Red Riding Hood. She knew that she was attacked by the wolf but she couldn't quite put her finger on what was cause and what was effect. An innocent goes to bring food to her grandmother, the wolf attacks her and dresses up in her clothes and kills the grandmother. Did Little Red Riding Hood save her granny? Did the wolf blow the house down or eat the bear's porridge, did he push Humpty off the wall or wait for the boy to start crying? She urgently needed to pop a pill, which would no doubt pile on to her ass.

She took another pill. She was an absence, a big cruiser slowly heading towards the iceberg, ready to sink without trace. She popped another pill. *Strike a match and combust, get into the car, edge out at a crossing and somersault into oblivion.* She popped another pill. *Let the wolf eat me, let me know my place on the food chain, anything but this slow death by breathing.* She popped another pill. *Sit me by the fire and let me melt, catch me in the tuna nets, let bearded fishermen spear me and throw me back in, put electric plugs in my bathroom.* She popped another pill, drowsy. *Let my newly cleaned white curtains act as my tunnel and John has locked the door and Chrissie is catching shadows.* She popped another pill. *The wolf as Red Riding Hood wore too much lipstick, microwave me to a crisp, open the door, Jim Jones what do I do next? Where are all the others? I can hear the rain but of course it doesn't matter now, parts of my body are malfunctioning but it feels right.* She popped three more pills. *Chop my wooden head in half with an axe, axe, what a great little word for Scrabble, I need water but I haven't the energy to get up. Is this a cry for help? No, I could just scream; do I want to live? I don't know but I want another pill, turn on the telly,* Neighbours, *good, soon I'll lose consciousness, all together now, with a little understanding, you and me for ever and ever . . .*

John sat down with his solicitor Cathal Nolan beside him at his desk. They had known each other since their schooldays, although they were never friends. In fact they barely spoke, coming from different ends of the tracks. Cathal was a front row person, John sat nearer the back. As children they were worlds apart, but as adults they had bumped into each other at a business function and realised they had more in common than they thought. They still weren't friends but John threw a lot of business Cathal's way and in return, Cathal dealt with his strange requests.

'It's a will you want then?'

'Yeah. I thought it was about time . . . You know, you can't be too careful.'

'Ah, you've got plenty of fight in you yet.'

'Listen anyway. I don't want to have to go through all the formalities of witnesses and the like, so if it's okay by you I'll just tell you what to leave and to whom.'

'That's fine, I can make it official back at the office. So who are the lucky people?'

'Right. I'd like to leave the house and fittings and a weekly sum of two hundred pounds to Michelle for the rest of her life.'

Cathal did a quick calculation. 'That could amount to another forty grand.'

'That's fine . . . I want the business sold and all my employees given a year's wages with an extra ten grand going to Helen.'

'I'll need her surname.'

'Jesus, what is her surname, Prendegast or something . . . You'll be able to find out, Cathal.'

'And the proceeds of the business go to whom?'

'Dominic Richards. He's a writer and this is his address.' John handed him a card.

'You're looking at around a hundred K when it's sold off . . . What gives?'

'Sure, what's money? He's the only one who has given me any sort of happiness or understanding.'

'Have you got any insurance policies or pension?'

'Yeah, I've got an insurance policy, there's about sixty grand tied up in that. I'd like that to go to my folks, but there's stipulations; the money has to pay off their mortgage, credit union and any other outstanding bills. The remainder has to be spent purely on leisure pursuits, holidays, that kind of thing. None of it is to be spent on carpets, curtains, settees or any other so-called household fittings.'

'Are you serious?' Cathal was chuckling.

'Deadly. I know them, they'll blow the lot on stupid shit and be as miserable as fuck.'

'Fair enough . . . Now that just leaves cash.'

'I've got over a hundred K in the building society. I want my brother Paul to get twenty grand, the only stipulation this time being . . .' John fidgeted around in the drawer and fished out a brown envelope '. . . he has to read this diary first.'

'What is it?'

'It's my state of mind when I was fourteen. I want him to know he made my life a misery then and it might help explain why I haven't kept in touch. I want another twenty to go to Jodie Craven, plus the bench in the back garden.'

'Bench?'

'Yeah, I had it shipped over from Edinburgh, she'll know the significance. I want twenty thousand to go to Dublin Aids Alliance, no hidden clauses . . . Another twenty to that tramp who begs outside the Londis shop on the High Street. The only thing I know is his name is Jim.'

'And if you don't mind me asking, why is he such a benefactor?'

'He's nice.' John shrugged his shoulders. 'He never had a chance, I'd like to give him a start.'

'But do you think that's a good idea? He'll just drink it away.'

'So what? If that's what gets him by, so be it.'

He pointed a finger at Cathal. 'There's little tinges of right-wing tendencies coming into your conversation, friend.'

'Hey, what can I do? The Christian Brothers drummed it into me. But you know, it's your money, you do what you like . . . That leaves you with twenty grand to play with. How about the woman who carries the crucifix around O'Connell Street?'

'Ha ha ha. I want it to go to Peter Bulger.'

'Red's brother?'

'That's right.'

'I didn't know you were friendly.'

John shook his head. 'We're not. But let's face it, having to put up with Red all his life, he deserves every penny.'

'True. I heard Red was back in town, I got an invite to his opening on Wednesday. . . Have you seen him?'

'Yeah, too much.'

'Has he changed at all?'

'Not so you'd notice.'

'Can you imagine his sales pitch? "Hey, buy this shirt or I'll punch you in the fuckin' earhole".'

They both laughed. Cathal was turning into a friend. 'He's an awful runt isn't he? Did I ever tell you about the time he dunked my head down the toilet?'

'Sure, he did that to everyone.'

'Yeah, but because I was the new boy, he shat in it first. I was sick for a week, he was a bloody nightmare. It's weird how you can laugh about it now.'

'I'm not laughing. The thing that got to me was, we all used to cower around the bike shed thinking one day he'd get his comeuppance . . . But he never did, did he?'

'Ah, John the only consolation is that he has to live with himself on a day-to-day basis.'

'But that's the strangest thing . . . He loves himself, he's a deity unto himself.'

'We shouldn't be wasting our time with him . . . Anyway, I'll get all this legitimised and I'll get you a copy to sign, so if you could avoid fast buses in the meantime . . .'

'Have you not got a blank one I can sign now?'

'What's the urgency? I can get you a proper one within a couple of days.'

'Let me sign the blank one. I'm superstitious, and anyway I trust you.'

'Fair enough. And I'll work out all the fractions so we can stay in line with how we share out your bounty at the time of death.'

'Yeah yeah yeah.' John got up to usher him out.

'How's Michelle's health at the moment?'

'Ah, you know, up and down, but she's alright. How is your family?'

'I made the mistake of telling the kids that we're taking them to EuroDisney. Now first thing every morning it's "Will Daffy Duck be speaking French? Are Mickey and Minnie still together? Where do they keep all the Dalmatians?" It's a nightmare.'

Cathal packed his papers into his briefcase and John unlocked the door for him. John's deed for the day had made him feel noble and selfless. He took pride in being able to be a provider after his death. It went some way to making up for his inadequacies during his life. Cathal put on a brave face but he was deflated. He thought it was sad that John knew so few people. He felt the same way when executing old women's wills, the ones who leave everything to cats' homes. He wanted to sneak a look at his children who took up a fair weight in his wallet and he made a mental note to invite his parents around for dinner on Sunday.

As they walked to the front door John was sharing a story about their mutual acquaintance Simon O'Donnell. He didn't get to the end of it because Michelle's comatose mouth-foaming presence came into view, insisting on more urgent action. John, lost for words, joked grimly, 'I think I've another forty grand to play with.' Cathal, uneasy, visibly crumpled. An ambulance arrived within forty-five minutes, the ambulanceman assuring John that she was in no immediate danger and they'd pump out her stomach and keep her in hospital for two or three days to recuperate. John waited until the ambulance had disappeared and then went back into his study. He had calls to make.

CHAPTER 12

Seven-thirty a.m. Tuesday, the answering machine winked its red eye at John offering the statistic of the last caller. That would explain his dream. John was on death row in an unknown country, although all the prison wardens were of Mexican extraction and they kept calling him OJ. He had been on his holidays in foreign climes and had driven on the wrong side of the road and knocked down a cyclist. The case went through the courts quickly. The jury dispensed with verdicts of guilty or not guilty and instead held up gymnast-type scores, John scoring 8.9 from all of them which in dream world was a hanging offence. As he was being taken down a waitress came to take his order for his last meal. John ordered something elaborate only to be given six cold Yorkshire puddings. Just as he was about to eat the first one he was strapped to the electric chair. There were about thirty people smiling at him on the other side of the glass, including his mum, dad and brother, the Aston Villa football team and Derek Daly the former Formula One racing driver. He saw his mum and dad whisper something to his brother when suddenly the chair swung backwards leaving him horizontal. His brother appeared above him with a large dollop of spittle hanging inches away from his mouth, ready to drop on to John's face. Then the phone rang. He had been reprieved, and he was awake.

He pressed the play button on his answering machine.

'Hi John, Red here, sorry for ringing so early but I have a massive favour to ask. Our Uncle Eamon can't make it to the funeral and we're short one pallbearer. I know it's a strange request but I was wondering if you wouldn't mind helping us to carry the coffin because I don't want anyone I don't know lifting her into the grave. If you could call us the second you get this message I'd really appreciate it. Thanks very much . . . Bye.'

For fuck's sake, this guy really takes the biscuit.

John lit a cigarette to give himself time to reflect on the decision he'd already made. The nicotine rush was countered by a coughing fit which resulted in a solid cremed green piece of lung phlegm swishing around his mouth. He spat into the pedal bin and studied it for a long time before confining it to history. He rang Red and agreed to his request, gobbled up a bowl of Start, showered, shaved and put on his best black jacket. He spent the next twenty minutes trying to find his one tie. His first chore of the morning was a visit to Michelle.

Michelle was in a private room in the Adelaide hospital. She sat up on her bed, her face a Halloween mask, her eyes dead and dopey.

'Howya feeling this morning, love?' John asked her, kissing her softly.

'Weak,' she said, weakly.

'They say you can come home the day after tomorrow.'

She half-smiled which was as much of a gesture as her energy would allow.

'What have they got you on now?'

'Just painkillers.'

'Look, you're obviously not up for a visit at the moment. I've brought you some magazines and one of those puzzle books you love so much. I've to go to Mrs Bulger's funeral, would you believe it I'm shoulder-bitting her. I hope she's lost some weight. I'm not exactly renowned for me physical attributes, am I? Is there anything else I can get you?'

Michelle tried to move a little. Her voice was croaky.

'I want you to stop seeing Jimmy. He leads you astray. That's when things started going wrong. Let it just be us two from now on, that's when we're at our best . . . No outsiders, we're a good team.'

She reached for John's hand. He wanted to comfort her but he couldn't take her seriously because she sounded like one of those cancer victims at the end of a TV movie who wanted to make her peace. At the same time he also had to weigh up the fact that he didn't want to tip her delicate balance. His compromise was a friendly nod and an 'Everything's going to be all right.'

He wanted to talk to her, tell her the truth but there wasn't much of a point. *Michelle you're on your own from here on in.* He wanted to shake her. *You're on your own, kid, we all are. Jimmy, I'm Jimmy, you're Jimmy, can you not see? That's the problem, my dear. I can't face up to myself either; Jesus we're a right pair, we're better off without each other.* He wished he could speak out loud, get these things out in the open, stop the stupid pretence; but no, that would be too simple. Instead he had to shove them back into his head, to decay and boil with the other confusions. He was glad she was weak and the visit could be contained. He left the magazines on the bed and kissed her unblinking face. Michelle's response was to summon up all her energy to blurt out a detailed account of her night with Red. John didn't react, knowing this was the last time he'd see her.

'Take care, Michelle.'

She watched him become a blurred dot.

John had to go to the Allied Irish Bank in Baggot Street to make his transaction. It was nine-fifteen and he had to be in Treetown for ten-thirty. A steady queue of shopkeepers formed an orderly line. John had an appointment with the branch manager, the fortyish Mr Lyons. He'd arranged on the phone for five grand cash to be made available. He had to listen to words of caution from Mr Lyons who was endeavouring to tell him that his money would work better in different accounts. Even though it was a simple transaction, Mr Lyons kept going over the bare facts as though he was playing for time. John thought that his slowness was in the hope that he would tell him why he was taking out such a large sum of money, but he resisted the pressure to offer an explanation.

'And how would you like your cash, Mr Palmer?' Mr Lyons finally asked him.

'Politely.'

Mr Lyons didn't register the joke and John was embarrassed. 'Fifties will do fine.'

John briefcased the money and Mr Lyons shook his hand to close the business. As he got to the door of the office, all hell broke loose. Four balaclavaed men came running into the bank and another man who'd been in the queue pulled down his hat and jumped over the counter before the alarm system could be activated. He pulled a bloodied syringe out of his jacket and held it to the jugular of one of the counter girls.

'Do as you're told if you don't want Aids.'

The biggest of the men stayed at the door while another two also jumped over the counter leaving the one with the sawn-off shotgun on the customers' side of the bank. He appeared to be the leader and kept giving his men instructions at the same time reassuring the members of the public who were caught up in the mêlée. He had three stock phrases: 'Nobody move, nobody gets hurt', 'Hurry up, hurry up' and 'We'll be out of here before you know it'. John was frozen to the spot, but Mr Lyons started to edge back towards his office. The gang leader ran at him, hitting him full on the face with the butt of his shotgun. The crack of the bone amplified the fear in the room. Mr Lyons fell to the ground, holding his already gushing nose. The leader placed his foot on his chest. 'I'd get that seen to, pal,' he said. He pointed his gun at John, motioning him to join the other customers. John did as he was told. Mr Lyons was shouting, 'You've broken my fucking nose, you bastard,' much to the annoyance of the leader who hit him full force in the face again, the gun crashing down on the hand which covered his nose. Nobody could bear to look at the bloodied mess.

'This isn't a fucking cartoon . . . Nobody else budge 'cos there's an awfully long waiting list in the hospitals these days.'

The clerk with the bloodied syringe to her neck couldn't take any more and vomited all over the counter, much to the raiders' disgust. John was on the verge of puking himself; whenever he saw anyone be sick it always made him want to vomit and it was plain to see that she'd had an egg and bacon buttie for her breakfast. The bank robbers were in and out within three minutes. On their exit the leader handed the distraught woman some Alka Seltzer, quipping, 'I'd lay off the fatty foods if I was you.'

Once they were gone, everyone looked at each other in disbelief. The shock began to take hold and the fear which they'd had to keep under wraps was let loose. The whole building seemed to be trembling. The police arrived and statements were taken and sweet tea was drunk. From the thieves' jokey nature, the Gardai knew exactly who was responsible, but they also knew that their chances of catching them were minimal. They became suspicious of John when he tried to excuse himself from the proceedings because of the funeral. It was known that the gang put one of their members in as a bystander in case things didn't go to plan. They also surmised that the raiders had had prior knowledge of the bank and its procedures. John's lasting memory was of Mr Lyons being stretchered out crying at the top of his voice, 'Those bastards, I can describe those bastards.'

John got back into his car and it took him ten minutes before his breathing regulated. His hands and legs were still shaking too much for him to drive away. The press liked to glamorise the gangs as modern-day Robin Hoods, and on occasion John himself would give them a silent thumbs-up for one of their cheekier heists; but coming against them first hand, he found the thuggery and malice disturbing. He did not understand their utter contempt for other human beings, their evil streak destroying innocence; an outrage which of course would be tolerated by the public. The gangsters were aware of this. They played on the fact, terror being their weapon. John wanted to drive off into oblivion there and then, be taken away from everything he knew. The hue of his existence faded further; but he still had unfinished business to attend to.

John made it just in time for the funeral Mass. He sat at the back, Red giving him a nod of relief from the front pew. There were only fifteen people in the vast church, John's parents among them. The atmosphere was similar to a Scottish second division football game. The attendees were there out of a robotic loyalty. John, rattled from his morning experience, eyed the coffin, a cheap heavy shiny wood with brass-plated handles. The wreath that lay on top of it was big and cheerless.

At the end of the service John was ushered forward. Peter patted his back and briefly introduced him to the other pallbearer, their Uncle Stan – Aunt Mary's better half. There was an awkward shuffling for positions, the brothers taking the front, and since they were the tallest the coffin sloped down towards the other two. The wreath slid down onto the floor where an altar boy rescued it from under their feet.

John, still shaking, felt pain in his shoulder straight away. He noticed that Stan, another thin man, let out dignified deep breaths which made John feel less isolated. Their progress was erratic and slow and John became uneasy when he sensed movement from within the coffin. He tried to placate his mind. The last time he had lifted anything heavy had been at least five years ago when a snooty delivery man had left a 1960s fridge on his doorstep with instructions to handle with care. Now he pretended that Mrs Bulger was the fridge. She would have been just as cold. He half-winked at his parents as he passed them in the courtyard. His mother wore a face of pride, no doubt picturing herself being carried by her son.

The men managed to get the coffin into the hearse, Stan's stoic face giving way to tremors. He was aware that John was struggling too and this brought the two of them together. They stepped aside and rode in the second car behind the brothers and aunt. The respectable silence was broken by Stan.

'They must have dressed her in her duffel coat or something; we'll need to get ourselves a stash of steroids or something.'

John smirked, but already Stan was annoying him by

ending each sentence with 'or something', a habit which he continued all the way to the graveyard. The journey from hearse to grave was mercifully short and the rain forced the priest to race through the rite. A couple of gravel-faced gravediggers busied themselves digging a couple of plots away. Once the burial started they stopped and smoked out of respect. Red, Peter and Mary each threw a handful of clay into the ground and shuffled off to a corner. The priest acted as host, shaking hands and offering salvation with his mix of poor education and Bible-speak. John sidled off to his parents to offer some comfort to his mother who had begun to sniffle. His father, dry-eyed, said what he thought was appropriate to nobody in particular.

'She had a good innings. She was very sick. She's better off dead.'

His parents asked about Michelle.

'She's a little under the weather,' was all John would say.

Father Burns, who had been their parish priest of old, made a bee-line for the Palmers. He'd been very popular in his time but had disappeared under a cloak of mystery. There'd been rumours of an affair with his housekeeper, who had left at the same time, but most of them knew that he'd gone because his drinking was getting out of hand. There'd been a joke at the time, that the Eucharist ceremony became known as the 'hair of the dog' part of the Mass. John had always despised him, ever since he'd served under him as an altar boy, when he'd taken his hangovers out on the boys and snapped at them in front of the congregation.

'Hello there,' Father Burns began. 'Mrs Palmer,

you're looking tremendous, and is the boy there still a handful?'

His mother played along. 'Worse than ever, Father.'

Father Burns looked at John admiringly. 'Ah, he's not the worst of them by a long stretch,' he said, putting his hand on John's shoulder. 'I always thought you had the makings of a priest in you, John.'

John was embarrassed. 'I don't know about that, I could never drink that early in the morning.' He regretted it before he'd even finished saying it because he knew he'd hit the target. He sneaked a look at the priest and all he could see was a broken man. He wanted to apologise, but figured that that would deepen the wound. He felt even worse when he heard the priest mutter to himself, 'We're all human.' Father Burns wandered off, his confidence dented beyond repair.

John's parents frowned their disapproval but John was too busy watching the wretched skeleton of a man he'd helped dehumanise a little more skip the formalities and sneak off into his car and quickly drive away. The car jittered and heaved as if it was sobbing. John was typical of sensitive types: he had an ability to adhere to the most insensitive of acts. This day was already one of extremes and he wondered if it wouldn't be a better idea to jump in with Mrs Bulger and have done with it. His new pal Stan snapped him out of his malaise with 'Are you coming for a drink or something?' This had the desired effect: Stan had restored his faith in man's limitations.

Back at the family house the guests were down to eight. The buffet consisted of ham and cheese and onion sandwiches. The brothers held centre stage and busied themselves taking nips of whiskey in old western style. The others stayed in their little sub-groups, having subdued conversations. Stan was sandwich monitor, balancing the plates and offering the grub. John was having polite conversations with people he barely knew, when Stan, acting as saviour, came by with 'Will you have a sandwich or something?'

John took one to make sure he didn't have to enter into any more conversations. He took a large bite out of his cheese and onion sandwich to discover as it meshed around his tongue that its main ingredient was a huge hardened blob of foul-tasting margarine. For the second time that day he wanted to vomit and had to swallow the whole thing down his gullet to avoid a splattering of the walls. He grabbed an orange juice from the mantelpiece and necked it down in one, only to realise that it was the undiluted variety that hadn't been watered.

A couple of kids were jumping on the sofa helping everyone take their minds off the solemnity of the events at hand. The more booze that was drunk the lighter the tone became. Stan tried to get the party going, asking, 'Is it a wake or something?' Grief gave way to remembrance as sweet little tales of the dead were told with nobody paying the slightest attention to truth. Peter again thanked John for the carrying, half apologising for shifting most of the weight on to him.

They'd been talking aimlessly for twenty minutes when Red approached, half-cut, hugging John and using his hold to force him into a corner.

'Love your mother, John,' he slurred. 'Don't make the same mistakes as me . . . Look at all these people, what do they know about the likes of us?'

He said this too loudly and stopped to take in his surroundings. John tried to convey a look of 'ho-hum' on his face, but Red was off.

'They're all waiting to die, they are the living dead, but we're different, we've got some get up and go . . . haven't we, John?' He poured himself another whiskey, spilling much of it onto the carpet. He swung his hands wildly, adding to the spillage.

'Hey, hey where's Michelle? She's a lovely girl she is, you're a lucky man.' He stopped to belch. 'You know I lost my virginity to her . . . ? Well, most of us did.'

Peter, who was listening, tried to intervene. 'Alright, Alan, enough. John doesn't want to hear this.'

Red pushed Peter away. 'What would you know, he's my friend . . . I'll tell him what I want, that's what friends do.'

Peter took John aside. 'I'm sorry about this, John. I suppose it's all catching up with him.'

'That's alright. I understand.'

Red grabbed John by the shoulder, which was already sore, and started to mimic his voice.

'That's alright, I understand . . . You always let people walk all over you, you've no spunk in you at all; is that why Michelle won't sleep with you?' Red's face curled up into an expression of soured menace and he sneered at John with utter contempt. John remained calm, even though he wanted to poke a dart into Red's eye and watch him deflate into the pool of ordure he knew him to be. He hid his hatred as best he could, all the time fighting the anxiety that always crept up on him in the presence of danger.

He could tell that Red wanted to punch him, was waiting to jump in on the slightest flicker of response.

'Why doesn't she sleep with you John, are you gay?' Red finished off his glass in one and annoyed at getting no reaction pushed John regardless. John tried to hold his ground but fell backwards. Peter broke his fall and, stepping forward, slapped Red hard on the face. 'Enough, okay?'

Red was too shocked to react. Instead he cowered a little, taking a step back. His strange sense of self came to the fore.

'Well he started it,' he complained.

Peter became arbitrator. 'What are you talking about?'

Red pointed at John. 'He never fought back . . . whenever there was any trouble he'd run away. What sort of a man is that? He's pathetic.' He moved closer to John. 'Remember that time Brookfield came down for that ruck, we took them on, where were you?' He tried to get Peter to side with him by making him his confidant. 'I'll tell you where he was, he ran home to his mammy. He even ran away from the girls.And he was shit at football.'

John was biding his time. He turned to Peter. 'I'll make him a coffee.'

The tension in the atmosphere had left only Stan and Mary in the room, who were tidying up. John, alone in the kitchen, went exploring for the coffee and its paraphernalia. As he poured the hot water into the mug he turned his head to make sure nobody was looking. He took the two acid tabs and put them into the mug, and then using a rolling pin, crushed the two Ecstasy pills and swept them with his hand into the brew. He didn't know what effect this cocktail would have but he figured it would be nice to get Red loved up.

Half an hour later Red was calm but had started gnashing his teeth. Peter had asked John to baby-sit Red since he had to drop Stan and Mary home. Red wanted some music but the only cassette they could find was Chris de Burgh's greatest hits. Red was soon tapping and singing along to 'Lady in Red', and laughing at the implications of the title. John let him have his own way and Red began to warm to him.

'You're alright John, you are. I'm sorry about earlier on. I shouldn't drink whiskey, it doesn't agree with me.'

'Nothing does, Red.'

Red let this pass.

'So your mother's dead then. I guess you're all on your own now, both your parents dead, just you on your own against the world.' John said this with a smiling friendly face and could see that Red was becoming confused, his eyes glazing over and sweat appearing on his upper lip. Red kept touching his chest with his hand, repeating 'The music's very loud, isn't it?'

John persevered. 'She's probably in a better place now. Do you believe in heaven, Red? I imagine if it doesn't exist that we'd just rot away . . . This would be it, it's over, kaput, no more life, just darkness.'

Red was shuffling about in his seat.

'Or worse still, heaven does exist, which means of course that hell exists as well. Imagine going to hell, Red. But you'd have to do something really bad to go there, wouldn't you? Like break one of the Ten

Commandments. Thou shalt not steal, thou shalt not commit adultery . . . did you ever break any of them, Red?'

Red was at the beginnings of his first panic attack.

'You know, I think in this day and age those two are probably allowable. I'd say the main one now which is still unforgivable is murder, you know, the taking of someone else's life. Did you ever do that, Red? Did you ever kill anyone? Someone called Pat maybe. A big strong lad like yourself now, I'm sure you'd be capable.'

Red was off. 'What do you know about that . . . ? Jesus, I feel really weird.'

John feigned concern. 'In what way?'

'I dunno. I'm getting hot flushes up and down my body . . . Can you get me some water?'

'Sure, no problem, in a minute . . . Why are you looking at the wall?'

'It seems to be . . . moving nearer to me. It isn't, is it?'

'Nah, it's just your imagination. Death affects people in different ways.'

'Can you stop talking about death, it's freaking me out.'

'It's best to face up to these things, get them all out in the open . . . Any troubles or doubts, get them out now.'

'Fuck! I can't feel my arms or my legs.'

'Shall I put "Lady in Red" back on? You've been in many a lady, haven't you, Red?'

'No . . . no, don't. I don't like it any more . . . Jesus, John, help me, I don't feel well.'

Red's eyes were starting to roll.

'What can I do?'

'Do something. Anything.'

'Ah, you're a big strong lad. You'll manage okay.'

Red stood up and started to pace. He was shaking. 'I need to lie down. Will you take me up to my room?'

'Sure.'

'And will you stay with me?'

'No problem.'

'Thanks, 'cos my brain's gone.' He slapped himself on the forehead. 'I'm frightened.'

'Welcome to the human race, Red.'

'John, please. Please make it stop, I don't like this.'

'Come on, just lie down. You'll be able to sleep it off.'

They managed to get to Red's room, John holding him up with his hands. Red's whole body was going into spasms to the extent that John's body was shaking a little as well. John slipped him onto the bed and the cat let out a blood-curdling shriek, sending Red over the edge as he curled up into a ball, repeating 'Dana's got my mother's eyes.'

John didn't enjoy Red's suffering but he considered it necessary. He wanted him to experience the mental torment that he had so far been able to bypass all his life. John knew he was being cruel but in essence all he was doing was making Red face up to his own abyss. He was causing a physical trauma, and if Red weathered it he would come out a better person. But he was like porcelain and the cracks were beginning to show. He was a mite scared himself, watching at first hand how fragile the brain could be. He had to remain emotionless, deal with it as a straightforward experiment, otherwise he would cave in and let Red's demons run amok in their carefree manner.

'Come on Red, just deep breathe, close your eyes.'

Red's voice was trailing off into a whisper. 'I'm frightened to close my eyes.'

'Why?'

'I see worse things then. I keep seeing my mother, and she doesn't love me.'

The curtains were pulled and the lights were off, there were only tiny particles pushing in through the cheap fabric of the curtains.

'I keep seeing my mum's eyes on monsters, lizards, snakes.'

'Surely you're not frightened of monsters?'

Red sat up. His whole body was sweating. His eyes would close until the images came too close then he would sit bolt upright, eyes wide open, and take a terrified slow look around the room.

'Have I gone mad? Is this what it's going to be like for the rest of my life? Because I can't take this.'

'No, Red, you'll be alright. You probably just have to atone for your sins. Do you believe in God?'

'Yes.'

'Do you think you're a good person?'

'I can't handle this conversation.' Horrified by another image he violently shook his head. 'Ah, fuck, please talk about something else.'

'Okay, no problem. How are you feeling now?'

'Like I've no control . . . Like I'm trapped, like there's danger everywhere, I'm paralysed from the neck down.' Almost crying but not able to, 'I can't feel my body. They're all coming to get me. Please, please talk about something else.'

'Sex, that's what men like to talk about, isn't it? Do you like sex, Red?'

'Yeah.'

'I'd say you're very good at it . . . When was the last time you had a really good fuck?'

'A while ago.'

'And when you have sex does it matter if you love the other person? Or is it a matter of just a good fuck?'

'I'm sweated through. Can you take my shirt off?'

'No, you're better sweating the whole thing off. Do you mind if I smoke?'

'Just keep talking to me. Will you hold my hand?'

'I don't think that would be appropriate. Let's just talk . . . You've just got to think positively.'

'Okay.'

'Do you think when you came into this world, you know, when you were conceived . . . do you reckon your parents loved each other?'

'I suppose . . .'

'Or maybe it was a case of your Da, now if I remember he was a bit of a drinker, and if the rumours were to be believed he had a fierce temper which he took out on your mother—'

'Why are you doing this to me?'

'Doing what? We're just talking, chewing the fat . . . Wasn't it you who always said "sticks and stones may break my bones but names will never hurt me"? That was one of yours, wasn't it? I remember, because there was that one time you said it to me . . . Yes, I was in my treehouse, you know, the one it took me three months to build, funnily enough with sticks and stones. But it wasn't a very solid structure, was it, Red?'

'Can you leave this for another time?'

'Oh come come, this is a good time . . . get all that

badness out of you. Anyway, there I was in my treehouse, you know, not bothering anyone, when I heard this commotion outside. And then in pops yourself. You gave me a bit of a start . . . Mind you, you always did, every time I saw you.'

'Did you do this to me, you bastard?' Red suddenly interrupted, grabbing at John who pushed him back down.

'No, Red, you did this to yourself. And you're missing the point. There's no more time for excuses, you just have to face up to things, you know, head on. So anyway, it's you and me in the treehouse, and you're shouting down at somebody, and what do you have, Red? A posse of admiring little girls. And you, Red, you had to impress them, didn't you? I tried to run but you collared me and then – I won't go into detail, even though I remember it vividly – but you took my trousers off, and then my underpants, my stupid Y-fronts that my mother bought me. I remember you were humming that striptease song as you threw the clothes down to the girls one by one. To be fair to you, you could always hold a tune. And then when I was naked, you asked the girls, did they want to see me. Can you imagine how I felt at that moment, Red? I'd say something like what you're feeling now; you know, you'd rather be dead.

'I was reading somewhere recently that some people admit to having happy childhoods. So what do you reckon, Red? Do you think society is to blame? No, it isn't. You're to fucking blame if the truth be told. Happy days, eh? So there I was like a caged animal . . . trapped . . . Maybe that's why I like animals to this day, Red, because you treated me like a dog.'

John came to the end of his cigarette. 'Have you an ashtray?'

'Put it anywhere.'

'Well, I won't flick it in your face, if that's what you mean. That would be too easy, wouldn't it, Red? Picking on the helpless, that would justify your evil deeds. But the treehouse, what happened at the treehouse, maybe you could finish the story . . .'

'You jumped out and broke your arm. You always took everything too serious. It wasn't my fault.'

'Ah now, Red, you make that sound like I had any choice. Let me put this to you . . . how are you feeling, by the way?'

'Pretty shit.'

'And what if I was to tell you it would get worse, this predicament of yours . . . like much worse, that this was only the beginning. Would you not jump out that window there to escape it?'

'It's not going to get worse, is it? Please tell me it's not.'

'That depends on you, Red. Don't I keep telling you, you're on your own now, master of your own destiny. Sticks and stones, Red. I've very brittle bones, me – lack of calcium I suspect. There I was, treehouse destroyed, me splattered in a heap. Oh, the physical pain of the break . . . oh, it hurts, no doubt about that, but that was nothing to the total humiliation of lying there naked, a shy fourteen-year-old in front of all those girls. That took the focus of the pain . . . Tell me this, Red. When you saw me there, did you feel any remorse?

'I didn't mean for you to break your arm.'

'But the rest was okay?'

'It was a bit of childish fun. We're adults now, I didn't know any better.'

'Still not getting through to you is it? But who do I blame, you or your upbringing? Let's bring it full circle back to sex. What chance did you have with your parents?'

'Leave my parents out of it, my mother is barely cold.'

'Oh come on, I'm not having a go at your parents, I'm just trying to understand you. You were brought into this world after your Da filled his belly full of beer. He probably slapped your mother into submission until he shoved his alcohol-fuelled sperm into her. You no doubt got a few slaps in the womb along the way, and then hey presto, nine months later you appear. Unwanted, existing only because of the church's rules. I've only two more things to say to you. One is going to make you feel a lot better. But unfortunately the other little thing I have to say is going to make you feel a lot worse. Which would you like to hear first, good or bad?'

'Please stop this, will you? I'm freaking.'

'Good or bad?'

'Good.'

'Your voice is gentle now, as if you were capable of tenderness . . . Good news first then. You're not going mad. You will wake in the morning, a little hazy no doubt, but you'll have your senses back. And to be fair . . .' he looked at his watch. 'I'd say you're over the worst of it. Because I understand that fear, and you'll be delighted to know you've survived the worst. The intensity and the images will start to fade; you're what they would term in the drugs world "coming down". The warning which should be heeded is that reality can be a lot scarier. Especially now that you know it is possible to lose control. Some people deal with this knowledge very well. Others . . . don't fare so good. Tomorrow will be a very interesting day.'

'What did you put inside me?'

'Does it matter? It's all stuff that can be got at any time.'

'I can't believe you put something inside me against my own will.'

'What, like the way you put your cock inside Michelle against her will?'

'She wanted it as much as me.'

'I don't think so, Red. What is it about weak and damaged people that attracts you? Did you think, "ah, it's only John's wife, what's he going to do about it"?'

'It wasn't like that.'

'Imagine, Red, as you were raping somebody else's wife your mother was dying, probably at the exact same time. Maybe she sensed it. I suppose it will be something to remember her by.'

Red had lost the power of speech and squirmed into a tighter ball.

'Red, you're always at pains to know why I don't sleep with Michelle. It's not because I don't love her . . . I do, dearly, I find her very attractive. As you know yourself she's a beautiful woman. It's not even the usual marital problems of being bored with the sex. You see myself and Michelle have never had sex . . .'

Red tried to stop him but John hushed him.

'But you're part of it now, Red, and that's the bad

news . . .' They heard the key in the front door. 'Your brother has got impeccable timing. So I'll leave you to get some rest. You'll need all your energy for the grand opening tomorrow. Take care.'

'What's the bad news?'

'Oh, I nearly forgot . . . Yeah, Michelle, she's HIV positive.'

Red went white. Behind him John could hear him scream as he shut the door. Peter came up the stairs alarmed.

'Is he okay?'

'He's not taking today very well . . . Probably needs some sleep.'

'Thanks for looking after him.'

'No problem. I'll see you tomorrow.'

John arrived home to find Chrissie assuming her tiger persona, dashing from curtain to curtain. The rest of the house was mute. Dust particles were having a field day. The lights were off, and only the flashing red button of the answering machine signified life. John turned on the music centre which lit up like an airport runway, giving the house a pulse. He lay down on the sofa. Chrissie, calmed by his presence, was doing her press-ups on his chest, her substitute for her mother's breast. John lay completely still for ten minutes to give her this comfort. He was wide awake. Red, he figured, would be just about dozing off now. He felt no guilt about his badness but he was surprised no sense of achievement beckoned forth either. Hadn't he done it all for the little people? So why did he feel shit now, this wasn't making sense. It was a battle of Goliath proportions; and thinking of that fable, it was typical that they focused on the action: we never get to hear the extent of David's emotional kickback. The movies show us the before and the direct after-effects, when the real story is the gradual trying to creep back to normality. *What happened to the Chief after the credits of* One Flew Over the Cuckoo's Nest? *Does he open up a chewing gum shop or did he suffer the consequences of his actions? Okay, it was symbolic that he thought for himself, took hold of his own actions, but I don't want to be a symbol. I just want the quiet life, so why do I feel hollow now? I've joined the race, I'm involved, situations are out of my control; I feel calm and capable, but of what? I'm frightened of my own actions. Am I in step with my own destiny?*

These thoughts disturbed him which in turn dominoed on to Chrissie who jumped off his chest to find a more tranquil setting. John went to his study to reread some of Dominic's stories, looking for clues. He had one more attempt to read the wine-soaked page of his latest piece. *Right, I'm going to go for it, I'll confront. But who, though; me, him or both?* He read for two hours, sipping at the ideas, coming to minor conclusions. The phone rang, making him jump. He picked it up quickly to stop the ringing.

'Yes?'

'Hi, it's Paul.' He could smell the urgency. 'Did you not get my message?'

'No, I've just got in. How are you? I haven't heard from you in an age. What time is it in LA?'

'Listen, I'll get straight to the point. I'm in terrible trouble.'

John remained calm. 'What's up?'

'I've been done for drink driving. I need five thousand dollars to pull me through.'

John left a long silence for Paul to fall into.

'I need bail. There's a fine. I have to pay for repairs to my car, I have to pay for re-schooling. It's a fucking mess. I wouldn't ordinarily come to you but I didn't want to worry the folks . . . Can you help me?'

'No.'

Paul ignored this. 'I wouldn't ask, but I'm in a right pickle.'

'You're working, aren't you?'

'See, that's half the problem. I need the car to get to work, otherwise I'll get the sack.'

'No, my point is you're working, you've got a good job, where the fuck's all your wages?'

'Look, that's neither here nor there.'

'That's a very blasé attitude, isn't it? You've been pissing all your money up against a wall and I'm supposed to rescue you . . . There's no way I'm gonna help you. Firstly anyone who drinks and drives deserves everything that's coming to them. And secondly I haven't seen nor heard from you in two years, so to be fair, we're not that close.'

'Jesus, you're my brother. We're family, for Christ's sake.'

'Where are you getting off on your big Italian ideas . . . ? It just so happens the same two jackasses fucked and we popped out, that's the extent of our relationship. I look forward to seeing you some time.'

John hung up and played back his messages.

'Hello, Mr Palmer. It's Joan O'Keefe, Pat's mother, and there's a bit of a problem about tomorrow, but we should be able to see you at the sports shop around five. I hope that's okay with you because that's the earliest we can make it. Thanks again for all your help. We'll see you there. God bless.'

No problem, I'm sure Red will be delighted to hear from you.

'Hiya Johnny it's your brud here, long time no hear . . . listen come here, could you give us a ring back, I want to pick your brain about something.'

John could trace the signs of panic in his brother's voice.

'Hello, Michelle, it's Doctor Smiles' office. You missed your four o'clock today. If you could ring me tomorrow and we could reschedule . . . Unfortunately Doctor Smiles is no longer with us but we're going to refer you to Doctor Hunter. Hope to hear from you at your earliest convenience.'

John was still wide awake and wanted a task to tire him out. He grabbed the *Evening Herald* from the door mat and double-taked at its headline: BANK RAID MANAGER NAMES NAMES. It transpired that Mr Lyons had been the gang's inside man and the idea had been that he wasn't supposed to get hurt. He was so incensed by the broken nose and the fractured jaw that he'd agreed to turn state's evidence. He and his family were already under a twenty-four-hour guard and the case was being rushed through the courts. It was a major breakthrough for the police, since this was the biggest crime family in Dublin and its leader was among those currently 'helping them with their enquiries'.

Fuck, this was pretty sensational . . . Fair play to the Lyons chappy. Another victory for the little people, that's if he isn't got at. The tape he'd been playing turned over automatically and as the second side started John realised he hadn't been enjoying it. He pressed 'stop' and took it out of the machine. It was a compilation from the New York duo Suicide and he'd had the tape for years, a throwback to when he pretended to be a punk. In big black marker he'd written on it, 'The Suicide Tape'. No doubt it had been the happiest period of his life. He decided to use the tape to make a new compilation of his favourite tunes. He started to gather stacks of CDs for his perspective soundtrack. The phone rang again and John knew it would be his father trying to make him change his mind with less persuasive ways than a horse's head in the bed.

'Hello?'

'John, it's your dad here.'

He played along. 'What's the urgency?'

'Listen, I've just had your brother on the phone. He's in a right state, can you not help him out, even a grand?'

'And what makes you think I've got that sort of money around? Just because I've given you money in the past doesn't mean I've got it in abundance.'

'Are you saying you haven't got it?'

'That's beside the point. You know my feelings on drink driving.'

'I guess I'll have to get a loan from the credit union.'

'That doesn't work with me, I'm not going to give in to emotional blackmail. I'm thirty now, I'm responsible for my own decisions, so I'd appreciate it if you stayed out of my affairs, okay?'

His father played the diplomat. 'Yeah, I know. I'm

sorry. It's just I don't think you realise the trouble he's in.'

'That's just fine and dandy isn't it, having someone to turn to. He's my older brother, shouldn't he be looking after me?'

'Look, it's late. You're probably tired, but see what you can do, son. He is your brother; blood is thicker than water.'

John dismissed him. 'Well, mine is thinning out. Goodnight.'

It was at times like these that he didn't care for families. He would usually try and understand their side of the argument and look at the struggle that they had rearing children but when their small-mindedness came into play, it validated his reluctance to become close. The sleepless nights of his bonded guilt were always thrown into confusion after talking to them. His dad's Biblical readings of media opinions; his mother's this-might-be-the-last-time-you-see-me plays for affection; their lack of love which kept them together; their tedious one-upmanship for favouritism; the utter ennui of their lives which they wanted to force-feed onto the siblings; the adjourning of their existence for which they wanted witnesses: even with all this, they never took the hint that he might have outgrown what they knew. *For better or worse – Christ, I didn't take any marriage vows, I was left with no choice of the outcome.*

With so many relationships falling asunder, surely it would make sense to be able to break up with your own parents. 'Hi Mum, listen I'm sorry to have to tell you this, but I've found someone else and I'll be ringing her every Sunday from now on . . . Yeah, and she'll be telling me about her neighbour's varicose veins and kidney complaints from people I've never even heard of; so *ciao* for now.' That would be ideal, you would be given a recovery period rather than ongoing unease. But was he being fair? Did he ever give the relationship his best shot, a total commitment? No, because in his parents' presence John always suffered from converphobia: the fear that there were better conversations going on elsewhere.

Red woke feeling groggy and his vision had a blue hue. The occasional body tremor was a reminder of the night before but his overriding emotion was simply relief at having normality restored. His head was an empty vessel, a background ringing in his ears made his balance shaky, and the overwhelming effect was one of premature ageing. There was no outward sign that he'd been through a trauma and survived. There was a need to look at his surroundings anew, a cautious rebirth. Never again would he take anything for granted, and for the first time in his life, he needed his mother. Corners were turned with expectant horror, as if he was riding a horse, the depressing eventuality being that it was only a matter of time before he fell off. The big question he had to prepare himself for was, would he be able to get back on? Now he just wanted to hide under his bed. He had to force a piss out of himself, and as his circulation got going he felt the Aids virus flushing through his system: the ringing in his ears was the virus's humming.

Over breakfast he tried to force some toast down his throat but his body wanted to be left alone. He should have been starving but his stomach muscles, suffering from aftershock, refused to sound the rumble. Peter talked about full breakfasts and the opening of the shop. It was all too much for Red and the only conversation he could muster was 'I'm not feeling too well.'

He hoped that Peter would pick up on this because any infinitesimal change would edge him towards hysteria. Putting sugar into his tea was too mammoth a task and it worried him that the sneaky looks he was taking at Peter weren't adding up to the normal picture. Peter looked different, as if he'd been replaced by a bad lookalike. It was a stupid thought to have but his brain was only dealing in extremes. Supping tea might freak him out: he was more comfortable picturing an axe in his brother's head. His new little voice Mr Severe Man was battling for control; there was a coup in his head. Mr Trusty Old Me was wounded and weak but still giving his all; this put him more at his ease until the new voice ordered an attack of the heebejeebes. The adrenalin shot up Red's body, the virus following suit. The only thing he could do was get up and get the fuck out. He responded to Peter's look of concern with an abrupt 'Not now, please.'

Outside he prayed for some relief, the bitter wind helping make sense of the shivers. Every person needed to be avoided as he walked the marathon walk. Deep breaths helped for split seconds before flushes and terror made even walking an impossible task. He saw a bunch of kids playing football and he wanted his childhood back, no matter how bad it was. He wanted to curl up into a ball and let the kids kick him into the haven of unconsciousness. He had to avoid buildings and traffic because not living was starting to look like a better option. The voice kept probing him, *How the hell are you going to deal with the opening of the shop?* His reserve was fading fast, wanting to slap and reassure him. *Time's a great healer*, counterblast, *that's what your mother used to say to you*, mmm comforting thought, yeah stay with this, this is a blessed remission – *not a fucking chance mate, time's a great healer, your mother's wise words, she's fucking dead, didn't do her much good.* You can get through this, look for solutions.

Red knew he was out of his depth, bobbing in an eternal sea, not even allowed a dignified drowning. The only way around this mess was to get pissed, get so far out of it that the drink gene would take over. But the thought of going into a pub . . . he shuddered at the very idea. He fell to the ground and like a dog he started to scratch at the clay, *bury me alive*: getting nowhere he pounded and shouted and cried and fell asleep. He awoke two minutes later, his first conscious thought coming from the severe guy: *welcome back to your reality.* Oh for Christ's sake, how long; I can't take this, I really can't, bump me off. Heart, if you have any heart, explode. He needed to see John, he'd have some answers, he was the only one who could help. He turned and started to make his way back to the house. He hid in some bushes nearby, waiting for Peter to leave. He couldn't talk to the lookalike. He looked at his watch, barely taking in the information. The shop opens in half an hour. This is the greatest day of my life. He shook his head in disbelief, his body still masquerading as a hard beat techno dancer. He saw Peter getting into his car; he hoped he would have the sense to open up for him. Once he was out of sight he went to the house. Getting the keys into the door was proving impossible. He laughed in despair; he was tempted to boot the fucker in but he persevered. Inside he went straight for the whiskey and gulped from the bottle, willing on rapid inebriation. He paced the room, swallowing on each breath. The shakes were wearing down and yawns were welcome signs of tiredness. Then the first level of drunkenness gave him back his fighting spirit: his senses were opening up.

'Yes,' he said as he clenched his fists. 'I can handle you.' His cockiness was coming back. 'Give it your best shot, now, I don't know what I was worried about. Come on, torment me now, I demand it.' He sat down hoping to nod off. 'See, I took you on and I've won. You didn't bank on Red being made of better stuff, did you? I've always been a fighter; didn't count on that, did you?'

It was false bravado, because he knew full well what was coming next. He might as well have pushed the button himself. Panic.

CHAPTER 13

John had cash and now he needed to get his hands on some drugs. He was dreading having to hook up with his old school chum Diamond Dave but it was the only contact he knew since Jimmy was well and truly out of his life. He had known Dave the dealer for years: a fortunate name, considering his occupation. Dave was totally open about his activities, and his house was directly opposite the cop shop. He was known as Diamond Dave to all and sundry, not because he was a nice guy, but as folklore had it he once stole a diamond ring from a high society old dear, and when she started screeching for help he had punched her windpipe with it. John knew he was capable of such sick actions: he was your bona fide nasty piece of work.

John parked around the corner from the drug dealer's house. There was a space just outside but that was too dangerous. To get drugs off Diamond Dave there was a very strict procedure. You rang him from the payphone outside his house and spoke in code. John dialled the number.

'Murder Squad, what body are you looking for?'

'Hi, Dave. We'd just be happy with one of his hands at this stage.'

'How many limbs do you want?'

'Three please.'

'Well if the price is right, come on down.'

He was a sick bastard alright. John rang on the bell. Dave's door was reinforced steel. It was supposed to be explosive-proof and would take at least twenty minutes to smash open, always giving him time to flush the evidence. A miniature Dave opened the shutter and looked at John. In a strong Northern Irish accent he shouted, 'It's alright Dave, it's laughing boy.'

John heard five bolts being unlocked before he was let in. Dave, who looked wasted, had his head between the biggest pair of breasts he had ever seen. The woman had the face of a horse and undeniably heroin eyes. John was reminded of a chamber of horrors. Dave gave them a final noisy suck before he greeted John with his toothless grin.

'Long time no see, laughing boy. You couldn't have come at a better time. We're celebrating our rival gang's big bust. Saves us having to do a hit, eh?'

John couldn't avert his gaze from the breasts. Dave noticed this.

'They're whoppers alright, she's an awful cunt but

what can you do? We couldn't fit a bouncy castle in here so she was the next best thing. Do you want to have a go?'

'Nah, you're alright Dave. I've got my good shoes on.'

Dave cackled, lighting up his manic face, the result of years of not getting the joke.

'Do you hear that, Razor? Good shoes on.'

Razor, who was swinging on a hammock in the corner, grinned.

Dave put his arm on John's shoulder. 'Are you still putting the fun in funeral, laughing boy?' He laughed at his own joke, the same one John heard every time.

'Yeah,' he answered. 'I've gatecrashed quite a few lately.'

The fun they were having.

'Is it the Parnell you're after?'

'Yeah.'

'Razor, would you ever get off Mary's bra there and sort the man out. I'll tell you one thing laughing boy, you couldn't have come at a better time. It's good shit this, the land movement was never in better shape.'

'The three acres will do me fine.'

'Do you want a sample?'

'I trust you, Dave,' John assured him, wanting to get out of this circus as quick as humanly possible.

'That's very nice of you, laughing boy. I'll tell you what, when I go straight I'll be sure to come to you for a reference.' Dave was off with the cackle again. Razor chopped out three lines on Mary's breasts, using a razor. John stared over at the grotesque tableau and when he saw the little red marks on her breasts he felt physically sick. The clowns did their lines and cracked a few more jokes about tits before John was out of there with his business done. Diamond Dave didn't let him down and gave him his usual parting shot:

'Keep working out, laughing boy.'

There was utter confusion at the sports shop. A buzzy queue had formed outside and Peter, who hadn't got any keys, was forced to go looking for Simon O'Donnell who had the other set. Once it was open the shop was a hive of activity. Dublin football jerseys were its biggest sellers, followed, for some reason, by darts. A lot of kids browsed and took advantage of the free Pepsi that was on offer. Peter tried his best but he had no experience of this kind of work. He fancied he had rung up a lot of the wrong bills and he just hoped it would all tally up at the end of the day. Simon stayed with him until after the lunchtime rush, wise-cracking his way into people's affections as he subliminally made them part with their money. The usual briefcased salesmen vultured their way over to Peter, vying for his business, taking advantage of the euphoria of the opening day. The local paper came down and took pictures of smiling kids, knowing already that their cover shot would be one of the misspelt name.

Any major problems Peter encountered he managed to soft-pedal his way out of by saying the owner would be here soon. Red made an appearance around four o'clock, dressed in his best suit. By then the business had levelled off to the occasional customer. Peter had intended to give him a bollocking but he could tell that he was in a mess. Red had used every ounce of courage, dutch and otherwise, he could muster to come into the shop. He knew he was a walking time bomb but the experience was dulled by the tranquillizers he had found in his mother's drawer. Peter was unaware of the scale of his angst and assumed it was a final coming to terms with their mother's death. He tried to lighten the mood with news of sales and pre-orders but Red's lips remained pursed: a slight nod of the head was his animated best. Peter was shocked when Red asked him for a cigarette. He handed his packet over without saying a word and when he lit the cigarette for him, he could see Red's hand shake. This made him slightly edgy too. The customers seemed to notice Red's shaking hands and Peter told him to smoke it in the backroom because it didn't look good for business. Red half shuffled into the storage room. The cigarette made him dizzy and he found the taste stomach-churning but he was grateful to have something to do with his hands. He sat on a box, swinging his legs back and forth, chain-smoking, hoping for cancer, happy that the waves of nausea were offering him another distraction.

John appeared at the sports shop at four-thirty. He had a chuckle at the sign as he mentally prepared himself for whatever demons were about to break loose. He was taken aback to see Peter behind the counter.

'How's it all going?' he greeted him.

'Very good, very good indeed. If we can get half this business on a regular basis we're well on the way.'

'That's great news. And has there been any problems?'

'Ah, you know . . . teething ones.'

'Where's Red?'

'He's in the back.' Peter threw John a concerned look.

'Is everything okay?' John asked him.

'To tell you the truth, I'm a bit worried about him,' Peter confided. 'He's taken Mam's death very bad. It only seemed to hit him yesterday, he's like a different person. I think he should maybe see a doctor.'

'Ah, I'm sure it'll just blow over, it's a traumatic time. Is it okay if I go and see him?'

'Please do, see if you can cheer him up.'

John walked into the dark of the storeroom, the lit cigarette signalling where Red was. He turned on a light and Red squinted up at him, and seeing John, cowered. The most alarming thing, as far as John was concerned, was how normal Red looked. The suit he wore helped to maintain the illusion of wellbeing. John sidled up to him.

'How are you?'

Red, who was fast becoming a consummate smoker, snarled, 'How long is this going to last?'

John knew exactly what he was talking about but he played dumb.

'What do you mean?'

Red looked him in the face, pleadingly. 'This feeling of fucking crisis.'

'Once you acknowledge it, it starts to go away.'

'Will I be able to get back to the way I was?'

'No, never.'

That made Red jumpy again. John tried to appease him.

'Don't let that worry you. Consider this the second phase of your life . . .'

'And what phase are you on, John?'

'The third. Which is unfortunately similar to the beginning of the second.'

'I don't understand these riddles.'

'Look, Red,' John explained, sitting down beside him, 'put simply, this is you facing up to things, no more coasting along, no more brute forces. What I'm giving you, and you should be thankful for, is awareness of your limitations.'

'Why did you do this to me?'

'Besides the obvious? . . . I was just jumping for the stars, Red, keeping a step ahead of my destiny.'

'I'm not into all that astrology shit.'

John laughed.

'Don't laugh at me,' Red warned him.

'I can't help myself, Red.' John smiled at him instead. 'It's just hard to comprehend how thick you are. I never fully realised.'

Without warning Red punched John hard in the mouth. An instant thick lip blew up. 'Don't fucking laugh at me,' he repeated.

John covered his mouth with his hand to gauge the extent of the injury and to block a further punch.

'And that's the thanks I get,' he said, nodding his head and spitting blood. 'Did that make you feel any better?'

'A damn sight better. See, that's your problem, John, you could never hit anyone; and not out of a sense of tenderness, as you would like to believe, but because you couldn't. You can't fight so you cower away.

Dreaming up your little dreams.'

This time he punched him full on the back of the head. John was getting nervous. 'That's reality,' Red was saying. 'The weak ones get hurt. See, I hit you but you can't hit me back, that's the way it goes. Where's the fairness there? You might know what you've put me through but now *I* know what *you're* going through.'

He grabbed John's hands. 'Look, your hands are shaking, you're shitting yourself, and I feel better.'

He punched him on the ear. 'That one will sting for a few days.'

He kicked him in the groin. 'But you'll feel the immediate effects of that one.'

John was on the ground, not knowing what part of his body to protect.

'My only regret is that I didn't hit you harder and more often. See, I've already found a use for my adrenalin,' said Red as he kicked him full on the stomach. John wanted to cry for mercy and would have done if he had had the strength. He was winded, his whole body pulsing out pain; he could barely breathe and there was no denying Red's strong argument. Red picked up a golf club and lunged it into the small of John's back. 'Hole in one! Hole in one!' he kept repeating as he pelted away. 'I am Tiger Woods.'

John knew he was in serious trouble now and there was every chance he would die. Consciousness became a light switch which Red was flickering.

'Give me Aids, would you?' Red spat.

The only thought John could stay with was that Red was out of control with rage. He started to hear indistinguishable voices as his body went numb. He saw the club hit his body again but he couldn't feel it.

Then it stopped.

Peter yanked the club away from Red and took hold of his arms, pinning them behind his back.

'What are you doing?'

Red struggled with his brother, getting in a few more kicks.

'This piece of shit has been asking for it.'

Peter pulled him away.

Red raged on. 'Your superior vision of the world is a little more blurred now, isn't it? You think you're so smart, sticks and stones.' The room was filled with hatred; Red for John, John for Red, and Peter for the situation. It was pure and all-consuming. As John and Red tried to regain some aspect of composure, both resenting Peter's stance of 'can't you settle this like adults?' Peter brought matters back to the mundane.

'Look, Red, we've a bit of bother outside. There's two young fellas who insist on talking to you.' Peter escorted him out onto the shop floor, coming back to take care of John.

'Are you okay?'

John muttered, 'Have you got any Ibuleve cream?' Peter lifted him up as gently as he could. John's body was a jigsaw of different pieces which probably had a few missing. Peter grabbed the first aid kit and quickly established that nothing was broken. John was starting to resemble a mouldy peach.

'It looks like you're going to be okay,' Peter assured him. 'But it's not pretty. What happened?'

'Red was just putting his point across.'

Out in the shop Red was greeted by two scruffy fourteen-year-olds with crew cuts and serious expressions. They were wearing what looked like their Confirmation suits. Red's adrenalin was still pumping on full.

'What do you want?' he asked them brusquely.

'That's no way to talk to your business associates,' the taller one said as he spat on the ground.

'Look, I haven't got time for this. What the fuck are you talking about?'

'Hey Rocko, get straight to the point will ya?' said the short one.

'Well it's like this, Mister,' the tall one began. 'This area, lot of chancers around here . . .'

The shorter one joined in the pantomime. 'They'd have your eye teeth out before you'd know it.'

'Worse still is the steady increase in arsonists. But that's where we come in. We can give you protection against that sort of thing.'

Red was angry and Simon O'Donnell, aware of what was happening, stepped into the shop and stood by the corner, watching. Red wasn't in the mood for taking any shit.

'Get out of my shop,' he ordered his two unwelcome visitors.

'Certainly Mister, no problem. I'm sure you're very busy, with it being your first day and all. We'll come back tomorrow for the first instalment of five hundred pounds, and then that'll be collected monthly there on in.'

Red seized them by the neck and knocked their heads together. Then he grabbed hold of their ties and forcefully threw them off the premises, warning them never to darken his door again. Outside, the two youths regained their composure and simply nodded at Red in mockery before they disappeared. Simon O'Donnell, looking worried, went over to the counter.

'You're an awful gobshite you are, Red, you shouldn't have done that. You just put up and shut up with that lot.'

'What, let a couple of kids walk all over you? I don't think so. That's the only language they understand; you meet force with force.'

'No, you've got it wrong, mate; it's the parents you're dealing with. They only let the kids do this to keep them off the streets. My advice is to run after them, apologise and give them the money now. Everybody else does.'

'Well, it's about time somebody stood up to them.'

'That's very noble of you, Red. About as noble as one of Henry the Eighth's wives.'

'Thanks for the advice. But if you wouldn't mind, I have to close up.'

Simon shrugged. 'It's your funeral,' and he was gone.

The shop was empty except for a middle-aged couple who were eyeing up the Gaelic football jerseys. Red went over and spoke to them.

'Can I help you?'

'Yes, we're supposed to meet John Palmer here.'

'Well, I'm sorry, he's indisposed at the moment.'

'Do you know where he is?' the man asked optimistically.

'He's out the back, but this shop is closing now.'

'It shouldn't take long.'

Peter had sponged and dressed John into a human state but he was still having trouble breathing and it hurt when he made any movement. Red came in and winced at the sight.

'There's a couple of people out here to see you, and I'd appreciate it if you could conduct your business elsewhere.'

Peter helped him up and he limped out. He saw the couple and approached them with a handshake.

'Mr and Mrs O'Keefe?'

They nodded.

'Pleased to meet you, I'm sorry for all your trouble.'

Looking at his bruised face, Mrs O'Keefe blurted, 'Are you okay?'

'I will be.'

Mr O'Keefe, who was pacing a little, was keen to get down to business. 'I believe you have some news for us.'

Red came towards them, saying briskly, 'Can you do this somewhere else, please?'

'Not really, Red, 'cos this concerns you as well.' John beckoned Peter over. 'I think you might find this interesting, Peter. And it's quite apt that this discussion is taking place here.' All eyes were on John who had to lean on the counter for support. 'This is Mr and Mrs O'Keefe,' he began. 'They have come up from Wexford looking for information about their son. I never knew him myself but as far as I can make out he was a decent type, trying to make a living for himself and his girlfriend.'

Mrs O'Keefe interjected. 'He'd never hurt a fly, he was mad for the football.'

Red was becoming impatient. 'Look, this is all very touching, but I really do need to close up.'

'Not yet, Red. Because this is where you enter the story. Now Red was very keen on the football as well. In fact the two of yous knew each other. You played on the same team.'

'Look, I don't know what you're talking about here.'

'Oh, you do. You were very close. Too close, in fact, because, Red,' John pointed at him, 'you even slept with his girlfriend.' Mrs O'Keefe looked distressed. John continued. 'You have a habit of doing that, haven't you, Red?'

Red was beginning to twig what was going on.

'Yeah, Peter, you see, your little brother there fell in love with the boy's girlfriend. In fact she's his fiancée, but she's still in America, isn't that right, Red? Being held for questioning. What happened was that the poor lad found out about all this and a fight occurred, leaving the unfortunate fella on a life support machine. Now Red, not content with battering him, knew that the boy had saved a lot of money, working all hours to save up for his return to Ireland. Red decided that he'd take that as well – and hey presto, there's the money for the sports shop.'

John softened his voice. 'I hope this hasn't been too hard on you, Mr and Mrs O'Keefe, but this is the man you're looking for. This is the man who killed your son.'

Red was working himself into a state.

'I never killed anyone. I barely hit him. I was defending myself, it was just a fight.'

Mr O'Keefe stared hard at Red.

'Our boy was put on a life support machine and now he's dead.'

Mrs O'Keefe took a step towards him.

'Why did you do it, son?'

Red's eyes darted everywhere; he was the makings of someone trying to turn themselves inside out. He looked to Peter as his saviour, but Peter, who was deeply shocked, refused to look at his own brother, turning instead to John.

'Shall I call the police?'

'Peter, you don't believe them, do you? They'll send me back to America, I'll be put in prison, don't let them do that.'

The couple's stony staring had Red rush-releasing pictures of his future, a future that was too horrific even to contemplate. Peter took hold of Red, who offered no resistance. The couple wanted to accompany them down to the police station, not for revenge but to put this regretful chapter of their lives to sleep, to see it out, to be able to mourn their son properly. John, still in pain, felt like Columbo at the end of a case, everything wrapped up neatly in a box. Bad men are locked away so that the good get a better night's rest. As the others departed he was left deflated, knowing he still had to deal with his own sorry state.

They walked to the car park, passing the two youths from earlier on who smirked and headed back into the shopping centre. Peter put Red in the front seat and the O'Keefes took the back. Nobody said a word. As they were leaving the car park the sound of an explosion made them all jump and behind them the front of the sports shop disintegrated in a shower of glass. They stopped the car and stared at the blaze. The two youths walked past them, smiling and pointing their fingers at Red, who was incapable of any emotion. There was no more running and the glue of his bones was loosening.

Michelle had rung home continually once she'd been told of her discharge but there was never any reply: all she got was the answering machine.

Eventually she took a taxi and when she opened her front door the stack of mail and the musty smell told her that the house had been uninhabited for at least two days. She heard Chrissie crying and went to her aid. She found her beside her new automatic food bowl, which was closed. She fiddled with the dial of its electric timer, trying to find out why it wasn't working. Chrissie refused to take her eyes off the contraption. When Michelle turned it upside down she saw that it had no batteries in it. She fed Chrissie and made herself a cup of decaffeinated coffee. The doctor had warned her against the proper stuff. Out of the pile of mail there was one addressed to her. She opened the package and out fell a video of *The Tin Drum*. Attached to it there was a note in John's handwriting: *'Darling, at last I've found it, hope springs eternal, never stop looking. Love John.'*

John had booked himself in to one of Dublin's plushest hotels. He treated himself to the best suite, food and services. He wanted to see if he could enjoy money; or his own company for that matter. He knew the answer before he even started. He called out an escort service for a massage with extras. He wanted to be as vulgar as money would allow. His body had healed to the extent that slow movement was comfortable but sex was out of the question. The phone rang and a sexy voice asked for his room number. It didn't bode well, since in his experience sexy voices were never accompanied by sexy women. He was nervous and swallowed a glass of wine in one. A knock on the door and the bubbling beauty turned out to be a sagging aunt. She asked John what he wanted and he half expected to be handed a little toy. He asked her to take her top off and massage him. Her tits were no great shakes and he watched as she oiled her hands and quoted the price list. Impulsively John started talking.

'Kiss me.'

'No, sir. I don't kiss the customers. We don't like to get involved.'

'I'm not a great kisser, so there's no problem there.'

'No sir, I don't do that.'

'I'm not a dirty old man, I don't want to fuck you.'

'Are you one of those people who just wants to chat all night, get things off your chest?'

'No, I want you to tit fuck me and then suck me dry.'

'That'll be another thirty pounds, sir, and I will be using a condom.'

'That's okay.'

She went down on John, rolling the condom on with her mouth. John watched with arms folded behind his head. He could barely get it up as she sucked on the rubber. She was making no effort at all to be sexy. She was probably thinking about her shopping list. After five minutes she came up for air.

'I don't think this is going to happen, sir. Is there any special quirk that gets you going?'

'Well you could stick your finger up my arsehole, that usually does the trick.'

She did it, amazing John, who asked, 'Are you allowed to kiss the customer's arse?' It made him laugh until it hurt. The ageing masseur packed away her oils and asked for the basic fee of thirty pounds. John gave her a fifty, still laughing, and told her to get some shopping on him. Alone, he knew he could never become the sort of high-flyer who lived for pleasure. He'd tried several ways of living, aware that he wasn't much cop at any of them. He started to write up the final section of his diary.

Maybe I'm immune to people. I find them terribly hard work. With Red well and truly out of the picture I assumed I'd be exorcised of him and my troublesome childhood but no, the memories are as vivid as ever, and worse still I know I've lowered myself to their level. I am no better. I wonder is this hatred of others purely a projection of my own self-hatred? I don't want to be a distraction for others yet I treat them that way. I wanted all and gave nothing. I pushed when pull was signposted, I blackened my whites, was glib when cheeriness protracted itself onto me. Have drowned good feeling in cheap booze, smoked to clog, was still picking at scabs, cheated with the diceman, had run on the spot for too long, kissed witches and shoo-shooed angels away, had kept my hand in the fire for longer than necessary and now missed the heat, where others climb the mountain to stop and smell the roses I was in the gutter smelling of piss. I was always rushing around the next corner without acknowledging that it was a circle. I never took in the information that it was always the same things I was seeing. I needed help but had no one to turn to, no shrink or twelve-point plan was of any use to me. The allergy which had started with my parents had contaminated all. There must be an organisation for those of us who are addicted to isolation but hate themselves. I know there must be millions of these organisations but unfortunately they are all over-subscribed to the sum of one. As a teenager I had always confused the word anonymity with animosity and now they have merged to create my personality. And to the breech, let me become another statistic, another sad deluded fool with bollocks for brains and no balls. There must be a better place, a place where we can tell the heavy breathers to be quiet, where smells have adjectives we don't comprehend, where there is no need to dream. Do you think this would be okay to put on the dating agency form? Do you think I might pull? The ones that I know will at last know that they didn't know me and I will fade away and the money I leave them means that they can wipe away their tears with expensive hankies and take solace in the fact that I'll be able to cry.

John finished writing his diaries and put them into a big brown envelope and posted them to Dominic. He took the suicide compilation tape out of his bag and chopped out a huge line of cocaine and made his way to the car. The sunshine was giving him a tremendous send-off and the hotel had valeted the car and sprayed some false freshness into it. The tape went on and he was buzzing from the Parnell and The Beloved started hitting classic pop notes offering a hint of foreboding before his beautiful voice asked to be delivered out of his sadness. Pedestrians became his video. The singer finds someone to pull him through; he's in love. It won't last, but enjoy it anyway sucker.

John went a little faster and wondered where he could meet all the beautiful people now walking the streets. Maybe they didn't exist: they were merely a projection, there purely to fuel his lonely fantasies late at night. Next on the tape came Bawl, and he notched the volume up again. The singer's lovely Dublin tone smacked of adolescent angst. The permissible angst, the one that others tolerated and understood. John's was in the category that others judged it painful to be around. Vintage Bowie came on to tell John they had five years left of crying. *Not me, pal.* He accelerated and dabbed his finger into his bag of blah blah blah. The Floors sussed that Jesus lived longer than Kurt Cobaijn. Yea and me too.The Charlatans sneered back into his life, making him take corners carelessly. Bronski Beat had him singing along in a squeaky voice, remembering his earlier doubts about his own sexuality. He thought of sex and couldn't remember ever enjoying an orgasm; he enjoyed the run-up but the wet patch always offered the shape of diluted love. More pretence; yes, his decision seemed to be the right one. What did rapists get out of their evil deeds, the power of disgust? Radiohead's 'Creep' was a celebration of self-hatred. A couple of songs faded as John took in his surroundings. The more remote the area the uglier the people became; not distorted, but their faces were shaped to convey a droopy muted dissatisfaction. More songs of disdain: The Wedding Present crying over unfaithful partners, The Fugees resenting inequality, The Divine Comedy letting the imagination rip into poncey romance. Nick Cave sang of doomed relationships. *Hey, are these guys telling the truth?* Another dip into the bag and he was near to his cliff-top destination. Maybe his final jump would give some kids an event to talk about or Chitty

Chitty Bang Bang might save him. Pavarotti blasted out feelings of intensity before The Whipping Boy's cry for help. Morrissey swooned gently about getting what he wanted for once in his life. Julian Cope thinks the greatest imperfection is love while The Wannadies reckon it's you and me always and for ever. The Parnell, the music and the sense of absolution made him euphoric. It felt good to be nearly dead. Tiny things sprang to mind: yellow bon bons, completing a crossword, a smiling face, one of Dominic's fables; fuck, what did happen in that story? There are so many questions that still need to be answered. *I can't kill myself, that would be too obvious. My story isn't finished, it's just that I'm no longer a child: he died back there, not me.* The new adult John, released from his childhood, thought of the six-million-dollar man. *We can rebuild him, we have the technology. Now I'm new, not different but new and looking forward to this next struggle.*

He got out of the car and went to the public phone box. He dialled Dominic's number and was glad that the answering machine came on.

'Hi, it's John Palmer here, I hope you remember me. I've dropped something in the post for you. But the reason for this call is, I was wondering, what happens next?'